Advance Praise for
Hong Kong 20/20

'*Hong Kong 20/20* is a journey, both bleak and invigorating, through one of the world's most extraordinary political experiments twenty years after the handover. It is opinionated, combative, energising, and unlikely to be available in a Xinhua bookstore near you.'
 —Tom Phillips, China correspondent, *The Guardian*

'Twenty years after Hong Kong's retrocession, its creative writing remains in robust health, as contributions to this new PEN anthology rousingly testify. The compendium's stimulating cocktail of critical essays, poetry, short fiction and cartoons is to be relished both by those who know Hong Kong well and by those who wish to know it better. Together these pieces lend a vibrant collective voice to the city's linguistic and cultural cosmopolitanism and pluralism and highlight its refusal to metamorphose into "just another Chinese city" or to forgo its unique identity. Every word on every page challenges official dogma on what "loving Hong Kong" really means and on who is permitted to do so and how.'
 —Michael Ingham, author of
 Hong Kong: A Cultural and Literary History

'With original and imaginative interventions into a range of intellectual and personal positions, this anthology brings together our city's leading activists, intellectuals and writers who speak out against the deteriorating situation of the metropolis and contemplate its uncertain future. Their lucid and ingenious writings open up new vistas in our understanding of our past and present relations with China and the world.'
— Lo Kwai Cheung, director of Creative and Professional Writing Programme, Hong Kong Baptist University

'PEN Hong Kong's stirring collection of literary pieces delves into the city's past and explores its future. Timely and insightful, this anthology provides a fresh perspective on questions of identity, citizenship and change.'
— Phillipa Milne, manager of the Hong Kong International Literary Festival

'"Borrowed place, borrowed time" was a phrase coined to describe colonial Hong Kong in the years before its return to China. Now a different clock is ticking, and it is twenty years since the 1997 handover. This collection of stories, poems, essays and cartoons is a vivid stock-taking of where Hong Kong is now, and where it may yet be going. These "reflections" are themselves a reflection of the people of the city—diverse, spiky, resilient, always surprising, wonderfully talkative.'
— Douglas Kerr, professor of English, University of Hong Kong

'Hong Kong is one of the world's greatest cities. It will be at the centre of some of the political and intellectual arguments of the century ahead. My own bet is that the success of Hong Kong's pluralist citizenship will come out on top whatever the challenges. Reading many of the contributions [in *Hong Kong 20/20*] confirms me in that view.'
    —Chris Patten, the last governor of Hong Kong

'Seldom before have so many of the clearest-eyed observers provided such a broad set of essays, poems, short stories and cartoons about Hong Kong's evolution. Anyone passionate about the city's future, or even just curious, should read it.'
    —Keith Bradsher, Shanghai Bureau Chief,
    The New York Times

HONG KONG
香 20/20 港

Reflections on a Borrowed Place

A PEN Hong Kong anthology

BLACKSMITH BOOKS

Hong Kong 20/20
Reflections on a Borrowed Place

A PEN Hong Kong anthology

ISBN 978-988-77927-6-5
Copyright © 2017 PEN Hong Kong
www.penhongkong.org

Published by Blacksmith Books
Unit 26, 19/F, Block B
Wah Lok Industrial Centre
37–41 Shan Mei Street
Fo Tan, N.T., Hong Kong
Tel: (+852) 2877 7899
www.blacksmithbooks.com
First printing June 2017

Cover and layout design by Melvina Mak
Cover photograph by Michael Kistler

For Hong Kong,

and all who share it

when a pen draws the horizon
you're awakened by a gong from the East
to bloom in the echoes is
the rose of time

in the mirror there is always this moment
this moment leads to the door of rebirth
the door opens to the sea
the rose of time

Bei Dao
'The Rose of Time'

Table of Contents

Essays

Poetry

Fiction

Cartoons and Sketches

Introduction

What would it mean for Hong Kong to write itself in its own language? This is the question culture critic Rey Chow asks in Jennifer Cheng's 'Umbrella Poetics'.

We are thrilled to offer this anthology to mark the twentieth anniversary of Hong Kong's return to Chinese rule. We have curated a mix of poetry, fiction, non-fiction and art by some of Hong Kong's most prominent literary and creative minds. We have also assembled young, emerging voices. We hope this collection ignites conversation about the city we share and love.

They say that literature and art come to the rescue of civilisation again and again. Now, more than ever, Hong Kong needs its writers, poets, journalists, academics and artists to articulate what it means to belong here, and to address what Hong Kong signifies as we navigate anxious years and watch China's promised 'one country, two systems' crumble before our eyes.

Who are we? What do we want? As Stephen Vines notes, these questions of identity are 'bolstered more by negatives than positives'. That is fine by us, as long as Hong Kong continues its struggle to speak its mind—and even change it.

Chip Tsao reminds us that the end of British rule in Hong Kong did not breed a Mahatma Gandhi, Aung San Suu Kyi or Ho Chi Minh. That's true, but we now have a fresh new generation, filled with a uniquely-Hong Kong panache and ready for change. They have shown us that Hong Kong is, above all, ever-evolving and ever-ready to reinvent itself.

Tammy Ho Lai-Ming sums it up well: Hong Kong was born many times, first as a fishing village, then as a British colony and now a Special Administrative Region. In the summer of 2014, it transformed yet again into a very special place, as hundreds of thousands of citizens took over large sprawls of the city and let umbrellas and tents bloom like flowers. What seems unthinkable and implausible today can, according to Joshua Wong, become a political reality tomorrow.

No wonder we care so deeply about this tiny speck of land, whether we are locally-bred, or of impure origins and of mixed-up backgrounds. Louise Law Lok Man observes that we work to 'build and share, receive and contain', and we long for 'fine and fair freedoms'. So Mei Chi is right to say that we see clearly when there is a 'discrepancy between the text and the visuals'. We know in our bones that 'belonging is, after all, a kind of longing'. We may not be able to explain why we have unfolded our homes on these rocks; but since we are here, we would like to state our case.

Xu Xi's fictional character Loong Hei boldly declares in his op-ed, 'what I am is a Hong Kong yan... [and] all I have to be is a writer from within, who can and must record this transit'. To use Tang Siu Wa's words, we must 'keep on telling the story and breaking through the information blockade'. Or else we just may, like the castaway in Jason Y. Ng's short story, devolve into beings who 'abandon defences... and disappear into an abyss of numbness'.

That is precisely why a group of us established PEN Hong Kong in 2016 to stand against what we see as an assault on freedom of expression in our city. PEN Hong Kong has watched and worried as the space for creativity and expression in Hong Kong continues to shrink. Our mission is to reverse this trend, to spread our love for the written word, and to work with our peers in PEN chapters around the world to protect free expression anywhere it is under threat.

The burst of voices in this anthology is a result of that goal. We hope it stops you in your tracks, as if 'a hundred-year-old turtle had crawled out to proclaim some good news'—to use Eddie Tay's metaphor. Some of these pieces are pessimistic, others hopeful. We aim to offer a diversity of viewpoints and interpretations of past and present—and a range of visions for the future. As in Leung Ping-Kwan's phrase, we 'write with a different colour for each voice'. Our anthology's forty-one contributors include some who work in English and some who work in Chinese. We plan to translate this collection in its entirety into Chinese to echo and honour Hong Kong's dual heritage.

This book is a celebration and also a declaration: we will fight to maintain our city's role as a safe harbour for those who would use the written word to speak truth to power, to effect change, to spread love, or just to make the world more bearable.

In these pages, you will find us, writing ourselves.

Anthology Editorial Committee
PEN Hong Kong
June 2017

Foreword

Timothy Garton Ash

What is the right metaphor for Hong Kong? A litmus test for the future of freedom in Asia? A hinge on some giant bronze door between East and West? A semiconductor between two world cultures: Anglophone and Chinese? A magic mirror in which everyone sees something different—the British their own troubled colonial past, some mainland Chinese a possible better future, Hong Kongers many different self-images? A mix-up club, a lighthouse, a weathervane, a great observatory?

The correct answer would seem to be 'all of the above—and more'. That is why I love coming to Hong Kong, a place where you can mark the passing of five days by the English cricket score method 卌 or the Chinese zing ideogram 正.

This fascinating anthology contains many diverse genres, tones and voices, some upbeat, many concerned, a few downright pessimistic. Indeed, anyone who cares about freedom of expression—and its close siblings, freedom of information and academic freedom— must be deeply concerned at the way these are under threat in Hong Kong. Yet equally impressive is the new dynamism of civil society and the mobilisation of a younger generation. Since the evolution of the relationship between China and the West is the pivotal geopolitical question of our time, it follows that if things go well in Hong Kong that will be a good sign for the world, and if things go badly... need I go on? Our hope must be a new synthesis, not a sharpening antithesis.

An anthology like this needs no larger political or historical justification. If it contains texts that are interesting, well-written, astute and evocative—and it does—that is more than sufficient reason to read it. But as it happens, Hong Kong 20/20 sheds light on a vital hinge, semiconductor, litmus test and mirror.

Timothy Garton Ash
Historian, commentator & author of
Free Speech: Ten Principles for a Connected World

Foreword

Kevin Lau Chun-to 劉進圖

In the decades since China and the United Kingdom signed the Joint Declaration on the Question of Hong Kong in 1984, there has been no shortage of watershed moments—moments that awaken generations, crystallise their identity and compel them to make sense of their city and re-examine their relationship with the sovereign state. There were the Tiananmen Square protests in 1989, the handover in 1997, the SARS outbreak and the mass July 1st rally in 2003, and the Umbrella Movement in 2014. Those who wish to wake up are already wide awake; and those who don't, won't, no matter how hard we shake them.

A single question keeps weighing on our young people: what is to come after this awakening?

The answer, I believe, is enlightenment.

Enlightenment is to search for answers, develop independent thinking, challenge conventional wisdom, debunk prejudices and superstitions, cultivate a worldview, establish a tenable belief system and ultimately construct a durable and incorruptible set of ideals and mission.

But how do we transition from awakening to enlightenment?

Without a doubt, the answer varies from person to person. But I'll always put my faith in the written word. Reading enables us to formulate thoughts, push the boundaries of the status quo, explore our self-worth and craft our personality. Good writing, whether it is essays, fiction or poetry, expands our horizons and shapes our worldview. There is no shortcut to enlightenment—the only way to get there is through reading broadly and thinking deeply.

There is no better way to mark another important moment in our history—the twentieth anniversary of the handover—than a collection of literary pieces. It is a perfect tribute to Hong Kong.

Kevin Lau Chun-to 劉進圖
Former editor-in-chief, Ming Pao

Translated from the Chinese by Jason Y. Ng.

Acknowledgements

Members of the PEN Hong Kong Anthology Editorial Committee—Tammy Ho Lai-Ming, Jason Y. Ng, Mishi Saran, Sarah Schafer and Nicholas Wong—would like to thank Michael Kistler for the cover photography; Melvina Mak for the cover and layout design; Gregg Schroeder for his copy edits; Martha Cheung, Lucas Klein, Suzanne Lai, Henry Wei Leung, Jason Y. Ng, Gordon T. Osing, Chris Song and Aurora Tsui for their translation; the family of Leung Ping-Kwan for permission to reprint three of his Hong Kong poems; and all the distinguished contributors who have lent their unique voices to mark this important milestone in Hong Kong history.

Timeline of Key Events

1841	Britain occupies Hong Kong Island
1842	China cedes Hong Kong Island to Britain
1861	Britain occupies Kowloon Peninsula
1899	Britain occupies the New Territories
1912	Sun Yat-sen founds the Republic of China
1927–1936	Chinese Civil War
1931–1945	Japanese invasion of China
1941–1945	Japanese occupation of Hong Kong
1946–1949	Chinese Civil War continues
1949	Mao Zedong founds the People's Republic of China
1966–1976	The Cultural Revolution in China
1967	Leftist Riots in Hong Kong
1984	China and the United Kingdom sign the Joint Declaration over the return of Hong Kong
1989	Tiananmen Square Massacre in Beijing

1997	Hong Kong transitions from a British crown colony to a Special Administrative Region (SAR) under Chinese rule; Tung Chee-hwa becomes the first chief executive of the SAR
1997–1998	The Asian Financial Crisis
2003	The Severe Acute Respiratory Syndrome (SARS) outbreak strikes Hong Kong; 500,000 citizens take to the streets to oppose an anti-subversion bill; Tung resigns and Chief Secretary Donald Tsang Yam-kuen becomes the second chief executive of the SAR
2007–2008	The global financial meltdown
2011	China becomes the world's second-largest economy
2012	Leung Chun-ying becomes the third chief executive of the SAR; student activist Joshua Wong leads a mass protest to thwart the government's attempt to introduce a 'national education' curriculum
2014	The Occupy (Umbrella) Movement erupts
2015	Five booksellers from Causeway Bay Books are allegedly abducted by mainland Chinese authorities
2017	Carrie Lam Cheng Yuet-ngor becomes the fourth chief executive of the SAR

ESSAYS

China's New Colony

Stephen Vines

T he torrent of rain started early on June 30th, 1997, the last day of British rule over Hong Kong; it was un-relenting right up to the point where People's Liberation Army troops sitting stiffly on flatbed trucks crossed the border at the stroke of midnight. Drenched to the skin at the Sha Tau Kok border point, I watched the vehicles stream by as cheering local crowds celebrated their arrival. This was a genuine manifestation of enthusiasm, which served as a salutary reminder that the reunification of Hong Kong with the Motherland struck a deep cord of hope in the hearts of local people despite the fact that many of them came from families who had fled the mainland.

Alongside the genuine enthusiasm were the manoeuvrings of the bigwigs who were clamouring to establish their place in the new order. Rita Fan Hsu Lai-tai, an Executive and Legislative Council member under British rule, who was to emerge as one of the sycophants-in-chief of the new regime, smugly noted that the rain was cleansing Hong Kong of over 150 years of British imperialism. She had already ar-ranged for her Commander of the British Empire medal to be safely tucked away in a drawer as she manoeuvred herself into a position as one of the new regime's closest trustees. She became the first president of the Legislative Council and presided over its business for more than a decade.

Fan was not alone because almost all the pillars of the post-British colonial regime were exactly the same people who had been pillars of the old order. The real Communist Party loyalists, clandestine party members operating underground in Hong Kong, were firmly told by their bosses up north to remain in the background because Beijing wanted to give an impression of continuity. In a nation where power and control comes second to old-fashioned ideology, the real believers were not as highly prized as they might have been. So they were left in the shadows as the new masters revelled in discovering so many willing hands among the people who had occupied leading positions in the old regime.

In fact the grey men in Beijing found much to like about the old regime and under the slogan of 'fifty years no change' carefully set out to preserve every aspect of British colonialism that once served the purpose of maintaining London's control over Hong Kong and could be pressed into service to ensure subservience to Beijing.

In many ways this replication of colonialism reached absurd levels, as one of the first acts of the post-colonial government was to introduce a new honours system to ensure that baubles could be handed out to trustees replacing those bestowed by Her Majesty The Queen in London. The new system of so-called Bauhinia awards more or less mirrored the old imperial system, whose recipients were mainly confined to tycoons, loyalists and civil servants.

More significantly, steps were taken to ensure that the legislature would remain largely powerless and would be detached from the executive arm of government. Crucially, the colonial system of functional constituencies was retained in the legislature, giving disproportionate voting rights to unrepresentative business and occupational groups who occupied half the legislature. Equally important was Beijing's embrace of the old system that made the Hong Kong Government a subservient mechanism in relation to the colony's distant rulers.

> I have been surprised by the speed with which some of my predictions have come to pass as China's promise of giving Hong Kong a 'high degree of autonomy' is eroded by the day.

Observing the laborious process of the handover of power led me to write a book entitled *Hong Kong—China's New Colony*, published two years after the handover. In some ways even I have been surprised by the speed with which some predictions contained in that book have come to pass as China's promise of giving Hong Kong a 'high degree of autonomy' is eroded by the day. Even quite minor government decisions are now referred to the Central People's Government Liaison Office and Beijing has abandoned all pretence of not meddling in elections, most recently instructing its loyalists to vote for Carrie Lam Cheng Yuet-ngor to become the fourth chief executive, a poll that is confined to a maximum of 1,200 electors, most of whom are in the loyalist camp.

The crucial improbability of a one-party state genuinely permitting autonomy lay at the centre of doubts I had back then and this has proved to be the case.

However, with the perspective of twenty years since the establishment of the Hong Kong Special Administrative Region of the People's Republic of China (snappy titles have never figured in the DNA of the Chinese Communist Party), I now appreciate that the description of Hong Kong as 'China's new colony' is insufficiently nuanced and I believe that I have missed a crucial element here: the evolution of civil society since 1997. The growth of political parties, grassroots campaigns, social media and public participation in protest has, arguably, transformed Hong Kong in ways that seemed inconceivable back in 1997.

Although this level of engagement was hard to predict it is not so unusual for immigrant societies to move from a more inward focus on immediate economic concerns to wider social concerns as they become more settled. A high percentage of the population has now been resident in Hong Kong for three generations, a stage at which this transition is more likely to take place.

To understand how much has changed requires a look back at the 'good old days' when the passivity and reluctance of Hong Kongers to engage in public affairs was a given allowing the canard to grow that Hong Kong people were only interested in money.

This was never true but it helped the former colonial regime foster the myth that it needed to be all encompassing because it ruled over a place where there was no appetite for any real form of self-government. The legend ran that in return for competent governance the people would be happy not to be involved. This view of things sort of made sense because the bulk of the Hong Kong population made their way to the colony to escape the chaos of China's revolutions, especially the lunacies unleashed by the Cultural Revolution. They were not inclined to be that concerned about participation in government.

The Brits knew a great a deal about the structure of government but were less sure-footed in their attitude towards the people they ruled. They were torn between making their colonial subjects identify with the imperial regime and simply containing them, regardless of their preferences, as long as they accepted rule from London. In Hong Kong, unlike in places such as India, the colonial administration focused on containment and made minimal efforts to inculcate a sense of 'Britishness' on its subjects.

The incoming Chinese administration has understandably proved to be much more interested in enforcing a sense of Chinese identity. This flows in part from the empty ideological coffers of the Chinese Communist Party that has been stripped of its belief in class struggle, forcing it to rely on a form of extreme nationalism as its claim to legitimacy.

This nationalistic stance is accompanied by worrying manifestations of paranoia over the foreign influences that have allegedly come to rest in China's most international region, a place ruled by foreigners until just twenty years ago. The ideological mission of the new rulers has been to expunge this 'foreignness'.

And here lies the paradox because while the majority of Hong Kong people have been perfectly happy to identify themselves as Chinese and very few of them even dreamt of identifying as British, the pressure to identify closely with mainland China has caused an enormous backlash and given birth to a far stronger Hong Kong-specific identity, especially among younger people.

In some ways this identity is bolstered more by negatives than positives. Thus, Hong Kongers tend to feel a closer identity with this place when the mainland authorities move to undermine the autonomy they themselves promised to honour, such as when the local government tried to step up indoctrination of school students to foster greater identity with the Motherland in the thwarted attempt in 2012 to introduce a patriotic curriculum in schools across the city. When the naked power of the Chinese state was on display with the abduction of people from Hong Kong for detention on the mainland, the sense of local identity hit new peaks.

There are also negative aspects to the growing attachment to a distinct, non-mainland identity, which are manifest in a sense of Hong Kong superiority towards 'less sophisticated' mainland compatriots, giving rise to ugly demonstrations against people coming across the border and buying goods in Hong Kong.

The reality is that Hong Kong is a very different place from the rest of the China, including Macau, the other Special Administrative Region. Superficially it seemed as though apartness was defined by the relative prosperity of Hong Kong but more fundamentally there was rule of law, freedom of expression and a growing self-confidence of the people which was reflected and reinforced by a distinctive local culture that has become more assertive as attempts are made to put it back in its box.

Seen through the prism of a one-party state that values control over practically everything else, any challenge to the dictatorship can be viewed as an act of anti-patriots. However, the reality in Hong Kong is that some of the most patriotic people are also opponents of the government. It is not a coincidence that the main organisation that coordinates the annual memorial rally for the 1989 Tiananmen Square Massacre is called the Hong Kong Alliance in Support of Patriotic Democratic Movements of China.

> The reality in Hong Kong is that some of the most patriotic people are also opponents of the government.

When the massacre itself took place, Hong Kong more or less ground to a halt as hundreds of thousands of people poured into the streets in silent protest. There was an impressive sense of identity with those who lost their lives, were arrested or rounded up. Only later, but not much later, did this sense of solidarity morph into one of real fear, prompting local consulates to be besieged by Hong Kongers seeking to emigrate.

By 1997, eight years after the massacre, these fears subsided and many of those who emigrated returned to Hong Kong, others quietly put their foreign passports in safe deposit boxes as part of rather elaborate plans for escape should the need arise.

The handover came and went and nothing really terrible happened so even more people returned to Hong Kong and although the memory of the massacre did not disappear, the pain dulled. As ever, people focused on their immediate concerns, leaving wider political issues simmering.

In the two decades since the handover, what could have been no more than simmering discontent has been, on every occasion, transformed into movements of mass discontent by the government itself. Most notably, in 2002, the government introduced anti-subversion legislation by way of enacting Article 23 of Hong Kong's mini-constitution, which is called the Basic Law. This legislation contained clear and disturbing threats to civil liberties and was shelved the following year, after a mass mobilisation of citizens which also forced the resignation of the first chief executive of the Special Administrative Region, Tung Chee-hwa.

The defeat of this attempt to curb Hong Kong freedoms was a precursor of other movements, some of which were successful, such as the movement to defeat political indoctrination in schools. Others that focused on preservation of the local heritage were less successful. And of course, continued protests have failed to produce a democratic form of government.

Although the protests were seemingly disparate, a pattern began to emerge; they increasingly became movements asserting Hong Kong identity and preservation of a way of life that was under threat from growing 'mainlandisation'.

The generation born after 1997, which grew up under Chinese rule, appeared to have less interest in the mainland and was focused on Hong Kong itself. They had ambitious dreams of establishing a democratic Hong Kong with a far greater degree of self-government. Yet again it was the government that helped crystallise this movement after China issued instructions in August 2014 to limit plans for the election of the chief executive by universal suffrage to an election that would be pre-screened, so as to ensure that only candidates approved by Beijing would be able to run.

This ruling by the Standing Committee of the National People's Congress made it very clear that the promise of free and fair elections was a sham. The extent to which this ruling undermined a genuine form of universal suffrage came as a shock, quickly followed by a mass mobilisation that led a month later to the Umbrella Movement that literally brought the centre of town to a standstill during long weeks of occupation of the streets by protesters.

Significantly, this protest was led by young people who more or less shunned the traditional pro-democracy movement. A new generation of protest leaders had arrived and, as is the way with new generations of protest leaders, they spawned more extreme elements who were so disillusioned by the former protest leaders and were so contemptuous of the government that some of them were prepared to embrace violent protest and convinced themselves that the fate of Hong Kong could only be settled on the streets.

The Umbrella Movement was eventually 'defeated' and the streets were cleared, but the sentiments it produced and indeed, the leaders it threw up, most certainly did not disappear. The majority of Hong Kong's law-abiding citizens may not have liked the idea of violence on the streets but, especially among the young, a new appetite for change took hold.

That appetite for change has since been manifest in the election of the new protest leaders to the legislature and their success in winning a host of other elections. Society has become more polarised and while the hard-line government of Xi Jinping in Beijing appears to believe that Hong Kong needs to be taught a lesson, it cannot quite work out how to do this.

The net result is an uneasy stalemate that leaves 'China's New Colony' hard to run, where dissatisfaction with the government is very high and where the potential for disruption is ever present. The government in Beijing fondly imagined that if it merely took over the colonial ways of keeping Hong Kong under control, it could somehow retain a subservient entity on its southernmost tip, albeit with some cosmetic concessions. History nevertheless has a determined habit of moving on and creating new realities.

It is hard to predict how this will pan out, but the idea that the status quo can be prolonged for much longer is clearly a fantasy.

Ma Ma Land

Chip Tsao

China's paramount leader, Deng Xiaoping, puffing his cigarette and spitting into a spittoon placed in front of him to humiliate British Prime Minister Margaret Thatcher in Beijing in September 1982, is widely rumoured to have thrown his logic bluntly in her face: 'What you British could achieve in Hong Kong, we Chinese also could achieve. And we can do better than you.'

Deng meant: Sure, the Brits turned a few barren rocks into the Pearl of the Orient since they took Hong Kong by force in 1842. Well done. But when the Chinese take Hong Kong back in 1997, we will amaze the world—you kicked off with a Chaucer, we will outdo you with a Shakespeare.

For a long time, it seemed the tiny Communist Party chief, whom Thatcher later described as 'cruel', had been prescient. Deng died five months before the handover, at age ninety-two, never fulfilling his promise to take his first step onto Hong Kong soil once the Chinese flag again flew over it. But Hong Kong thrived, with hot cash flowing in and out, and became an even more crucial link between the world and mainland China. Business remained business. China was committed to capitalism at full throttle of GDP growth with hot cash spilling over and flooding the West. Deng's political descendants did not confiscate all private enterprise. They did not shoot a single landlord, or send entrepreneurs to labour reform camps to break their capitalist will. 'One country, two systems', as Hong Kong's setup was called, protected troublemakers too. Beijing allowed the city's two most notorious democracy activists, Martin Lee Chu-ming and 'Long Hair' Leung Kwok-hung, not only to live, but to lead demonstrations and candlelight vigils.

The Basic Law—a mini-constitution drafted by Beijing—is supposed to serve as a thin layer of rubber to screen out a widely-feared virus during intimate physical contact between the two contradicting systems. All freedoms, plus an independent judiciary inherited from the British vintage era, are guaranteed. But democrats have been protesting that it has been punctured stealthily with a needle by Beijing. Mainland Chinese agents are being sent to Hong Kong under cover as bankers, businessmen and academics. A power base called the Central People's Government Liaison Office is seen as reducing the power of a supposedly 'highly autonomous' Special Administrative Region (SAR) government of Hong Kong into something like the Vichy regime in 1942 France.

China thwarted democratisation. It never allowed universal suffrage as it promised Hong Kong in the Basic Law. The Communists picked a succession of puppet chief executives to lead us: the failed Shanghai businessman, Tung Chee-hwa; the self-proclaimed 'caring capitalist', Donald Tsang Yam-kuen; and then an eccentric called C.Y. Leung—a British-trained building surveyor and a clandestine Maoist who seemed to take a Nero-like pleasure in setting fire to the system of Hong

Kong and watching the community blaze. The Basic Law promised that Hong Kong people would rule Hong Kong, with a 'high degree of autonomy', in matters other than military defence and foreign policy. Now, Hong Kong's elites are left with a one-party Leninist state and a nepotistic capitalism that is stricken with corruption. So Hong Kong hovers. The gap between the region's expectations and what China is willing to offer has never been so wide.

For a long time, Hong Kong was a money-making entrepôt, flourishing and comfortable. Unlike the situations in India in 1947, Burma in 1948 or North Vietnam in 1956, Hong Kong returned to China in 1997 during peacetime, not after a world war, and peacefully, without civil uprisings organised by fervent and violent nationalists calling for decolonisation and independence. It did not breed a Mahatma Gandhi, Aung San Suu Kyi, or Ho Chi Minh. Hong Kong never had, or needed, a Lee Kuan Yew—the Cambridge law graduate and Machiavellian who led Singapore out of colonialism and the Third World, sidestepping Communism. When the handover came, billionaire businessman Li Ka-shing was Hong Kong's public hero and Money the Only God. Business as usual.

Until now.

Twenty years later, iPhones replaced Nokias, and Emoji supplanted English as the global language. Bin Laden's terror has been replaced by the threat of ISIS. The new generation wakes in the 'international financial city', claustrophobic, boxed in their partitioned rooms, locked in layers of high rises and shrouded in the smog that spills over from the mainland. They are surrounded by buzzing troops of mainland shoppers who spend cool cash on jewellery, property, private hospital beds, kindergarten seats and untainted milk powder. Apart from being victimised by a most merciless form of Chinese capitalism, young people's resentment builds as Chinese President Xi Jinping's Maoist cult of personality and his tighter grip on freedom of expression also spill over into the territory. Officials of the SAR government attempted to impose an education campaign designed to instil a sense of 'national identity' into the brains of children who are not well-off enough to apply for emigration to the West despite their love of Western values, while the rich claiming to be patriotically loyal to the Chinese emperor all have either a green card or a Canadian or British passport safely hidden in their pockets.

These Hong Kong kids share their fury with one click. Frustrated by the deadlock over democratisation as promised in the Basic Law, young students occupied central districts for more than a month in protest of China's hypocrisy and bullying. Yellow umbrellas were held and tents set up on streets, only to be dispersed by tear gas. The Umbrella Movement in 2014 linked Hong Kong with the globalised campaign of protests by the iPhone generation from Tunisia to Thailand and Taiwan—definitely a virus spread by the cynical CIA, a belief strongly held by a furious Beijing.

But can the young generation save Hong Kong from those who, as the last British governor of Hong Kong, Chris Patten, once said, might give Hong Kong away bit by bit in exchange for personal gain? Those who have grown rich here are the VIP guests at banquet halls in Beijing. With a bubbling economy and growing foreign reserves, the supreme masters in Beijing are never short of red packets (*lai see*) to hand out to those who side with the Motherland. The masters reward the Hong Kong business elite's loyalty with investment projects. China controls the chief executive and the economy. The rich are happy to relinquish Hong Kong's autonomy to please the new colonial master because they learn quickly who butters their bread. They march to the People's Republic of China's national anthem just as well as they danced the intricate galliard of 'God Save the Queen'.

Paradoxically, Beijing is anxious not to destroy Hong Kong and convert it into just another Chinese coastal city because it knows the value of the territory as an estuary for the outflow of Chinese money, what with Hong Kong's financial system linked to London and New York under common law. But when the heart beats, the blood surges through the entire body. So Beijing curses the 'Western powers', especially the United States, for propping up the democrats to sabotage Hong Kong. Beijing occasionally itches to send its agents to kidnap a few, those deemed most dangerous and urgently-wanted on its list. And Hong Kong suffers as the 2047 deadline, when all promises made twenty years ago expire, tick-tocks nearer. With Britain's mouth watering over Beijing's investment cheques and the rest of the West dizzy from its own civil wars among political correctness, Muslims and Donald Trump, Western governments, media and liberals see the world with blurred vision. 'Turning and turning in the widening gyre, the falcon cannot hear the falconer,' a brave pro-independence Irish poet warned 100 years ago. Things fall apart. Hong Kong is gradually fading away.

> The rich march to the People's Republic of China's national anthem just as well as they danced the intricate galliard of 'God Save the Queen'.

Introduction to Cartoons by Larry Feign

'**H**istory is written by the victors.'
—attributed to Winston Churchill and others

Sadly, no one named Victor was available to write a history of Hong Kong's handover to China. So when the British newspaper, the *Independent*, decided to cover the story of Hong Kong's last hundred days under British rule, they chose to do so through the eyes of a cartoonist. I will confess an interest in this matter, being the cartoonist commissioned for the task, but even if it had been someone else, I would have seconded the idea. Hong Kong had been a den of absurdities for the previous ten years; those hundred days before the transition promised any humourist an embarrassment of riches.

I actually looked forward to the change in sovereignty. At long last people would talk about something—anything!—other than, 'So, what are you doing after 1997?'

Twenty years later, all anyone talks about is how much better things were before 1997. Well, maybe not everybody. Some simply don't speak such thoughts out loud. Others are paid fifty *mao* to write the opposite in online comments sections. Who's right?

The trouble is that there has never been a definitive version of Hong Kong history. The city was founded by scoundrels, populated by refugees. It wasn't until the late 1980s that more than half of Hong Kong's population had actually been born here. Hong Kong had always been a haven of convenience, to escape chaos on the mainland or to get rich and move on. There was no deep sense of belonging, no Hong Kong identity. History didn't matter. Covering Hong Kong's transition was like writing on a blank slate: every worst-case scenario rang true, but so did the best.

On the day of the handover, bauhinia flags flew, chests were beaten, speeches were given in Mandarin. Hong Kong was again a proud part of a strong and powerful China. A hundred and fifty-six years of humiliating history was at last avenged! The east was now, finally, fully red!

Then the next thing they did was build a Disneyland.

Is it any wonder that cartoonists make the best historians?

Britain Lifts a Finger

Larry Feign

Promises and Reality

Chris Yeung

To mark the arrival of the twenty-first year of 'one country, two systems', more than 300 events will be held in Hong Kong at an estimated cost of HK$640 million, more than nine times the HK$69 million spent on the tenth anniversary of the handover in 2007. The theme for this landmark year is, 'Together, Progress and Opportunity', and the celebrations are meant to foster a sense of unity among a politically divided populace.

On July 1st, the ceremonies to observe the return of Hong Kong to the communist-ruled Motherland will reach a climax, with the swearing in of Carrie Lam Cheng Yuet-ngor as the city's new chief executive. China's president, Xi Jinping, is set to preside over the inauguration of Lam, who is the first woman to hold the post since the handover. The occasion is meant to mark the beginning of a new era, with changes in policies on issues such as land supply, and to usher in an end to economic stagnation.

But the pomp masks a deep sense of disillusionment, doubt and fear held by many Hong Kongers over the fate of their city. The Hong Kong and mainland governments might be planning parties, but many Hong Kong citizens, especially those who are young and middle class, are dreaming of emigrating to a better place—and future. Many Hong Kongers, especially those in their twenties and thirties, are tempted to further distance themselves from the mainland, not integrate closer with the hinterland. Some are talking about independence for Hong Kong.

The mood leading up to the twentieth anniversary of the handover bears a striking resemblance to the mood prevalent in the city before the handover, when people braced for an uncertain future. On that July 1st, the emotion-laden departure of the popular last colonial governor, Chris Patten, and the crossing of the border into Hong Kong by the People's Liberation Army (PLA), caused many in the city to fret. But the stir those symbolic acts in 1997 caused

> The rising discontent over mainland interference in Hong Kong's affairs has disillusioned Hong Kongers.

was short-lived. For years, the people who chose to stay or had no choice but to stay were largely okay with the change of sovereignty. It was a case of, 'so far so good'. The PLA were almost invisible. The Central People's Government Liaison Office, formerly under the name of Xinhua News Agency, had stuck to its role of liaison and refrained from making comments on Hong Kong affairs, at least publicly. And following Deng Xiaoping's famous 'southern tour' in 1992 to reboot mainland economic policy, Deng's hand-picked successor, Jiang Zemin, presided over a long period of rapid economic growth.

But the 'wait and see' attitude is gone. Many have seen enough. The rising discontent over mainland interference in

Hong Kong's affairs—whether by attempting to indoctrinate students with patriotic texts or instigating the introduction of overreaching national security legislation—has disillusioned Hong Kongers. Deng, the chief architect of 'one country, two systems' and China's 'reform and openness' policy, would not have predicted the enormous and complex—and sometimes contradictory—socioeconomic changes and political turbulence that arose in the course of putting the city's capitalist system and the mainland's socialist system under the tenet of 'one country'.

As soon as he took power, Tung Chee-hwa, the first chief executive of Hong Kong, trumpeted closer integration with the mainland. One of Tung's best-known dicta was: 'If Hong Kong is good, China will be good. If China is good, Hong Kong will be even better.' China was a weak, underdeveloped, sleeping lion, devastated by merciless power struggles and political-ideological campaigns since 1949, until the Deng-orchestrated reform in the 1980s, when Hong Kong was taking off economically. The prosperity of Hong Kong, then one of the Four Asian Dragons, and its effective governance under colonial rule had provided a role model for China as it made a late start in modernisation. More important, the relocation of Hong Kong industries and the flow of investments first to Guangdong, then to the rest of the mainland, boosted the Chinese economy. However, flaws began to appear in the win–win formula of economic integration, as China grew stronger and mightier.

As China began riding a high-speed train towards greater economic and political strength and the ruling party gained self-confidence, Hong Kong was slowing economically. The Asian financial crisis erupted in 1997, followed by the world-wide bursting of the dot.com bubble in the early 2000s. Both events battered the Hong Kong economy. In the midst of the city's economic woes, came a list of government fiascos under the Tung administration: a scandal at a public housing project, the mishandling of the severe acute respiratory syndrome (SARS) outbreak in 2003, and a brazen attempt to introduce an anti-subversion bill.

After the ravage of SARS, the central authorities intensified their supportive policies to help reinvigorate the Hong Kong economy. To stimulate the ailing retail and tourism industry, Beijing relaxed restrictions on visits by mainlanders to the city. But this had the unintended effect of straining mainland–Hong Kong relations as the influx of mainland tourists over the years began to cause controversy, and tensions grew between the visitors and the locals. If the mainland economy had been dependent on the investments from Hong Kong to drive growth since 1979 and in the early years after the handover, the city's reliance on the influx of people (mostly tourists) and capital from the mainland has become clear in the past decade. Meanwhile, major mainland cities, in particular Shenzhen and Shanghai, have developed at rapid rates. Top Chinese officials predict that Shenzhen will overtake Hong Kong in about two years' time, in terms of its overall economic strength. The Shanghai municipal government, meanwhile, has set 2020 as the target year for its city to become an international financial hub.

With the nation's economy having leapt to become the world's second largest, the ruling party of China has adopted a 'going out' strategy to seek more financial and political opportunities through investment overseas. Not surprisingly, Hong Kong has emerged as a popular target for mainland investors. Several pieces of land listed by the government for secret tendering in 2016 and 2017 landed in the hands of mainland developers at sky-high prices. James Tien Pei-chun, businessman and honorary chairman of the Liberal Party of Hong Kong, warned in April 2017 of the 'infiltration of mainland enterprises' into various aspects of life of the Hong Kong people. Citing the example of mainland developers snapping up land at record high prices, he said many local consortia were unable to compete. 'Our various aspects of livelihood have now been closely intertwined with China-funded companies,' Tien said at a symposium hosted by *Citizen News*, a Chinese-language online media outlet. 'When a state is able to control the economic lifeline of a region, it will become doubly difficult for the place to have its own democracy and way of life. The central authorities will call the shots on everything.' Numbers speak. Mainland companies make up about 40 per cent of market capitalisation of the Hong Kong stock exchange in 2017. The corresponding figure in 1997 was 16 per cent.

The economic role and function of Hong Kong are increasingly in doubt amidst a rising mainland China. Put bluntly, the question of whether Hong Kong is irreplaceable has been raised and challenged. The central authorities and many mainland citizens seem to have taken a fresh view about the long-term strategic importance of Hong Kong in China's grand plan. Put bluntly again, some no longer think the city is still the goose that lays the golden egg.

The formula of 'one country, two systems' was originally conceived for the reunification of Taiwan. Under Deng's plan, it was to be the most practical and viable solution to end the decades-long separation across the Taiwan Strait. Beijing also hoped it would allow the smooth transition of Hong Kong from the hands of British colonists to the communist regime with a simple 'change of flag' and the replacement of a London-appointed governor by a locally-elected chief executive. The peaceful return of Hong Kong to Chinese sovereignty was meant to showcase China's rise and integration with the world.

Instead, the process of political integration under Chinese rule has proved to be tumultuous, riddled with friction and tension, controversies and crises.

One of the main controversies was the introduction of the national security legislation in 2003. Inserted into the post-handover charter known as the Basic Law, at a late stage of drafting, in the wake of the June 4th killings in 1989, Article 23 is deemed by Beijing to be the key provision that gives substance to the principle of 'one country' in the Special Administrative Region (SAR). Under the provision, Hong Kong must enact a law to safeguard national security by prohibiting acts such as subversion and sedition and theft of state secrets and it must also ban local groups from fostering ties with overseas political organisations. An attempt by Tung in his second term to enact such a law ignited a 500,000-strong march and led to his downfall in 2005; he cited health reasons for his resignation. The Tung administration withdrew the draft legislation and it has never reappeared on the legislative programme. Chief Executive-elect Carrie Lam said she had no intention to dust off the plan.

The Communist authorities decided after the 2003 march that their hands-off approach was wrong, ignoring criticism of their failure to honour the promise of 'Hong Kong people ruling Hong Kong'. Shocked and bewildered by the uproar against the Article 23 legislation, they felt adamantly that it was 'perfectly right and justified' for Hong Kong people to enact a law to safeguard national security. To Beijing, that Hong Kongers have resisted doing so shows their 'hearts have not yet returned to the Motherland'. The mainland government attributed resistance against Article 23 to Hong Kongers putting too much emphasis on the notion of 'two systems' and too little on the principle of 'one country'.

> The Communist authorities decided that their hands-off approach was wrong, ignoring criticism of their failure to honour the promise of 'Hong Kong people ruling Hong Kong'.

Since then, Beijing has tightened its grip on Hong Kong affairs. Mainland scholars of Hong Kong who had moved on to other research topics, were regrouped to conduct fresh studies on the SAR. The united front led by the Central People's Government Liaison Office in Hong Kong—the *de facto* Chinese consulate in the SAR—has been broadened and deepened. Officials from that office (known as *Sai Wan*, or the 'Western District' where the office is located) in charge of overseeing local affairs have been active in attending events. Pro-establishment legislators in Hong Kong routinely receive phone calls from the Liaison Office to chat about policy, at times getting advice from the mainland officials on how they should vote at Legislative Council meetings. There also have been credible claims that the Liaison Office has manipulated the city's District and Legislative Council elections in recent years. The alleged interference included lobbying for support of Beijing's political protégés and persuading others not to run to avoid a split of votes. The overzealous approach of the Liaison Office in lobbying votes for Carrie Lam, who was understood to be the 'only candidate' Beijing supported in the 2017 chief executive race, triggered protests even from within the pro-establishment circle.

Several years after the massive protests over Article 23, the Hong Kong Government announced a compulsory national education curriculum scheduled to begin in September 2012. Many Hong Kongers were rightfully nervous that the mainland was trying to brainwash students. Parents and students protested and after a ten-day sit-in outside the government headquarters, officials backed down. Like the Article 23 bill in 2003, the national education plan was shelved. Several pro-Beijing figures in contact with mainland authorities said the Chinese leadership blamed the prior administrations and that of Chief Executive C.Y. Leung for not standing firm on matters key to the principle of 'one country'. The officials reportedly feared the Hong Kong government compromise on national education had given rise to the pro-independence thinking prevalent in society, especially among young Hong Kongers.

According to a poll of the city's political sentiments conducted by the University of Hong Kong once or twice a year since the handover, public support and trust towards Beijing was high for a time after 1997. Public trust towards the central authorities was even higher than towards the Hong Kong Government during Tung's term. The feeling of patriotism surged during the Beijing 2008 Olympics and the Sichuan earthquake in the same year. But the Hong Kong public's support of Beijing began to decline from its peak in 2008 in the wake of several widely reported human rights abuses by Beijing as well as other mainland scandals, including episodes of poisoned food and tainted baby formula. In

2009, Beijing sentenced the writer and political activist Liu Xiaobo to eleven years in prison for inciting subversion after he co-wrote *Charter 08*, a document that called for constitutional reform in China (Liu won the 2010 Nobel Peace Prize). In 2012, the June 4th activist Li Wangyang was said to have 'committed suicide' at a detention centre in Hunan province, shortly after he gave an interview to Cable News Hong Kong during which he talked about the annual June 4th commemorations in Hong Kong and the 1989 crackdown in Beijing. By the end of 2015, five publishers from Causeway Bay Books, known for its publication and sale of books that purportedly revealed secrets of power politics in Beijing, went missing. They eventually turned up on the mainland. Bookshop owner Li Bo 'returned' to the mainland without going through the city's immigration checkpoints, sparking speculation that he had been abducted. He denied that claim, but did not reveal details of his 'return' to the mainland. The saga stoked fears that mainland security agents had enforced mainland law in Hong Kong, which was prohibited under 'one country, two systems'.

Conflicts in mainland–Hong Kong relations grew sharper after C.Y. Leung became chief executive in 2012. Leung, a building surveyor by profession, was groomed by the Communist authorities from the 1980s to play a role in the transition of Hong Kong. Partly because of that, Hong Kong people never trusted him. His hard-line stance towards the pan-democrats (those in the pro-democracy parties) has worsened the city's political divide. His failure to persuade Beijing to abandon or revise restrictions issued on August 31st, 2014, by the National People's Congress Standing Committee (NPCSC) on the chief executive election resulted in the 79-day Umbrella Movement. Under the so-called

'8/31 Decision', a candidate needs to secure the support of at least half of a Beijing-friendly 1,200-member committee before he or she can be qualified for the 'one person, one vote' election. Protesters were angry about the restrictions and demanded genuine universal suffrage in electing the chief executive. In June 2015, the pan-democrats rejected a subsequent government universal suffrage blueprint that was based on 8/31 Decision.

In March 2017, 1,194 Election Committee members cast their votes for the next chief executive. Carrie Lam beat former financial secretary John Tsang Chun-wah, 777 to 365. Woo Kwok-hing, another candidate, received twenty-one votes. Labelled by pan-democrats as 'C.Y. 2.0' and ridiculed by Tsang as 'Society Splitter 2.0' for her hard-line style, Lam was praised by Xi during a meeting with her in Beijing in April 2017. Both Xi and Premier Li Keqiang expect her to resolve longstanding problems and deep-seated contradictions in Hong Kong. Concerns over these problems and contradictions were first raised by former Premier Wen Jiabao in 2005 during a visit with the then-Chief Executive Donald Tsang Yam-kuen. Twelve years on, there is no doubt the city is still troubled by conflicts and contradictions in mainland–Hong Kong relations as manifested in political disputes over universal suffrage and over local issues such as a widening income gap, persistent housing problems and a lack of upward mobility.

In his bid for the 2017 chief executive post, John Tsang campaigned on three principles: trust, unity and hope. He was the more popular candidate according to opinion polls, but was defeated in the casting of ballots by the Election Committee stacked with pro-Beijing members. Although he was never known as a fighter for democracy, the phenomenal rise to fame of a career civil servant could be attributed to his success in articulating the hearts and minds of Hong Kongers. After twenty years on a roller coaster, people felt an affinity with his calls for trust, unity and hope. The 'John Tsang phenomenon' has been a subject of much soul-searching among pundits and in society at large.

Twenty years ago, jittery Hong Kong people braced for uncertainties over the sovereignty change. Twenty years on, Hong Kongers are once again confronted with anxieties, this time arising from the gulf between promises and realities under the twenty-year-old 'one country, two systems' constitutional experiment. It seems that nothing has changed and everything has changed.

The Mix-ups

Louisa Lim

Growing up in Hong Kong, the ghosts whispered through our lives. The susurration of the spectral chorus was a constant invisible hum, like the blood-engorged mosquitoes trapped inside our mosquito nets at night. My first encounter with the ghosts came when I began primary school at age five, just weeks after our arrival in Hong Kong.

My new school was Glenealy Junior School, whose mission was to provide a thoroughly colonial education to the children of expats. Our first lesson consisted of memorising the Lord's Prayer, undoubtedly the brainchild of our school founder and headmistress, Miss Doreen Handyside, a stout childless spinster straight out of Roald Dahl. An avid golfer, she had a head of tight curls piled high, and darting, beady eyes primed to spot naughtiness, which she handled smartly with a staunch whack across the palm with a ruler.

I didn't care. That first morning, I was triumphant in my new yellow-and-white-checked cotton dress, with my brown satchel proudly slung across my chest. I had longed to go to school for years, and I was surprised and thrilled that so many of my classmates had the same sepia skin and chestnut hair as me. In the English countryside, my Singapore-Chinese father had been such a rarity that the postman asked my British mother if she had married an Eskimo. Now, suddenly I was part of a tribe that I hadn't even known existed. I was vibrating with a heady mix of excitement, trepidation and joy. But straight away, the school ghost ruined everything.

I first heard about her the same way I heard about menstruation and our-parents-being-Father-Christmas: in solemn, fervent whispers from my elder sister, Emma. There was a door just inside the girls' bathroom that opened onto a vertical shaft, she said, and legend had it that a young cleaning amah had tripped down the shaft—or had she been pushed?—and fallen to her death. Now she haunted the toilets where she had bled to death, alone and in pain. From that moment on, my days were spent strategizing how to avoid being by myself in the haunted restroom. On the very rare occasions when I went alone, I would sit on the lavatory, weeing as fast as humanly possible, my heart thumping and my palms sweaty as I glared at the grey Formica stall, willing the ghost amah not to float through the locked door.

She was so real to me that I could see her neat black bun and grey cotton trousers as she conscientiously swilled water round the pale pink-and-green-tiled bathroom floor, pausing to rinse her tattered grey mop in a red plastic bucket. Sometimes I even saw the baby she carried in a sling on her back, its head lolling on the small fat neck that was soon to be snapped. The chubby infant was so real to me that over time I couldn't remember if she had been an integral part of the legend or my own fevered addition.

In my head, I imagined transfixing the rest of my class by spreading the Legend of the Amah in hushed, horrified whispers. I know that I didn't. Just the thought of the phantom amah gripped me with a clammy kind of dread that squeezed my heart like the ghost-that-sits-on-your-chest-at-night. The slightest word would have dispelled this paralysis, but a suffocating blanket of fear and lassitude rendered speech impossible. I was so terrified of the ghost amah that I succumbed to the spate of knicker-wetting that hit my class. At home, I sat on my mother's lap and sobbed with shame. When she asked me why I hadn't gone to the bathroom, I didn't tell her about the phantom amah. I knew that, as a no-nonsense Brit, she wouldn't understand.

She briskly discounted the existence of ghosts. But we knew better. The proof was all around us. Walking to school, we smelled pungent wafts of burning incense from the small red shrines sunk into the walls at the entrances of apartment blocks. Sometimes sticks of incense were impaled into a single orange. These were offerings to the dead, since smells drift over temporal boundaries into the ghost world. Aromas can sate the hungry ghosts, the dead abandoned by their uncaring offspring to vengefully roam the earth, famished for all eternity. During the month-long Hungry Ghost Festival, the malevolent spirits were mollified by tiny pyres of paper money in square metal tins beside makeshift shrines of candles and food offerings. The small conflagrations punctuated the pavements, thickening the sticky dusk across the island.

My father not only believed in ghosts, but had seen one himself back in Singapore. On a dare, he had gone into a dilapidated colonial mansion with friends. On the way out, they had passed an old man in the entrance hall. When my father mentioned how odd it had been to see someone else in the house, it transpired no one else had seen the old man. When they went back to check, the old man had vanished. No one doubted it was a ghost. Spirits were a part of my father's world; family legend even included the tale of a photograph of his dead mother, which came to life to scold a daughter-in-law for her laziness. The talking photograph was only partly effective, since it terrified the daughter-in-law so much that she ran away. We clamoured for the frisson of his ghost stories, but he rarely told them when my mother was around.

Our small world was suspended between the two cultures. My parents had transgressed racial norms, and continued to quietly do so. Though ethnically Chinese, my father had managed to snag a position as a colonial civil servant, so he became that most oxymoronic of categories: the Chinese expat. My posh British mother, despite her execrable tone-deaf Cantonese, became one of the first experts on Hong Kong's local cultural heritage, spending her spare time trudging around abandoned study halls and dusty earth god shrines, a pastime we found unutterably dull.

Our parents' social world revolved around an unfortunately-named club for couples consisting of Chinese men and Western women. The Mix-up Club was born out of the social opprobrium that such pairings attracted, shunned by both Western and Chinese communities, though it was later renamed the M Club to avoid being mistaken for a cross-cultural swingers' outfit. We often celebrated holidays with the other Mix-ups, the kids running wild as the Western wives swapped Chinese recipes and the Chinese fathers compared their children's exam results.

We walked the mile to and from school in packs. When we were feeling particularly brave, we would dare each other to run alone through the corridors of a house on Conduit Road haunted by a British sea captain who had leapt off the balcony to his death. Holding my breath, with all my senses vibrating, I would speed through the corridors in a flustered panic. The rhythmic slap-slap-slap of my white plimsolls against the floor echoed behind me, sounding ever more like the footsteps of a phantom pursuer at my heels.

Hong Kong has always been a city of refugees, outcasts and chancers fleeing communism, poverty or disgrace in one form or another.

Ghosts of another kind dogged the families at my school. Hong Kong has always been a city of refugees, outcasts and chancers fleeing communism, poverty or disgrace in one form or another. Over the four decades since we first met, my classmates' family histories have unspooled over pints of cold beer into stories that were operatic in their scope and tragedy. Tales of huge mansions lost by opium addicts, of ancestors forced to hide in the jungle, of family fortunes destroyed in fires that burned down entire villages, of children bought and children sold, stories of unimaginable public disgrace in a society where face is valued above all else. As insiders, we were privy to epic secrets. As outsiders, we shared them openly.

Those ghosts—and the fear of them—were a driving force. Our parents, shaped by their families' turbulent histories, wanted to pave our paths with solid exam results leading to respectable jobs. They hoped our diligence would smooth the stigma of their unorthodox matches. We were mongrels, neither true *gweilos* nor purely Chinese. We mix-ups didn't even have a proper name; Anglo-Chinese was too Victorian, Eurasian bore a ring of the Raj, half-caste was simply offensive.

Like ghosts, we flitted between two worlds, becoming inter-preters and intermediaries between the two sides of ourselves. We were people from the future who transcended the stale fixed identities of the past and whose worldview was formed by con-stant shape-shifting and code-switching. We never questioned our right to think of ourselves as Hong Kongers. To us, Hong Kong's unusual status suspended between British and Chinese rule made it the embodiment of our identity, while we were natural corollaries of its peculiar political proposition.

We had grown up in a place whose history was intentionally left blank.

As a child of colony, I was sent away at thirteen to a British girls' boarding school, my suitcases bulging with royal blue pinafores, a heavy navy cloak and the stiff straw boater that made up my new school uniform. From then on, homecom-ing became ritual. That split second of arrival stepping off the plane, ambushed by that familiar stench, feeling myself sliding back into kilter as the heat dissolved that brittle British mask of detachment.

Back then, I had no idea that any acceptance of our mixed race in Hong Kong was at best grudging, at worst purely aspira-tional. Our most important streets were named after colonial governors, but I had no idea the men we memorialised had pushed through anti-Chinese legislation that prefigured South African apartheid. The eighth governor, James Pope Hennessy, along whose eponymous road the bottle-green trams trundled, actually listed the ways the British distrusted the vast majority of Chinese residents as 'dishonest, potentially dangerous, malevolent, engaged in mysterious secret societies, foolish in their religious beliefs and only suitable to be clerks, shroffs, amahs, houseboys and coolies."[1]

In 1842, the Chief Magistrate William Caine, along whose road I used to walk, introduced a night-time curfew for Chinese alone that lasted for the most part of four decades.[2] The second governor, Sir John Davis, on whose Mount we used to hike, required Chinese to carry registration tickets or face flogging, a punishment not meted out to British residents.[3] Then in 1904 a ban was placed on Chinese and Eurasians living on the Peak by the colonial administrator, Sir Francis Henry May, who later became the fifteenth governor.[4] This last discovery was a stunning personal blow since I was distantly related to May and used to boast about this in the playground in happy ignorance of my ancestor's racist authoritarianism.[5] In fact, he was most famous for being the subject of a failed assassination attempt on the first day of his governorship.[6] We had grown up in a place whose history was intentionally left blank[7]. We did not learn

---

1 Wesley-Smith, Peter and Chan, Ming. K (Ed), *Precarious Balance: Hong Kong Between China and Britain, 1942–1992*, Routledge, London, 1994, Chapter 6.

2 Munn, Christopher, *Anglo-China: Chinese People and British Rule in Hong Kong, 1841–1880*, Curzon Press, Richmond 2001 page 131.

3 Eitel, E.J, *Europe in China*, Oxford University Press, Hong Kong, 1983, page 238.

4 Welsh, Frank, *A History of Hong Kong*, Harper Collins, London, 1997, page 342.

5 Ibid, page 360.

6 http://query.nytimes.com/mem/archive-free/pdf?res=9902E7D-61F31E233A25757C0A9619C946396D6CF.

7 Ma, Eric Kit-wai, *Culture, Politics and Television in Hong Kong*, Routledge, London, 1999 page 29.

of the Opium Wars or Treaty Ports, though glancing references were made to foot-binding and rickshaws as exemplars of Chinese cruelty. Through Miss Handyside and her ilk, we had internalised the colonial mindset without even realizing it. So conditioned had I become that it did not even hit me until the very first day that Hong Kong returned to Chinese sovereignty. By then, I was working in the newsroom of a thoroughly amateur local television station, stammering my way through stilted, utterly news-free reports on bridge openings and lantern festivals. As the handover approached, we knew we were ill-equipped to report on our transfer of sovereignty, though we had gamely planned hour after hour of live feeds.

I was supposed to be covering the story from Beijing, but I had resisted, making excuses because I couldn't countenance the thought of not being in Hong Kong. So I stayed in the office, getting strobe glimpses of the anachronistic pomp as I sped around the newsroom, frantically editing pieces and banging out host intros. I ran past screens showing the last governor, Chris Patten, dripping, as he made his defiant farewell address in the pouring rain. I was in the edit suites when the Democratic Party leader Martin Lee Chu-ming appeared on the balcony of the then-Legislative Council building, pledging that democracy would return to Hong Kong. I don't even remember where I was at that moment when the British flag slid down the flagpole, but I do know that I did not have time to process how this moment of transition could upend the fulcrum on which our lives balanced.

It was the next morning that I realised in a moment of sickening clarity just how great our lack of foresight had been.

The Pattens had already tearfully motored out on Her Majesty's Yacht *Britannia* and the foreign press were packing up. When I stumbled into work on July 1ˢᵗ, the newsroom was almost empty. The news agenda was sparser still. Our focus on the British departure had been so all-encompassing that we simply had forgotten to think about Hong Kong under Chinese rule. We had not mapped out any plans or themes going forward. We had reached the end of history, and, even though our story had not ended, we found we had nothing else to say.

I was sent to the Hong Kong Exhibition and Convention Centre with vague exhortations to look out for news stories. My cameraman and I ended up vainly running after Deng Xiaoping's son, Deng Pufang, trying to shout questions at him as he was wheeled speedily by. We were spinning in the wind, completely unprepared in every way for an event that had been scheduled for ninety-nine years.

Soon after, I left to work for the BBC, a job that ended up taking me to China for a decade. Each subsequent homecoming was further tinctured with trepidation. In that time, Hong Kong's landmass grew as its harbour shrank, while the soundtrack of the street tilted ever more towards Putonghua. My Hong Kong was, as always, in motion.

In 2014, I was glued to my laptop as thousands occupied the streets of Admiralty. After police fired teargas, one of the crowd chants was '*Heung Gong Yan!* Hong Kong People!' In the kickstream of my thrill at this defiant assertion of identity was the thud of recognition that this did not include people like me. Was I Chinese enough to be a Hong Konger? Could you even call yourself a Hong Konger if you weren't a native Cantonese speaker? Had I ever even been a Hong Konger? If not, where then was home?

My kind has always excelled at negotiation, but as the off-spring of tigers and lions, we fail at failure. We're bad at accepting defeat. I still claim Hong Kong as my hometown, but I see the day approaching when it no longer accepts me. The way I look, the way I speak, these are out of alignment with the forces that roil Hong Kong politics. Loving Hong Kong has become a political tool utilised by forces of nationalism that have no use for people like me.

My childhood vision of a place of racial harmony marrying East and West turned out to be a mirage. I had lived in a series of bubbles, each an act of will, painstakingly constructed by determined empire-builders both big and small. My hopeful myopia meant that I had not seen beyond the confines of my bubble, nor had I understood its fragility, for its foundations were fictions that bore no weight. But it was my Hong Kong, and I mourned my dispossession from the beautiful, impossible ideal of Hong Kong as a cultural and ethnic entrepôt.

As I thought about my childhood, I remembered how my days had been ruled by fear of the Ghost Amah of the Girls' Toilet. It was time, I decided, to finally make my peace with her by breaking the silence. My first step was to casually bring up the subject with my old classmates with a tone of practiced nonchalance. To my utter surprise, no one else remembered the phantom cleaner. I was baffled. How could it be that no one else could even recall the ghost that had terrified me for so many years? It was time to return to the source of the legend, my sister Emma. One winter's day, I rang her at her chilly home in Northumberland. When I mentioned the Ghost Amah, silence cascaded down the line. This was unusual for Emma, whose words usually tumbled out in unstoppable torrents. Finally, she spoke. 'You know,' she said haltingly, 'I don't really remember it. But I think I made the whole thing up as a joke. You didn't really believe it, did you?' That was the thing: I really did believe it. I had believed it all.

How I End up Here

Tang Siu Wa 鄧小樺

It was May of 2004 and I was doing some substitute teaching. Exhausted after morning classes and with no appetite for lunch, I was dizzy, sitting at someone else's desk, my head filled with tasks like student homework and teaching schedules. Too reluctant to carry out the to-do list I had drafted on scrap paper, I was surfing the web aimlessly when all of a sudden I came across a blog and realised the postings about June 4th had begun: every year, people set a schedule for themselves, counting down the transition from mid-spring to early summer when they start digging up personal and collective memories, like moist soil that loosens little by little, softly reminding each other to gather in Victoria Park. All of a sudden I was overwhelmed. What am I still doing? That time of the year has come. Tears rolled down my face. At the same time a clear voice rang in my heart, urging like a loyal, old-fashioned alarm clock: I must wake up before June 4th.

Waking up

I was in primary five in 1989. On the midday news I saw

three college students kneeling in front of the Great Hall of the People, the student in the middle holding up a huge paper roll. It suddenly occurred to me that something had gone wrong. Why should they be kneeling down? No government should let its college students wait for its response on their knees. It is the 1980s. How come we are still kneeling?

Later in college, I read that the gesture of 'kneeling' is closely associated with absolute monarchism.

But at that moment in 1989, it was that scene that revealed to me for the first time that some people were risking their fate for others, perhaps even for the so-called nation. I have no idea why a kid who had only read Chinese classics such as *Dream of the Red Chamber* could have thought of such things. And my young mind seemed to know that no one would understand how I felt. I didn't talk to my family about it. Deeply upset, I was inconsolable watching the TV news, tears burning in my eyes.

News on TV and in newspapers began to pour in. Mother and I lived in a room rented from a relative. The landlady, an old woman, began to cut newspaper clips every day. When 1.5 million protesters took to the street in Hong Kong on May 28th, everyone in the house joined the rally. We made a hat out of a painting of mine, the first time my own work was turned into a protest prop. There were frequent strikes and assemblies at school. Though I didn't remember anything the headmaster and teachers said, I listened to the song 'Blood-stained Glory' many times. A classmate who heard me sing it into the phone was surprised that I could actually sing. In fact I'm still a terrible singer to this day, but I've listened to the song so many times that I remember the lyrics and melody by heart, the way I would recite passages from books.

Growing up

What was it like at that time? I could recall some faint hopes—like starlight that sometimes sprinkled on our hair at night—that China might change. More and more people gathered at Tiananmen Square. The China that had gone through the catastrophic decade of the Cultural Revolution that put my ancestors through the humiliation of the Red Guards and left my aunt schizophrenic, might change. I've witnessed hope without bearing hatred. For this I can't but count myself as lucky.

Early in the morning on June 4th, I somehow woke up and saw the crackdown on television. I was shocked to tears. The whole street scene of the capital was turned upside down. Before that I just thought it must be very hot on the Square, not knowing what they were doing. It had never occurred to me that we would have to worry about them dying. I cried out of helplessness.

On a piece of A4 paper I wrote, 'INHUMANE BRUTALITY'. With nowhere else to post, I ended up posting it outside the window where we hang clothes to dry. My gesture was frowned upon by a young lady who shared the flat with us. 'You're that worked up?' Having experienced the Cultural Revolution, she was wary of expressing political opinions. The school summoned us for silent mourning on the playground, during which I cried my heart out. When we returned to the classroom, one of my best friends told me with indifference: 'I didn't know you'd fling yourself into it.' Did I feel misunderstood? I did not even feel that way. Sorrow surrounded me like an eggshell with a glowing aura: it doesn't matter, it doesn't matter at all. No one can really stop you as the source of sorrow lies in your heart. Things that come from within are invincible. You will be driven to accomplish a lot, including those things you did not believe you were capable of doing. There are people who sit and wait to be changed while you take action yourself.

There were strikes across different industries, voluntary flower presenting at the Xinhua News Agency in Wan Chai, unofficial funeral halls set up all over the city for public mourning. Though it may sound a bit like wishful thinking to suggest all these were of actual help, everyone was acting spontaneously out of inconsolable sadness. Sorrow leads to spontaneous actions. I imagine everyone in the city at that time carried an eggshell with a glowing aura like I did, one that grew inside.

My class teacher back then was an intern who loved Chinese but was not good at teaching and wore verdant green and light-yellow floral dresses. My fellow students were not particularly fond of her, yet she once walked over to talk with me about June 4th. As a result of the disturbance to the teaching schedule that year, no one really paid attention to schoolwork, thus I came first in the examination for the first time. Later I wrote a composition on June 4th for my secondary six literature examination and got the highest mark in class, despite the essay being marked as 60 per cent off-topic, though I forget now what the assigned topic was. Whether for exams or in creative writing, I've been writing about June 4th in a lyrical way. But the fact is I've been benefiting from the massacre right from the beginning, while all I've done in return is of no practical help but only confirms my sense of existence. In this sense, I'll always be in debt to June 4th.

In debt

In debt to whom? To the deceased. How strange that we are in debt to the living and the departed whom we do not know.

In 'Elegy for the Martyrs', a June 4th memorial song, there are lines that go like this:

> *Here I was trapped*
> *Couldn't fight with you shoulder to shoulder*
> *Now I just can't say how heartbroken I am*

I would understand it this way. Living in a relatively liberal city, Hong Kongers are not ignorant of the dark side of the People's Republic, and would secretly agree that Hong Kong, though small in size, is to a certain degree responsible for promoting democracy and freedom in China. While we Hong Kongers had always assumed our role to be a subtle, clandestine one, undertaking the endeavours gradually and in a winding way, it surprised us when millions of people under totalitarian rule stood up in 1989 for national reforms, with perseverance and sacrifices beyond our imagination. These forerunners awakened in us a belief we had always secretly held. When passion and idealism stitched up the break in history, we could not wait to follow. At that time the whole city was roused to action. We had the entertainment industry calling for benefit performances, college students and leaders from various sectors going to Beijing, and mountains of materials donated without a second thought. All these actions demonstrated a desire to 'fight shoulder to shoulder'. We were comrades. We had never felt so close to China. Yet when the critical moment arrived, it turned out that we could not meet our fate together.

We are indebted, therefore we shall keep on telling the story, breaking through the information blockade. Not only that. We have not done enough in our daily lives. We should have dug deeper into the issue, but we did not. C. and W., a young couple, told me that it had been twenty years, that they must do something. They wanted to return to Tiananmen Square and sit there for a whole night, doing nothing but smoking. C. thought of working on a collection of oral histories and W. of filming a documentary featuring our parents' genera-tion. Even ordinary citizens have their June 4th complex. W.T. told me her idea of compiling a poetry collection on June 4th. L. and I talked about co-ed-iting a book on the massacre when we were on the street after a typhoon. He suggested contrasting the 'before' and 'after' attitude of all those who did an about-turn; I said it sounds too much like telling tales. I want something on collective memories. It was the better part of a year before the twentieth anniversary of June 4th. We were surrounded by crowds of dragonflies that went out mating after the typhoon.

> We are indebted, therefore we shall keep on telling the story, breaking through the information blockade.

All these things could have been done, yet we didn't try. That's because our lives are bound by schedules, leaving no room for June 4th. It is not okay to have left no room for something we have cared so much for more than twenty years. We are lazy. We still owe something to June 4th.

We think we are indebted because we once regarded ourselves as comrades. For years this sense of indebtedness has been maintaining a sense of comradeship, which points to an imagined community formed by the living and the dead. A kind of publicness emerges wavering and flickering like candle flames. And thanks, to Yuan Mu*, our role becomes clear: we shall persist in the battle against lies by telling the true story. It is the scattered stories circulating among the folks that build up a sense of belonging to the country. June 4th narratives are characterised by identification with ordinary people and criticism of the regime, features that can be traced back to the nationalist concerns since the May 4th Movement in 1919.

But is such empty talk all I have to say?

Back to the Square

Every time I visit Beijing, I sit in Tiananmen Square to expose my skin to the sun that has not changed from that day. Apparitions there keep telling stories of the past even in broad daylight. L is not like me. He avoided Beijing for twenty years, for he could not bear that place. From his trips to Beijing in May

---

* Translator's note: Yuan Mu, Spokesman for the State Council of the People's Republic of China in 1989, claimed that no students or civilians were killed in Tiananmen Square.

and November in 1989 he still clearly recalls the bullet holes on residential buildings and the damage around the Monument to the People's Heroes. He said troops fired warning shots into the air and stray bullets killed many civilians who just popped their heads out from their houses to see what was happening. He always pauses a lot when he speaks of this, as if the recollection is unbearable, and I have to support him and his narrative with my imagination.

Every year in the small hours of June 3rd, a group of social activists and cultural workers gather under The Flying Frenchman statue, a man with one partial wing, outside the Hong Kong Cultural Centre, casually sitting on the ground, singing and reading poetry in memory of June 4th. It was in 2008 when someone brought us 'The Internationale' with new lyrics written by him. The last two lines made me burst into tears as if I was slapped in the face:

> *One day we shall be singing*
> *On Tiananmen Square*

The original version goes like this:

> *The Internationale*
> *Shall one day come true*

Ideals are forever calling us, even though the meaning of the word *internationale* is worn down—our country has become a foreign land.

Because of that song, I insisted on going to Beijing in 2009 no matter what. That night L. and I walked along the Square surrounded by exotic buildings with flashing light bulbs.

While the lampposts were still the old ones, there were no longer youth cyclists dressed in white with ribbon sashes streaming. I got what I wanted, humming, 'One day we shall be singing/On Tiananmen Square.' But I understood at once. With decent clothes and a foreign travel bag, and with hotel people waving at us, I would certainly be allowed to sing, because I looked in every way like a tourist. It seems that if you are a tourist you may do whatever you like. But why can I only return to the Square as a tourist?

Tiananmen brings me familiarity and comfort just as I'm at ease in graveyards, like a flower of destiny planted in the right vase.

Feeling utterly useless, I shed tears and stealthily wiped them away. The attempt to cover up only made me look more like a tourist. Even my voice turned cartoon-like. As for L., he was still mired in the abyss of speechlessness: night in Beijing means only one thing to him, and that is crackdown. We ended up having a quarrel that night, though I know we have the same map of the capital in our mind. Chang'an Avenue, Di'anmen, Muxidi, all these street names and places sound so familiar as the route taken by tanks entering the city was told over and over again. But then, what we shared would ironically further complicate our communication.

As I was travelling with a companion, I did not visit the Square again to do what I would like to do, like light a cigarette, take a drag, and stick it in the ground upside down, the ritual of mourning tacitly recognised in Beijing. Again I miss the Square. I want to be back. The colour of the lighting there reminds me of the dusky sky on the night of the crackdown. History clouds over the capital city, in which ghosts from different generations are singing songs of various tempo that merge into a gigantic undercurrent. June 4th often gives me the feeling that I'm together with the dead, so Tiananmen brings me familiarity and comfort just as I'm at ease in graveyards, like a flower of destiny planted in the right vase.

Sorrow

In my off-topic composition I quoted a line from Song Dynasty poet Yan Jidao:

> *Lotuses say not a word*
> *   when water flows in vain*
> *melancholy are we for the flowers*
> *   withering year after year*

I was, of course, quoting out of context, yet I'm glad I've been associating literary works about private affairs with June 4th since a young age. Yes, I would cry at the sight of anything about June 4th. Sometimes I cry my eyes out at the candlelight vigil, using up my tissues and messing up my sleeves, which probably shocks people around me. While it is June 4th that I'm crying for, such collective sorrow also stirs up my own misery and frustration that can be traced far back: unattainable dreams, ambitions beyond my ability, betrayals, impossible loves, exhaustion that wells up within me, and day-to-day conflicts and misunderstandings. All these flow through my bones one by one. I reckon that I've learnt to be sensitive to all these because of June 4th.

Victoria Park on the night of the candlelight vigil is a surreal space, a place filled with all kinds of meanings. Such an immense lake of sorrow emerges for one night every year amid the highly-efficient operation of a machine-like modern city. I believe those who throw themselves into the lake with friends after work and dinner arrive with the determination to leave everything behind, seeing the vigil as a 'come-or-die' occasion. Therefore, how could sorrow not be a source of motivation? Every year I would push myself so hard before June 4th, like I was taking an exam, and accomplish something different from what I had done, just as one may reach beyond oneself in the face of crisis.

I write about June 4th a lot. This time I thought of writing an article to sum up everything that has to do with June 4th and me, but I rejected the idea. When reality is going nowhere, it becomes tempting to sum up. If such temptation is eroding our motivation, resist it. The fight regarding June 4th is a long journey that will suffer setbacks again and again, and involves repeated efforts. If we cannot manage repetition, we won't be able to go on fighting. Thus the key would be to progress through repetition. We shall not expect a one-off solution, settle for mere emotional venting, forget what we once believed and possessed or give up imagining the future. Neither shall we tolerate evasions nor deem ourselves unique enough to steal the spotlight from the main issue. In this way we shall write history.

Translated from the Chinese by Aurora Tsui.

Loss

Oscar Ho Hing Kay

On Anger and Love in Post-Occupy Hong Kong

Timothy O'Leary

I remember watching a documentary at home in Ireland, when I was about eighteen years old, about Harvey Milk, the first openly gay city official in San Francisco, who was assassinated in 1978. The one detail of that film that has stayed with me ever since was a scene from a commemorative march after the assassination. The march was peaceful, perhaps even silent. As the mourners move solemnly through the street, a passerby begins to shout at them, 'Where is your anger? Where is your anger?'

Many years later, on October 6th, 2015, I myself co-organised a silent protest march at the University of Hong Kong (HKU). That protest was driven by strong emotions for me as well as for my fellow teachers and students. In my case, it was driven mostly by anger. In the following months, I participated in other protests, in which the anger, the shouting and the slogans were at the forefront. But I never felt comfortable at those events.

Today, three years after the Umbrella Movement, and two years after one of its many after-shocks hit HKU, the emotions unleashed by the movement and the stalled political reform process continue to move this city. Each of us, whether locally born, a permanent resident, or a temporary visitor, must decide how to process, reflect and act upon these emotions.

I spoke at my first political rally in August 2014. As head of the School of Humanities at HKU, I had made a public statement in support of the 511 students who were arrested at a peaceful sit-in on the night of July 1ˢᵗ. So I was invited to come to a rally to speak about the principle of civil disobedience, on the doorstep of Wan Chai Police Headquarters.

Back in August 2014, the disobedience in Hong Kong was very civil indeed. I remember a young police officer politely helping me to cross a cordon, so I could enter the backstage area. Long time pro-democracy activist Martin Lee Chuming spoke before me. He spoke in Cantonese, so I couldn't understand what he was saying, but he was speaking in a measured, reasonable tone. Then I gave a short talk on the philosophical basis for the idea of civil disobedience, with the help of simultaneous translation by student leader Alex Chow Yong-kang. People laughed when I made a joke about then-Chief Executive C.Y. Leung's lawlessness, so I knew they were following my speech. But the tone was calm, relaxed, and attentive.

After me, the firebrand lawmaker 'Long Hair' Leung Kwokhung spoke. As far as I remember, he was holding a copy of

Gandhi's writings. Satyagraha meets Che Guevara outside the Wan Chai Police Headquarters, and even though he spoke with more obvious passion than either Martin Lee or I had done, the mood was still calm, cool, almost academic.

The only ominous sign at that event was that some of the police were carrying odd-looking poles strapped to their backs that looked almost like samurai swords. Nobody I asked seemed to know what they were, but they later became well-known, the infamous 'Disperse or We Fire' crowd control banners mounted on wooden poles.

In late September 2014, I went to Australia to visit my daughters. I don't remember if Benny Tai Yiu-ting had declared the Occupy Movement, or Umbrella Movement, before I left; what I do remember is that I was in Canberra on September 28th when I heard the news that police had used tear gas. The emotions I felt in that moment were very intense. I felt a strong urge to go back to Hong Kong. This was driven by the sense of responsibility I felt towards the students who were leading the protests. Many students from HKU were of course involved, but it wasn't just about 'my' students, it was a feeling about all the students who were involved, from universities and secondary schools across Hong Kong. The same students I had seen sitting peacefully on the street outside Wan Chai Police Headquarters in August, eager to learn about the principles of civil disobedience, were now wearing homemade gas masks and brandishing umbrellas on the streets of Admiralty, Causeway Bay and Mong Kok. I didn't think I could do anything for them, and I wasn't planning to fight with the police myself, but I felt a strong urge to go back.

The next day, I went to the campus of the Australian National University in Canberra. One of the first things I saw was a small group of students from Hong Kong who had set up a table with a petition. I don't remember what the petition was asking for, or to whom it was addressed, but the students were handing out yellow ribbons to people who signed it. I was taken aback by the strength of my emotional response. I went straight up to talk to them, and I felt like hugging them. I wanted them to understand that I, too, was a Hong Konger, even though I couldn't speak their language. I signed the petition, took a photo with them, all of us wearing our yellow ribbons. When I met my daughter, I took her back to the table to sign the petition and got a yellow ribbon for her too. It felt like such a small and futile gesture, but at that time, it was all I could do.

That was the moment I realised I loved Hong Kong. Not in the sense of loving the food, the street life, the people, the culture— in a way that even a tourist might love a city—but in some deeper, more lasting way. I had now lived in Hong Kong longer than in any other place in my adult life; it had become my home.

In September 2016, I attended a seminar by a former Hong Kong University professor who was returning to HKU to talk about the current political situation. She began her talk by saying that she had 'a strong emotional attachment' to Hong Kong. I began to think about what that means exactly, to have a strong emotional attachment to a place. What struck me is that it means that all the emotions one feels about the place are intensified. Not just love, admiration, respect, but also fear, anxiety and anger.

Anger, anxiety and fear are quite often exactly the right things to be feeling.

There is a widely-received idea that the first of these (love, admiration, respect) are positive emotions, while the latter (fear, anxiety, anger) are negative. I have always found that characterisation to be inadequate. Emotions are emotions, they move us in all sorts of ways, sometimes in ways that can be called positive, sometimes negative. But no emotion is inherently either positive or negative. Anger, anxiety and fear are quite often exactly the right things to be feeling. In the summer of 2015, I began thinking about this theoretical question in the context of my own very real, steadily growing anger about what was happening at HKU.

Two things made me angry that summer. First, there was the escalating attack on the reported nominee for the position of vice president (Staffing and Resources) at HKU. Professor Johannes Chan Man-mun, the former dean of the Faculty of Law, was widely reported to be the nominee for this senior position, but he was being viciously attacked in mainland-owned media outlets (in particular *Wen Wei Po*). Professor Chan was dean when Benny Tai, of the Department of Law, founded Occupy Central with Love and Peace. Even though Chan had already stepped down from his deanship and was out of Hong Kong during the autumn of 2014, it seemed that he was being held personally responsible for nurturing the Umbrella Movement.

Second, it seemed that HKU Council was wavering in the face of this mounting criticism. Earlier, Arthur Li Kwok-cheung, a notorious pro-establishment figure, had been appointed to the Council by the chief executive, C.Y. Leung. Then, in August 2015, the Council postponed its decision on the appointment on the grounds that they needed to wait for a new provost to be appointed (an appointment which had still not been made by June 2017). All during August 2015, as colleagues began to trickle back to Hong Kong from holidays and research trips, there was a mounting sense of anger. My anger came from the sense that forces were at play that could undermine the university and were meant to inflict misguided revenge, and to teach a lesson—a lesson of fear—to academics and students across Hong Kong. The absurdity of the 'waiting for the provost' excuse seemed especially designed to elicit academic ire. How stupid did they take us to be?

At the same time, I was receiving calls from journalists asking me when the staff would do something. I had the same question myself, but I told the journalists that once everyone was back, something was sure to happen. Nothing did happen until September 29th, 2015. That night, the HKU Council voted to reject the nomination of Chan for the position. In the following days, I brought together a small group of colleagues from Law and Social Science to organise a protest. What was the mood on campus in those days? Anger, frustration and fear. I mentioned to a colleague that I was organising a protest, and she said something like, 'You can say goodbye to your career.' The protest we organised took place one week after the Council decision, on October 6th, 2015. The original idea of holding a moment of silence near the library had grown into a silent march across campus, with participants dressed in academic gowns or in black. There were no banners, no slogans, no shouting. There was to be one speech only, delivered by me, at the bottom of the Sun Yat-sen steps near the Main Library. As we made plans over the weekend, we thought maybe fifty to 100 staff would join us. Our fear was that nobody would show up because nobody cared. But, on the day, more than two thousand academics, administrators and students joined the protest.

There was something very eerie and moving about that march. As we set off, a huge wall of journalists and photographers backed away in front of us. We walked, slowly, silently, firmly, with the lunchtime crowds scrambling to get out of our path. If they hadn't heard about the protest in advance, they would have been bewildered by what they saw. Just before I left my office, one of my daughters rang me and asked if I was nervous about the protest and about the speech I was going to make. It was a well-timed question, because it forced me to pay attention to what I was actually feeling. What was it? Anger? Trepidation? Anxiety? My answer, as far as I remember, was that I felt grim determination. I think the photographs of that day convey that too. The faces are stony, set, serious, grim.

In January 2016, I spoke at a rally in Central that protested against the appointment of Arthur Li as chairman of HKU Council. Two elements of my experience that day frame my thinking about anger and politics. After I spoke, a leading figure in the pan-democratic camp remarked to me that she thought anger was the refuge of the powerless. I was a bit surprised by this, but I didn't really have a response at the time. Then, after all the speeches had been made, I was encouraged to take part in the protest march to Government House. I was given a placard to hold, but since it was written in Chinese and I couldn't understand it, I managed to hand it on to somebody else. Then I was asked to stand in the front row holding the main banner. I was a little reluctant to do this, but I finally agreed. As we set off, preceded as usual by the press and the police, we began to chant some slogans. These were all in Cantonese, except one: 'Arthur Li, You Will Pay.' Of course, I knew that this was an allusion to Li's reported intimidation of an academic many years earlier with the words 'you will pay'. But, despite my opposition to the system that allows Hong Kong's chief executive to appoint the chairman of HKU Council, and despite my belief that Arthur Li was not a good candidate for the position, I nevertheless was not comfortable walking through Central chanting 'Arthur Li, You Will Pay.'

Is this simply because I am a mild-mannered academic who is not used to marching and chanting anything at all? Partly, yes. But it is also because, even though I wasn't prepared to reject anger as the last resort of the powerless, I also wasn't prepared to give vent to my anger in this particular way.

In August 2016, a visiting American philosopher spoke in Hong Kong about anger and justice. I wasn't able to attend her talk, but I heard (perhaps inaccurately) that her argument was basically that anger is a bad thing—at least, a bad thing in the context of political conflict and struggle. There it was again, the idea that anger is a negative and destructive emotion, one that should be excluded from politics and from public discourse. But if we exclude anger from public life, don't we also exclude love? Is it possible to limit our strong emotional attachments to the so-called positive emotions?

The question, in public and private life, is not whether our emotions are 'positive' or 'negative', but how we deal with them, how we act on them, how we let them guide us. When the passerby at the Harvey Milk memorial demanded 'Where is your anger?' he didn't realise that there was already a great deal of anger there, silently, in the street. Anger doesn't always come in the form of shouting, abuse or violence, just as love isn't always gentle, caring and supportive. But anger, like love, can be hard to handle. As Aristotle recognised, 'Anybody can become angry, that is easy; but to be angry with the right person, and to the right degree, and at the right time, for the right purpose, and in the right way, that is not within everybody's power and is not easy.' We can add that being angry in the right way sometimes doesn't look like anger at all. Sometimes, in its silence, it might make people wonder

> If we exclude anger from public life, don't we also exclude love?

where our anger is, but that doesn't mean that it is any less present, both as a guide and a motivator. The challenge for all of us in a post-Umbrella Movement Hong Kong is to hold on to both our anger and our love, and to learn how to let them guide us—to the right degree, at the right time, for the right purpose and in the right way. Like love, anger is sometimes silent, but it moves us nonetheless.

Have Political Parties Reached the End of the Road?

Margaret Ng

G rowing up in post-war Hong Kong, we knew that parties, meaning political parties, were taboo. Party, or *dong*, meant the Chinese Communist Party. Kuomintang, the Nationalist Party, was a fading shadow meaningful only for Taiwan. The Communist Party was a real presence, the agent of the dreaded power across the border. We had a real taste of that power in the 1967 riots, which started as a labour dispute and was quickly turned into a violent disturbance organised by the local communist unions against the colonial government, lasting from May to December. From July on, bomb attacks were a daily scare and the city was brought to a near standstill.

I was then a student at the University of Hong Kong. The riots also woke us up to the need to think about Hong Kong's fate after 1997.

The taboo was broken by the Sino–British talks. Political debates about Hong Kong's future became a territory-wide concern. Small groups were formed by people interested in participating in politics in one way or another. It was soon the consensus that democracy could only be brought about by the development of political parties. In the aftermath of the Joint Declaration, the British administration in Hong Kong and the mainland government both tacitly condoned and encouraged this trend in anticipation of government in Hong Kong under Chinese sovereignty.

The Legislative Council (LegCo) was first opened to indirect election in 1985 and to direct election in 1991. In 1990, a number of groups in favour of democracy joined to form the United Democrats of Hong Kong. In 1992, Beijing loyalists founded the Democratic Alliance for the Betterment of Hong Kong (DAB). In 1993, the Liberal Party was formed by a group of business people and professionals. In 1994, the United Democrats combined with Meeting Point and was renamed the Democratic Party. The paramount objective was to achieve democracy for Hong Kong.

Yet, some twenty years after the handover, democracy seems to be no nearer. In 2014, during the Umbrella Movement, the thoroughly disillusioned younger generation condemned democrats for having done nothing to advance democracy. The Democratic Party took the most blame for betraying the cause by supporting 'democratic reunification' with China, but political parties were roundly denounced as unfit to lead Hong Kong's democratic movement.

Have political parties, then, come to the end of the road as fighters for democracy in Hong Kong? How have we come to this? What is the way forward?

Between 1985 and 1995, while both the Hong Kong administration and the Chinese government in Beijing were keen to encourage those they thought suitable to form political parties and stand for election, their objectives were opposite.

The outgoing British administration wanted to see democrats organise parties to push forward democracy in Hong Kong and thus prevent Chinese influences from taking control in the political vacuum. Beijing and its Hong Kong loyalists wanted a business-friendly, elitist and conservative party which would run Hong Kong under the dominance of a one-party system. This was consistent with China's long-term vision of Hong Kong as a commercial centre which steered clear of welfare politics.

The democrats started off by doing extremely well in district board and LegCo elections in 1991 and 1995. In 1995, the Democratic Party had the largest number of seats in LegCo[1], and its chairman, Martin Lee Chu-ming, was invited by Governor Chris Patten to join the Executive Council. However, Lee felt unable to accept because of the confidentiality and collective responsibility rules which would effectively prevent him from consulting his party over proposals raised in the Executive Council and compel him to vote with the government.

There were many reasons for the early success of the democrats in general and the Democratic Party in particular. The government's encouragement and international recognition were factors, but more importantly, they represented the predominant public will that democracy should succeed. The democratic cause called forth a generation of new politicians who were in their prime. By contrast, the pro-Beijing DAB was mistrusted, while the Liberal Party was active mainly in certain business-related functional constituencies.

---

1 The Democratic Party took 19 seats out of the 60 total.

But the democrats suffered a reversal of fortune after the change of sovereignty. To retaliate against Patten's huge expansion of the franchise of the functional constituencies, Beijing called off the 'through train'—meaning the continuance in office after 1997 of the pre-1997 legislature—and substituted a handpicked Provisional Legislative Council from which the democrats were excluded. In the period January 1996 to June 1998, laws were purportedly passed by this body to put the functional constituencies more firmly than ever in the control of the government. The election method was altered to prevent democrats from dominating, and the former elected municipal councils and district boards were abolished, resulting in the loss of political influence as well as resources for democrats. In spite of a great victory for the democrats in the 1998 LegCo election[2]—the first under the Chinese flag—in which the Democratic Party took twelve seats, the flagship party gradually sailed into stagnant waters. By then, the DAB was set to take over as the dominant party.

The position, post-1997, was this: Because of the dominant government-controlled seats in the functional constituencies, the democrats in LegCo remained in the minority despite getting an overall majority number of votes in the elections. At the same time, because of the split-voting system whereby a member's motion requires a majority within both the functional constituencies and the geographical constituencies to be carried, almost any motion of the democrats was doomed to be defeated. Unless the government was sensible in making concessions when good grounds were shown, stalemate

---

2 The turnout rate was 53.3 per cent; 1,489,705 voted, with the Democratic Party taking a 42.8 per cent vote share.

would be the order of the day in LegCo. In these circumstances, the democratic parties would have to fight hard not to appear entirely ineffectual. Pushing for political reform to bring about universal suffrage under the Basic Law became central to Hong Kong's autonomy as well as to the growth of democratic parties.

It was a conundrum. Without political reform the democrats would be at a perpetual disadvantage. Yet being perpetually disadvantaged made it difficult for the democrats to force through any political reform. It is fair to say that the lacklustre performance of the Democratic Party contributed to the gradual disillusionment of its traditional supporters. But it would not be true to say that the Democratic Party and other democrats did not try hard to push forward democratic reform. Their efforts took the form of pressing upon the government the clear sentiment of the public, in LegCo's debates and in peaceful protests. It also drew up for public debate options for the election of the chief executive and LegCo members that represented gradual progress in accordance with the principles of universal suffrage; moderate enough, in their view, to be acceptable to the government and to Beijing. Nothing worked. The government chose to simply ignore and stall.

> There was a growing conviction that in the face of so much adversity, unity was vital.

By the end of the 1998–2000 LegCo term, there was a pervasive sense that the Democratic Party had lost its direction and become bogged down. Another criticism against the democrats was their fragmentation. There was a growing conviction that in the face of so much adversity, unity was vital, and the Democratic Party did not have the leadership to lead the movement. In the meantime, in the favourable conditions of Beijing's nurturing and ample supply of resources, the DAB was able to grow and develop and gain recognition for its community work in spite of its pro-government stance.

Faith and morale were greatly revived in 2003 after the July 1st march and astounding defeat of the government's attempt to push through national security legislation. In the district board elections in November that year, the democrats scored a great overall victory, with the incumbent in Kwun Lung, a traditional DAB stronghold, ousted from his seat by a democrat outsider. It was widely feared by Beijing that the democrats might take the majority of seats in the 2004 LegCo election, but that did not happen. The democrats did little to take advantage of the revival.

Meanwhile, pro-Beijing groups took a strategic move to transform themselves. That year, the DAB, with its strong grassroots image, and the backbone provided by the Federation of Trade Unions, merged with the pro-Beijing and pro-business Hong Kong Progressive Alliance, a group originally formed solely for political expediency. With the merger came a blood transfusion in DAB leadership: the traditional leftist unionists gave way to younger industrialists, lawyers and accountants. Thus was accomplished the first step of Beijing's original objective of a party with a conservative middle class (though not yet elitist) image.

In response to the public's desire for new development, the Civic Party was founded in March 2006[3]. The Civic Par-

---

3 I hereby declare interest as a member of the Concern Groups and a founding member of the Civic Party.

ty had its origin in the Article 23 Concern Group formed by a group of legal professionals to resist the government's proposed national security law. Following the July 1st march of 2003, the group decided to focus on promoting universal suffrage, but when the Standing Committee of the National People's Congress in an Interpretation on April 6th, 2004 changed the rules for political development and then ruled out universal suffrage for 2007–2008, some members of the Concern Group agreed that a new political party should be formed to carry on the long-term campaign for democracy.

Interestingly, the new party was welcome in different quarters thanks to various kinds of misunderstanding. For example, certain Beijing officials believed that the core members, being an elitist group, had the potential to form the elitist conservative party Beijing had been looking out for. Alternatively, traditional supporters of democracy in Hong Kong hoped that this new force would supply the charismatic leadership needed to unify the democrats. The Civic Party's goal was merely to keep all those democrats who were disillusioned by one democratic party or another within the fold.

Beijing and Hong Kong democrats alike were soon undeceived. The real difference of the new party was that it was an even greater stickler for constitutional principles and less pragmatic than the Democratic Party. It also had no ambition to fill the super leadership role. Apart from generally strengthening the democratic camp in LegCo, the new party made two main contributions to the movement. The first was fielding one of its members, Alan Leong Kah-kit, to contest the 2007 chief executive election against Donald Tsang Yam-kuen, the Beijing-chosen candidate, to force open the small circle election into a competitive territory-wide election campaign, with television debates in which the public participated. From then on, the culture was set and there was no going back.

The second was to effectively force a referendum on the question of the abolition of functional constituencies. In January 2010, five LegCo members (including two from the Civic Party), representing five geographical constituencies, resigned their seats to trigger territory-wide by-elections, and to make each vote for the re-election of the resigned members a vote for abolition. The purpose of the referendum did not catch the public's imagination, and the result was not a success apart from the fact that the idea of referendum could not be erased[4]. For this, the Civic Party acquired a reputation of being radical on account of its partnering with the members of the radical League of Social Democrats in order to bring about the by-elections. The Democratic Party had backed out after initially indicating interest.

Events took an unexpected turn when Tsang challenged Civic Party leader Audrey Eu Yuet-mee as the spokesperson for the referendum to a debate on the government's proposals for political reform. Eu won the debate hands down. Immediately after that, Beijing officials in Hong Kong agreed to secret negotiations with representatives of the Democratic Party, and reached a compromise whereby five new district board seats, to be nominated by district board members from among themselves, would be elected by a broad franchise of every registered voter who is not a voter in any other functional constituency. On that compromise, the Democratic

---

4 The turnout rate was 17.2 per cent, with 579,795 people voting.

Party voted with the government, and on June 23rd, 2010, the constitutional reform package was passed by LegCo for the first time.

Just as the referendum cost the Civic Party a great deal of moderate supporters, so did the compromise alienate many supporters from the Democratic Party, especially among the younger generation. The compromise did not lead to a better relationship between democrats and Beijing and the Special Administrative Region government, nor to further democratisation. On the contrary, the next package to come out of Beijing, was the '8/31 Decision' (a proposal issued by the National People's Congress Standing Committee on August 31st, 2014) whereby Hong Kong people could vote for the chief executive but only from among two to three 'patriotic' candidates screened by a Beijing-controlled nomination. The proposal was the most uncompromising of all proposals, and directly led to the Umbrella Movement of 2014.

On June 18th, 2015, LegCo rejected the 8/31 Decision, with all twenty-seven democrats voting against it. Thanks to the fiasco of a failed boycott attempt, only seven pro-government votes were cast, while some thirty-odd members failed to vote. While this warded off the disastrous proposal and may have shown the power of democrats standing together, nevertheless the practical effect was that the Hong Kong system is no closer to universal suffrage and the impasse remains, firmer than ever.

The 2017 LegCo election saw traditional democratic parties make conscientious efforts to effect a change of guard and to place greater emphasis on localism in their manifesto, but the party structure remains much the same. Ironically, despite their strong renunciation of LegCo as dysfunctional, and their view that all democrats in LegCo should resign, many of the Umbrella activists, including those groups which strongly advocated self-determination or Hong Kong independence, formed parties and stood for election, with remarkable success. The tactics and conduct of the new blood differed from the old only in degree—with more drastic consequences to themselves. Beijing decided to take a tough stance, and issued an Interpretation of Article 104 of the Basic Law on oath taking, which has resulted in the disqualification of two duly elected members, and threatens to disqualify more.

The more interesting point is this: the denunciation of traditional political parties was based on the premise that each individual is autonomous and entitled to self- determination. Everyone is equal. No one has the right to decide or speak for anyone else. No one can put himself or herself forward as a leader, nor can be accepted as one. Political parties violate this principle by presuming to lead the democratic movement, and also by reason of their authoritarian structure. Elitism is anathema to the philosophy of radicalism which the Umbrella generation seems to embrace.

Of course there are logical flaws in this view: autonomy does not preclude leadership but only certain kinds of leadership, and it is for the autonomous individuals to decide what kind of leadership is compatible with their autonomy. But the more immediate question is, assuming this view is to be adopted, what then is to be the new model of decision-making? How is the democratic movement to be carried forward?

The Umbrella Movement has brought into focus a problem

which has been years in coming: that Hong Kong does not have the conditions for meaningful political party development, at least not for political parties of the traditional form[5]. Apart from the Beijing-approved DAB, no political party has a membership of more than a thousand. The old taboo is gone, but the old authoritarian mindset remains: that politics are for those in power. No one who does not seek power (eg through elections) or needs to maintain power has any interest to join political parties. This being so, it is up to such people to seek their own financial and other support. Further, political parties are perceived as powerful and should be subject to the same demands of the public as others—such as government officials—who are in power, and open to criticism when they fail to meet the demand. There are people of a different mindset, who believe that politics is the business of all citizens, and therefore it is in their own interest and to some degree their responsibility to support, financially and morally, the political party closest to their ideas, but such people are still in the minority. This minority is not to be scoffed at: indeed they have kept the democratic movement going. But their number is far from enough to overcome the serious difficulties, including the fundamental obstacle, namely, that under Hong Kong's constitutional arrangement, no political party which is not sponsored by Beijing can take over the government.

It may be that the way forward, difficult though it is, lies in two simultaneous lines of action. First, following traditional lines but changing tactics, parties should spend more

---

5 Joseph Lian Yizheng interestingly suggested that the basically Leninist parties in Hong Kong founded by elitist leaders on core ideologies should be changed into US-style parties which are relatively ideologically soft but strong as election machines.

time going to the community and seeking the community's support on every major issue, instead of immersing themselves in the increasingly meaningless and unseemly skirmishes in LegCo's precincts. Parties should wage battle in LegCo only after securing clear community backing.

> The old taboo is gone, but the old authoritarian mindset remains: that politics are for those in power.

Second, following the spirit of the Umbrella Movement, a new model of bottom-up deliberation and decision-making rooted in true localism should be developed. This should start with discussion among neighbourhood householders on affairs of the neighbourhood such as tree care and street cleaning, and expand to territory-wide issues such as public open space and town planning, and the monitoring and holding to account of district councils, LegCo and government bureaux. The expertise required and devotion to intense work needed should not be underestimated.

Of the two, in my view, the latter is far more exciting, but the two lines have the same foundation: unless everyone is mobilised, democracy has no future in this community. The only political parties which can thrive will be government-sponsored parties, and the system of government in Hong Kong will not be democracy but its opposite.

Handover

Harry Harrison

Hometown

Kris Cheng

Each spring, I face the same question about my travel plans.

'So are you going to *baai saan* this year? It's almost time you visited again,' my father says. *Baai saan*, or 'visit the mountain', means to visit Zhongshan city in Guandong province. More specifically—and importantly for my father—it means visiting the graves of my ancestors.

I have never understood this ritual. I have never spent more than three days at a time in Zhongshan. Zhongshan is known for its hot springs and for being named after Sun Yat-sen, the founding father of modern China, but that's about all. The trips for me consist mostly of watching older family members perform rituals on the hill to pay respect to my grandparents at the ancestral home—they trim the wild grass, place fruit and other gifts on the graves, fold paper money as an offering. They only need me at the end, to maybe pour some wine on the grave or bow. Then we have a roast pig with relatives. These traditions never meant much to me, except that I knew they were a way to pay respect to my father and my extended family. All of this seemed to be happening in such a remote place, far away in mainland China. But it is mostly because of my grandfather that I was born and raised in Hong Kong.

My grandfather, whom I never met, was a member of the ousted Kuomintang and a train station manager, according to my father. My grandfather did not like the Communist Party. One day, he badmouthed it and was later convicted as a counter-revolutionary and sent to a labour camp in the northeast province of Heilongjiang for ten years. He survived but lived in fear after returning home to Zhongshan. He died a few years later.

My father left China to come to Hong Kong in the 1980s because there was not much opportunity for him on the mainland. He was a teacher, but because of his family background he could never join the party, and therefore would not have been able to rise very far in his career. My father ran a label printing company in Hong Kong to feed the family and never really cared about politics. 'Those who suit their actions to the time are wise,' he often said, quoting a Chinese adage. He thought the young people in Hong Kong who joined mass protests against the express rail link and other wasteful publicly-funded infrastructure projects, or against the government in general, were a weird bunch. 'Why care about politics so much?' he would ask. 'Why provoke the government and end up like your grandfather?'

But to me, the answer comes naturally: if you are born and raised in Hong Kong, you care about Hong Kong's future more than anything.

My father and I grew up very differently. He is reserved in politics because of his father's history. He is concerned about the news but does not want to participate actively in events. He is probably representative of Hong Kong's older generation. He and my mother lived through the Cultural Revolution. My father saw firsthand the risks of speaking out, and keeps his opinions to himself. 'If there wasn't the Cultural Revolution, if I ever had the opportunity to study more, I would have been much smarter than you,' he often says over dinner. 'You can voice your opinion in a civil manner, but you don't want to be on the front lines.'

The younger generation raised here in Hong Kong did not really encounter that fear of repercussions for speaking out until recently. The Hong Kong we grew up in was relatively free—we had freedom of speech and we could join public debates, form our own opinions and our own identities. Not everyone

> My father saw firsthand the risks of speaking out, and keeps his opinions to himself.

supports an independent Hong Kong, for example, but surely young people are worried that if we cannot discuss this topic and others freely, things may go down a slippery slope—more topics may become taboo.

I was born on November 30th, 1989, in Hong Kong. My mother said it was a difficult birth, and she sometimes joked about having to watch the TVB channel's anniversary celebration from a hospital bed, where she had to spend the week or two leading up to my birthday.

I do not have any significant memories of political events before 1997. British-Hong Kong days were vague for me. I was never taught how to sing, 'God Save The Queen'. I did not know anything about the United Kingdom except that a relative lived there. I do have one memory from the night of June 30th, 1997, when my mum told me to switch on the television to watch the handover ceremony. I watched it because she told me to, but I didn't understand what it was about.

After the handover, the only difference I noticed was the gradual change of the postal boxes, from the rounded colonial red ones to the new rectangular green ones, an easy change for the young me to spot. The SARS outbreak in 2003 that killed more than 250 people here and frightened the world did not affect me or my family much. We weren't too afraid, although my parents did wear masks to work. For me, a student, it just meant a break from school. On July 1st of that same year, half a million people marched to protest the proposed national security legislation that would have defined sedition in vague terms and made it easier to arrest people for speech critical of the government. But I was still too young to understand the marching.

In the early days after the handover, years before Beijing tried to implement a controversial 'national education' curriculum here to teach us what it means to be 'Chinese', I remember little education about 'who we are', but only a subject called civics. Surely, we must have been taught about the Yellow and Yangtze rivers—the cradles of Chinese civilisation as many like to call them. And of course, we learnt the national anthem of the PRC, but I felt removed from these topics. What I remember most were lessons about not crossing the road on a red light, or not picking up money on the street that doesn't belong to you. I may not have a ready answer if I am asked, 'Are you Chinese', but

I surely can describe how to behave like a civilised person according to what the teachers taught us.

I was a good student and passed the first secondary school public exam in secondary five with flying colours, so I was allowed to skip the second public exam in secondary seven. Because I was basically free from studies, I think I was open to a political enlightenment. This relative freedom came for me during 2006 and 2007, during the protests against the demolition of the former Star Ferry Pier. Those who favoured demolition argued that the structure was a symbol of colonialism. Like so many other young people, I had no vivid memories of the colonial days. To us, the structure had come to represent Hong Kong itself, and did not need to represent the past. At that time, activists such as Eddie Chu Hoi-dick (now a lawmaker) and others used the term 'collective memory'. This term has now disappeared from local media, but at that time it made sense to me. I do belong somewhere, I do have an identity, and even though many issues in Hong Kong are quite distant for me, it is somehow my responsibility to care. The confrontation over the pier made sense to me from this perspective.

The movement to save the old Star Ferry Pier was often compared to the 1966 riots sparked by the fare rise of the Star Ferry (supported by the colonial government) that triggered the hunger strike of a twenty-seven-year-old man, So Sau-chung. Crowds of people supported So and his cause and riots erupted after he was arrested and sentenced to jail.

Only after the protests of 2006 and 2007 did my father tell me Mr. So was a relative of ours. He mentioned it after seeing an article about So in the newspaper, and he even asked me whether I could find a contact number for So (I did, but my father never called him). Apparently, So left his family and became a monk. Perhaps So's ordeal was another reason why my father did not encourage people to protest. But although I never met So, and he was only a distant cousin, I felt a historical connection to him and felt less alone.

In 2008, Hong Kong became a centre of debate over the Beijing Olympics (the equestrian event took place here). The Olympic torch passed through Hong Kong in May that year. As a first-year university student, I joined a group that planned to carry banners during the torch run through Sha Tin in the New Territories to protest the mainland government's propaganda, which seemed to exclude any room for criticism or even questioning what it meant to be Chinese. I had also just begun to become aware of some of the human rights abuses occurring on the mainland.

Some of our banners made fun of the overwhelming Chinese nationalism being pushed by the mainland and the Hong Kong Government. Others called for a more rational view of Chinese identity that would allow people to choose their own identity, and not have one forced upon them, especially one they were forbidden to question. One banner read, 'China is an inalienable part of Mongolia', poking fun at the statement made by mainland officials and pro-Beijing figures in Hong Kong that any part of the world that belonged to China historically must be a part of China now. Our plan failed after plain clothes police officers spotted us on the way to the protest site. The officers asked to see the banners but we did not comply. Some of us later stood on the kerb but the police asked everyone to leave and took the banners forcefully, saying it was for our safety and that 'it's a happy day' and that 'there's no need to talk about' the sentiments expressed on our signs. We left after that.

I was a typical first-year university student then, questioning everything I had been told, and the incident made me resent how an identity was being forced upon us. Why should we not question our own identity? Even if everyone identifies as Chinese, what exactly is the relationship between Hong Kong and China? Who can we be?

My father, meanwhile, doesn't doubt his Chinese roots. His bedtime readings are Chinese classic novels, such as *Outlaws of the Marsh* and *Romance of the Three Kingdoms*. He reads these over and over. He writes splendid calligraphy that I could never hope to replicate. I write commentaries in Chinese newspapers, but to him they are the work of an amateur. 'Hong Kong schools don't teach enough about Chinese history and culture. You are a university graduate. Didn't your schools teach you how to read and write classical literature? Your writing skills are appalling,' he says.

I am usually speechless when he says this. He never spent a day in the Hong Kong education system and would probably not understand that his standards for literature are simply too high for local students. But I understand where his expectations come from and just agree to disagree.

After my political awakening as a teenager, protests in Hong Kong continued, and in many ways grew stronger: The protests against the Guangzhou–Shenzhen–Hong Kong Express Rail Link in 2010, the national education curriculum protests in 2012, the HKTV free-to-air license denial incident in 2013 and the historic Umbrella Movement in 2014.

More young people joined these movements, as they continued to worry about Hong Kong's future under Chinese rule. I was an observer for most of these events.

My political concern did not waiver. But perhaps because of the subtle influence from my family, after university I chose to be on the sidelines as a journalist. I write in English to explain to a wider audience what I see from a local perspective—to help those outside Hong Kong and the Chinese speaking community understand these important chapters in our lives and our fears that the promises made to us in the Basic Law and in the Sino–British Joint Declaration of 1984 are being broken by our leaders. Our freedom is in jeopardy. My father still wishes I were in business and would stay out of politics, and probably a lot of other parents of children in my generation feel the same. But at least he respects my choice to do what I do and is happy that I keep a 'safe distance'.

In fact, my father is becoming more active in current affairs himself, even if quietly and indirectly. A few years ago, my father joined an association of people from Zhongshan. He explained to me he wanted to help his hometown, particularly the people there who helped him during the years of turmoil in China. He is an active member, often joining the trips back to Zhongshan to do volunteer work, or attending gala dinners to raise funds to improve the city. To show him the support he has shown me, I often tell him I respect his choice. But I also tell him he should

> My father still wishes I were in business and would stay out of politics, and probably a lot of other parents of children in my generation feel the same.

be careful of political involvement through the association, which often encourages members who live in Hong Kong to support pro-Beijing causes. At the request of his association, sometimes my father even turns up at some pro-government events. He maintains he is simply being pragmatic.

Sometimes I show him news reports of some pro-government protesters who were paid to show up, and jokingly tell him it was a bit foolish of him to pay bus fare out of his own pocket to attend. 'I don't like the Communist Party, more than anyone, but I am not opposing everything for the sake of opposing,' he answers. 'I support whatever is good for Hong Kong and my hometown.'

I may not fully relate to my father's emotional attachment to his hometown, but at the same time he may not completely grasp the concerns I have about mine, as we grew up so very differently. But I am thankful that we can talk about our disagreements honestly—at least I can understand how he came to hold his views, and maybe with time he will understand how I came to hold mine.

Safe Harbour?

William Nee

O n a cool spring night in 2007, I stood on the street across from Shanghai University leisurely browsing pirated books for sale. The stall sold illegal copies of the classics, such as *Romance of the Three Kingdoms* and *Jane Eyre*, alongside the year's best sellers like the *Harry Potter* series, all in Chinese. But many customers came to snap up the latest contraband from Hong Kong and Taiwan—books and magazines that offered insight into political personalities and purges on the mainland. The big story then was the downfall of the Shanghai party secretary, and people wanted to know details of the political infighting and corruption that the state-controlled media would never reveal.

Suddenly, a van pulled up and a handful of plain-clothes policemen jumped out. The officers quickly brushed by me, an unassuming American student, and scooped up handfuls of books. The officers muttered something, but after they left I noticed that only the politically-sensitive Taiwanese and Hong Kong materials were missing. Nobody, including me, had said a thing.

I had grown used to the silence. At the time of the book raid, I had been living in China for six years. I first worked as a lecturer at a small college in Henan province and later moved to Shanghai, using every spare moment I had to master Mandarin. In a few years, I went from being able to say little more than *ni hao* to being able to understand news reports and read Chinese classics and contemporary socio-political works. When my Mandarin reached a high enough level, I transitioned from full-time teacher to full-time student, studying international relations at the prestigious Fudan University and taking all of my classes in Chinese.

I was riding the wave of excitement in the mid-2000s—an era in China that some now refer to, only semi-ironically, as a 'golden era'. Although the country teemed with social problems, such as massive unemployment, a widening wealth gap and severe air pollution, it nonetheless gave off a sense of limitless optimism and energy. Economic growth was in the double digits. Industrialisation, privatisation, the world's largest rural-to-urban migration—all of the development that took decades in other countries, seemed to happen in China within a few years.

Reading modern classics in the original Chinese, such as Yu Hua's *To Live*, a book that depicts the enormous socio-political changes in China in the mid-twentieth century from a common man's point of view, or the contemporary books on the life of migrant workers and the struggle in the countryside, such as *Will the Boat Sink the Water*, made me feel as though I were inside the fast-changing juggernaut that was China. I also sought out the banned materials so popular with many mainlanders. During a trip to Hong Kong in 2006 one summer, I stocked up on 'forbidden fruit' books—

Wang Lixiong's epic, *Sky Burial*, on the history of Tibet; the Chinese version of the *Tiananmen Papers*, which exposed leaked Chinese government documents on the government's internal deliberations on how to handle the protests that erupted across China in the spring of 1989 and culminated in the tragic, bloody Tiananmen crackdown; and another book on the politics of 1989 and the Tiananmen Square protests. Over the next few months, I slowly pored over the books, looking up the Chinese characters I didn't know on Pleco, my new dictionary app.

And yet, when I showed these books to some of my classmates at Fudan—brilliant postgraduate students who could recite dynastic history and international relations theory—they reacted as though I'd tried to give them a vial of the smallpox virus. When I tried to initiate discussions, these students would mumble that certain time periods in China's past were 'complicated', and cut off the conversation.

As my studies continued, I became restless. I had spent years learning Chinese to better understand the culture, I was surrounded by brilliant people at an elite university, and yet, I couldn't have many of the meaningful conversations that I wanted to have. At times, I saw the results of the strident, xenophobic nationalism that the Communist Party had infused into its primary and secondary education system throughout the 1990s. Some professors at Fudan frequently let loose on fact-free rants akin to those I had become accustomed to listening to on AM radio in my grandmother's car during my childhood in the United States. Many students either agreed with, or were too nervous or too complacent to challenge, the teachers. I was starting to feel that mainland Chinese academia may not be the best fit for me.

Intellectually frustrated, I left Shanghai shortly after the incident at the bookstall ten years ago to pursue a master's degree in Hong Kong. I had only visited the city twice before moving here, but with its wonderful cafés, fabulous bookstores and jagged mountains, I could see why so many people considered it a nice break from the gritty and sometimes stifling environment of Shanghai and other parts of the mainland. In addition, the city had long provided a safe harbour for China watchers and students who wanted to freely observe and debate mainland politics, economics and society. My goal was to get a position where I could leverage my skills as a China researcher and analyst. Back then, Hong Kong's reputation as a free and open society had not changed much since the handover from Great Britain back to China in 1997. The mainland seemed, for the most part, to leave the city alone. And in fact, many China-focused non-governmental organisations not welcome on the mainland ran their operations from Hong Kong, where they could safely hold conferences, publish reports critical of the Chinese government and interview dissidents and activists passing through from the north.

> The city had long provided a safe harbour for China watchers and students who wanted to freely observe and debate mainland politics, economics and society.

Through contacts I made in my master's program at the University of Hong Kong, I landed a dream job as a public affairs and liaison officer at one of those NGOs, the China Labour Bulletin (CLB). Led by an exiled former Beijing labour activist, Han Dongfang, the organisation advocates for Chinese workers by promoting civil society, pursuing public interest litigation—in areas such as employment discrimination, occupational illness and injury—and enhancing workers' abilities to engage in collective bargaining with their employers. I worked closely with Han, and soaked up his experience as an organiser, campaigner and strategic thinker. In the spring of 1989, Han had established the first independent trade union in Chinese mainland history, which soon made him one of the people scapegoated by the authorities for contributing to the Tiananmen Square protests. After voluntarily turning himself in to the authorities, he was sent to prison, where they forced him to live with convicts afflicted with tuberculosis. Upon his release on medical parole in 1991, authorities banished Han from China. He first went to the United States, where he had surgery to remove a TB-riddled lung, but he refused to stay far away for long. In 1993, he came to Hong Kong to set up CLB. He and his deputy director, Robin Munro, one of the last foreigners to leave Tiananmen Square on the eve of the June 4th bloodshed, were exactly the type of dynamic people I had so desperately hoped to meet when I first came to China, and now they were my mentors.

Despite the problems on the mainland, we were optimistic at CLB: Chinese workers were underpaid, overworked, and sometimes subjected to harsh and even deadly working conditions, but increasingly they were fighting to secure their rights, and to make the system better. By 2008, the Chinese government had made concessions to workers through a raft of new legislation designed to protect the rights of individual workers and mitigate disputes. Furthermore, the government, under then-President Hu Jintao and then-Premier Wen Jiabao, was promoting the 'Harmonious Society'— and civil society organisations could argue that their work was contributing to this broader goal by addressing social discontent at the grassroots. The catchphrase 'Harmonious

Society' was often mocked on the internet—since *hexie* 'to harmonise', had become a slang word for the deletion of internet posts that ran afoul of the state censors. And every year there were tens of thousands of small-scale protests and disturbances, dubbed 'mass incidents' in official parlance, so one might assume that China was anything but 'harmonious'. And civil society organisations in China were frequently monitored or even outright controlled by the authorities. But overall, it seemed like there was a growing space, and sometimes even tacit official recognition, of the importance of the work of civil society. As the Chinese leadership appeared to be willing, at least to some extent, to address the social inequalities that had emerged—by strengthening some parts of the legal system and paying greater attention to the plight of disadvantaged groups—nongovernmental organisations could often operate within the space created by the 'Harmonious Society' campaign to contribute towards its goal.

From our office in Hong Kong, it seemed that NGOs could do important work. Universities continued to provide excellent analysis of social, legal and political trends. And while many noticed incremental pressure put on the 'one country, two systems' framework, overall, in my first few years at CLB, the Hong Kong system—supported by a free press and the rule of law—felt intact.

But things began to change—both on the mainland and in Hong Kong. It became increasingly clear that the rise of Chinese president Xi Jinping was being accompanied by a more hard-line approach to ideological affairs. Since I felt that a deteriorating situation required a strong and vocal defence of human rights more generally, I decided to make the move from CLB to Amnesty International—where I became proud to be part of the world's largest and most-recognised human rights movement. I was hired as a China researcher. I wrote research reports, urgent actions, op-eds and United Nations and government submissions and also did media interviews on issues related to freedom of expression, human rights defenders, social, cultural and economic rights, the death penalty and many other issues.

A secret document issued by the Central Committee of the Chinese Communist Party General Office in April 2013, the so-called Document No. 9, seemed to epitomise the government's new tough stance against human rights. It identified numerous 'false ideological trends', and positions to be rejected, such as 'Western constitutional democracy', 'universal values' (often a synonym for human rights in mainland discourse), 'promoting civil society', the 'West's idea of journalism', and 'promoting historical nihilism' or challenges to the historical narrative crafted by the Communist Party.

When the document was first published in the international press, there were intense debates about whether or not it was even genuine. But most doubts were put to rest when in 2015 the government put veteran journalist Gao Yu on trial and sentenced her to seven years in prison for 'disclosing state secrets', which were widely believed to be Document No. 9. In any case, it became clear that the government was acting on all the central tenets of the document: it crushed the nascent 'New Citizen's Movement', which included a diverse array of citizen-activists dedicated to promoting a new form of participatory citizenship and constitutional democracy. Civil society organisations, such as Yirenping and the Transition

Institute—which had previously operated without too many problems—were deemed 'sensitive' and shut down, and foreign NGO worker Peter Dahlin, a Swedish citizen, was detained in January 2016; a new law on foreign NGOs has made their operations and cooperation with their Chinese counterparts much more difficult. In July 2015, the government launched a sweeping nationwide campaign to question, detain or harass nearly 250 human rights lawyers and activists (at the time of this writing, five have been convicted and sentenced and four remain in detention awaiting trial or sentencing); and Chinese media outlets have been told that their 'surname is Party' and that they must promote the Communist Party's interests and abide by the 'Marxist View of Journalism'.

Since Xi Jinping came to power in late 2012, China has enacted or drafted a series of sweeping laws with a national security focus, which pose a serious threat to human rights. These laws, through vague and broad provisions, give extensive power to the government to silence critics and prosecute human rights defenders.

Hong Kong too began to change. In the few years since I had first arrived, it seemed to me that relations with the mainland had deteriorated remarkably. In my own experience, the cost of rent skyrocketed, and I felt the pain that most non-homeowners face dealing with rising costs in the city that the Economist Intelligence Unit recently named the world's second-most expensive. Clearly, economic disconnect, rising costs, the housing crisis and the perception that the current political system has been ineffective at tackling citizens' grievances has been a much-cited cause of the deteriorating situation.

However, it would be too simple to ascribe the discontent to mere economic problems, as there were also social and political changes. In 2010, Joshua Wong Chi-fung had risen to prominence leading the student group Scholarism in protests against a plan to implement 'moral and national education' in Hong Kong, which was seen by many as mainland-style indoctrination. In addition, many Hong Kongers were concerned that the central government's promise to allow universal suffrage for the chief executive election by 2017 would not be genuinely implemented. When the central government released its decision confirming this suspicion in 2014, it enraged passions of many activists in Hong Kong, and later that year prompted the Umbrella Movement, during which numerous groups and activists took to the streets.

At Amnesty International, our main role is not to agree or disagree with any particular demand concerning the details of the electoral system, since we are independent of any government, political ideology or economic interest, but we strive for a world in which all people can enjoy their human rights, including the rights to freedom of expression and peaceful protest.

Arguably the most serious breach to the 'one country, two systems' framework and Hong Kong's 'high degree of autonomy' after the Umbrella Movement was the infamous Causeway Bay booksellers case.

In mid-October 2015, four booksellers who worked at

In mid-October 2015, four booksellers who worked at Causeway Bay Books went missing in quick succession.

Causeway Bay Books went missing in quick succession: Lui Bo, Lam Wing-kee and Cheung Jiping in Guangdong in southern China, and Gui Minhai, from his home in Thailand. The bookstore, located in a small second floor shop in the Causeway Bay shopping district on Hong Kong Island, and its owner, Mighty Current Media, were well-known for publishing and selling salacious 'banned' books on political and social issues in China. The bookstore was popular with mainland tourists. As soon as we heard news of these multiple disappearances, my colleagues and I put out statements to journalists to voice our concerns, and I was on TV to discuss the possible worrying ramifications of the threat to freedom of expression in Hong Kong and the creeping reach of China's crackdown on dissent and human rights defenders.

However, it wasn't until late December 2015, with the disappearance from Hong Kong itself of Lee Bo, another bookseller at the same company who had been helping to campaign for his colleagues, that much of Hong Kong and the international community became outraged over the case. Suddenly, many of the activists, regular citizens and people from civil society I knew became enormously concerned about their own safety in Hong Kong. In early January 2016, no one knew where the five booksellers were. No one knew if they themselves might be next.

For the next few days and weeks, I followed the case closely, doing press interviews and other media work for Amnesty International on the changing situation. Gui Minhai was the first to reappear—although the circumstances were far from reassuring. On January 17th, 2016, Gui was interviewed on CCTV, China's state-run television network, 'confessing' to a crime he apparently committed in China over a decade ago. Absurdly, during the interview one could see changes in Gui Minhai's sweater, and the length of his hair, making it clear that the interview was conducted over different days. To make matters worse, the interview didn't even address some of the most important issues: what were Gui and his colleagues exact whereabouts? Had they been detained under Chinese law, and if so, on what charges? Did they have access to lawyers? Did Gui Minhai and Lee Bo—both foreign passport holders—have consular visits by diplomats of Sweden and the United Kingdom, respectively?

Over the ensuing months, one by one, all of the booksellers except for Gui Minhai came back to Hong Kong, cancelling their missing persons reports that had been filed with the Hong Kong police, and otherwise remaining quiet. Their unwillingness to talk—no doubt for fear of the repercussions for doing so—meant that no one really knew exactly what had happened.

But then one of them—Lam Wing-kee—decided to speak out to 'defend the rights and freedoms of human beings' by holding a press conference in Hong Kong. Lam said he had been placed in 'residential surveillance in a designated location', a form of secret detention that allows the police to hold criminal suspects for up to six months outside of the formal detention system—without access to anyone outside. The police are supposed to notify family members within twenty-four hours of imposing the measure, but do not need to tell them where their loved ones are or the reason for their detention. Lam alleged that he had to sign a document saying that he didn't need a lawyer, a common tactic often used in 'sensitive'—or political—cases.

As I worked on the booksellers' case, I couldn't help but reflect on the incident at the bookstall in Shanghai nearly ten years before. At that time, no one, including myself, said anything. We stood there in fear, all knowing the *qian guize*, the unwritten rules of the game. When something similar happened in Hong Kong, civil society and the international community stood up. Courageous people like Lam Wing-kee spoke out, and it made a difference, proving that the mainland's fear tactics would not always work.

This is the crucial point: defending human rights requires boldly speaking out. Going forward, it will be even more important to find the best way to do so, to continue speaking out without becoming reflexively anti-government or anti-China, for example. It is crucial to make criticisms based on facts and on international laws and standards. It will be necessary to recognise Hong Kong's diversity and to help mobilise different sectors of the community.

We cannot stand by silently while books, or even people, are whisked away. Without the courage to speak up, we risk losing our right to speak up at all.

The views expressed in this essay are those of the author, and do not necessarily reflect the views of Amnesty International.

Tai Hang Nullah

Gérard Henry

High tide in the nullah linking Victoria Park to Wun Sha Street in Tai Hang behind Central Library. Small fish coming from the sea used to make their way here. Sadly, it was covered by the Dragon Path.

Dignity and Shame, Or, a Personal Take on LGBTQ Rights in Hong Kong

Marco Wan

I t is Chinese New Year; a time of festivities, high spirits, good wishes and seemingly endless amounts of home-cooked food. More importantly, it is a time for celebrating family ties: catching up with relatives, paying respects to grandparents, marvelling at how much toddlers have grown over the past year, seeing the big smiles on children's faces as they receive their red packets.

It is after dinner on the first day of the New Year, and we're leaving the restaurant. As my elderly aunt stands on the pavement, she turns to me with a big smile and says, 'Your brother's children are adorable! When is it your turn? I want to receive the invitation to your wedding banquet before the end of my days.' I try not to roll my eyes. Here we go again. My uncle—more astute than my aunt—intervenes to save me from the awkward situation. He gives me a knowing glance, then says to her in his usual grumbly voice '*Aiya*, get in the car!'

I used to love Chinese New Year. I loved eating *neen go* and *lor bak go*. I loved receiving red packets. I loved playing with my cousins. Yet like many gay men in Hong Kong, as I grew older I experienced a growing sense of unease about the holiday. The question of marriage came up with almost as much certainty as the Lunar New Year cycle, asked by the same people, with the same hopeful look. It was no doubt well intentioned, but it hurt. It chipped away at my heart, just a little bit every year, a reminder that no matter how strong the bond between my partner and me, it would not be recognised as legitimate in the eyes of some members of my family, those very people who were dear to me. It was also a reminder that, regardless of my achievements, I would always somehow be lesser than everyone else in their eyes.

Over the years, I've come up with various responses to that question. I thought about coming out and lecturing everyone about the importance of equality and the right to marry. I'm a law professor after all. But what would be the point? My immediate family already knew about my sexuality (and was supportive), and I was not going to change the mind of my eighty-five-year old aunt anyway. Plus, it would create much embarrassment, the last thing you want at a family gathering on Chinese New Year's Day. To lecture my relatives would be to have no sense of occasion. I thought about responding with a sarcastic remark, but sarcasm only works when there is a common frame of reference. I thought about just brushing it off, but the more I tried to ignore the question, the more I was angry at myself for being too much of a coward to confront it.

> The question of marriage came up with almost as much certainty as the Lunar New Year cycle. It was no doubt well intentioned, but it hurt.

Since the handover, LGBTQ rights in Hong Kong have developed at a rapid pace. This is in part due to various high profile court cases, and in part due to wider changes in social attitudes towards nonconformist sexualities. In 2006, the courts equalised the age of consent for homosexual and heterosexual intercourse in the case of *William Roy Leung v. Secretary for Justice*, and one year later the Court of Final Appeal unequivocally stated that both the Basic Law and the Bill of Rights prohibited sexual orientation discrimination by the government in *Secretary for Justice v. Yau Luk Lung Zigo*. In 2013, transsexuals gained the right to marry in their new gender in *W v. Registrar of Marriages*. The case of *QT v. Director of Immigration*, which challenges the government's decision not to issue a dependent's visa to the civil partner of a British lesbian working in Hong Kong, is currently going on appeal, and at the time of writing the Court of First Instance had just decided in *Leung Chun Kwong v. Secretary for the Civil Service and Commissioner of Inland Revenue* that the government had to award spousal benefits to partners of gay civil servants who had legally married abroad, even though it was not obliged to allow joint assessment of taxes on the basis of that foreign same-sex marriage. The government will no doubt appeal the *Leung* case, but for now the mood is upbeat. The proceedings of both *QT* and *Leung* are taking place in the aftermath of the United States Supreme Court decision of *Obergefell v. Hodges*, which legalised same-sex marriage in the United States. Finally, a recent survey by the Equal Opportunities Commission indicates that there is majority support for enacting antidiscrimination legislation on the grounds of sexual orientation, gender identity and intersex status to regulate the private sector. Things are not perfect, but the landscape of LGBTQ rights is changing.

Yet every time I think about my aunt's question, I feel that these legal advancements do not quite get to the heart of the problem. Discrimination of course needs to be confronted, but the analysis of, say, the technical differences between direct and indirect discrimination or the nature of my Article 25 right to equality under Hong Kong's Basic Law seemed very far off the mark that Chinese New Year's Day. The paradigm of rights, while important and indeed powerful, does not quite capture the way in which a simple question from a well-meaning family member can hurt, year after year, again and again and again.

What is it, then, that is so poignant and yet so elusive about my aunt's question? I find some critical writings on *shame* as an analytical category helpful here. One way of thinking about the effect of this seemingly innocuous question is that it inflicts a sense of shame on someone who cannot satisfy its most basic assumptions about marriage. It sets up the institution of heterosexual marriage not only as something desirable, but as such an integral part of society that there must be something wrong, something queer, about a person who is excluded from it. Children are not the only people who receive red packets during Chinese New Year; unmarried adults do as well. The implication is that unless I get married, I will always be an overgrown child who fails to reach proper adulthood. Even though she didn't intend it as such, the question 'when is it your turn to get married?' (or variations thereof) is therefore really another way of saying 'shame on you for not getting married'.

> The question which assumes that everyone can (and should) get married underscores for me how alone I am in not being able to partake in the most fundamental aspect of family life.

The queer theorist Eve Kosofsky Sedgwick has written very insightfully on this very expression, 'Shame on you', and contrasts it with another expression at stake here, that solemn promise of 'I do' in a marriage ceremony. She points out that 'Shame on you' has a number of characteristics. It is impossible to do justice to her argument in this short essay, but I would highlight three points that she makes. First of all, she argues that unlike 'I do', 'Shame on you' has no subject: the 'I' is erased from the sentence, and one of the defining characteristics of shame is self-effacement.[1] The 'I'—that sense of selfhood—disappears from the sentence and there is only an exteriorised 'you', an object, an Other. Such is the effect of my aunt's question: by assuming that I could be part of the institution as it currently exists, it effaces a fundamental part of me from the family gathering. There is a sense in which I'm not fully there at the moment of utterance, because there is a part of me that simply cannot exist within the logic of her question.

Second of all, Sedgwick points out that shame isolates: someone who is shamed is traditionally cut off from the rest of society, and someone who is ashamed acutely feels the sting of the difference between himself and everyone else around him.[2] The question which assumes that *everyone* can (and should) get married underscores for me how alone I am in not being able to partake in the most fundamental aspect of family life. Since I cannot legally marry in Hong Kong, questions like this one turn Chinese New Year, with its emphasis on family, unity and sense of belonging, into an

---

1 Eve Kosofsky Sedgwick, 'Queer Performativity: Henry James's *The Art of the Novel*', 1 *GLQ* (1993), 1–16 (4).
2 Ibid., 14.

annual evaluation of my own relationship with my partner as something unworthy of legitimatisation as proper family life, and therefore as shameful.

Thirdly, and most importantly, Sedgwick posits that shame can take part in the creation of identity, or our sense of who we are and who we can become.[3] If society perpetuates ideas about the undesirability of certain people based on their immutable characteristics, then a sense of shame would gradually become an integral part of how these people understand themselves. Moreover, if you are shamed often enough, regularly enough, by those dearest to you, however subtly or unwittingly, then shame will also be built into the way you understand your own feelings, behaviour and existence. Bullies can damage us, but it is not necessarily the bullies and haters who make us feel most ashamed of our sexuality. It is those closest to us who can most painfully, deeply and disturbingly make us ashamed of who we are.

Sedgwick's analysis of shame brings me back, perhaps somewhat circuitously, to the law. The courts in Hong Kong have clearly stated that dignity is the lynchpin of equality. It is widely accepted that human beings are equal before the law, regardless of traits such as race, gender or sexual orientation, because there is an intrinsic worth common to humanity called dignity that must be protected. To erode one's dignity is to intrude into the very essence of what makes a person human. What is less commonly observed in the legal discussions in Hong Kong is the complex and inextricable link between dignity and shame: to shame someone can mean re-

---

3 Ibid., 5.

ducing them to something smaller, making them feel inferior or unworthy, causing them to hang their heads and lower their eyes, and, ultimately, undermining their dignity. Not all forms of shame directly translate into an erosion of dignity. When a fundamental right is blatantly denied to someone, very often that denial can lead to self-effacement, a sense of isolation, and damage to one's very selfhood. Dignity and shame are intertwined because the induction of shame can be tantamount to the erosion of dignity.

By restricting marriage to a man and a woman, the law perpetuates the view that LGBTQ people are not worthy of marriage, and therefore are lesser human beings compared to heterosexuals. To put the idea slightly differently, by denying same-sex marriage, the law plays a big part in the shaming of LGBTQ people: it suggests that our relationships are not as legitimate as heterosexual relationships, that our love is less noble than heterosexual love, that our vows cannot be taken as seriously or solemnly as heterosexual vows. It suggests that something about same-sex love is simply too undignified to be granted legal recognition. The legal denial of same-sex marriage creates the very society in which my aunt's question can be articulated: a question which so blithely assumes that LGBTQ people are too alone, or too promiscuous, or too maladjusted, or simply too shameful, to even think of qualifying for entry into the institution of marriage, such that no one in her family could possibly be one of *them*.

Given the complex entanglements between dignity and shame, I would suggest that shame is not something that we can simply get rid of through the fight for same-sex marriage or for LGBTQ rights more broadly. In other words, dignity and shame are not simply polar opposites: achieving dignity does not necessarily mean getting rid of shame. This is because, as Sedgwick has posited, there is much overlap between shame and sexual non-conformity: the one thing that sexual minorities have in common is the experience of being shamed at some stage in our lives: by our colleagues, by our friends, by our family, by society.[4] In a sense, shame is the bedrock of LGBTQ experience. Sedgwick goes on to argue that, given this centrality of shame, it is not realistic to attempt to excise shame from identity. Rather, shame should be harnessed as a source of energy for change, for reframing the debate about sexual minorities, for transforming culture, for reforming law and politics. Shame, in other words, can be a force or motivation for the LGBTQ movement.

What might that mean in relation to marriage? While some scholars would argue that a queer critique necessarily implies a wholesale rejection of marriage as a heterosexist institution, I don't believe we need to go that far. One way in which shame can be put to productive use is as a drive for the reflection and interrogation of the nature, history, and function of marriage. That is not to say that we would reflect or interrogate because we are ashamed—that would be too literal an interpretation of the work of queer theory— but that given the long exclusion of LGBTQ people from marriage, even if (or when) we achieve marriage equality, we would necessarily stand in a different historical relation to it. This different historical relation can in turn engender critical thinking about the assumptions, norms and structures inherent in an institution which society takes for granted. For instance, perhaps having been excluded from the trajectory

---

4 Ibid., 13.

of getting married, having children and starting a family for so long, when we do gain the right to marry we could think hard about whether the point of marriage is to replicate this trajectory, or whether there is something more fundamental to marriage than procreation. Another possibility is that our different relation to marriage provides a foundation for us to rethink the gender roles it traditionally imposed on society. We can harness shame not only as a force for championing equal dignity, but for critically engaging with the most fundamental ideas about gender and sexuality. This volume marks the twentieth anniversary of the handover; in another twenty years, family gatherings during Chinese New Year in Hong Kong will hopefully have become even happier occasions for being more inclusive and more diverse.

Reflections from a *Gweilo* on Being Out of the Loop

Michael O'Sullivan

I am a teacher, writer and academic who has lived in Hong Kong for nearly all of the second decade since 1997. Living in Hong Kong has enabled me to work in a highly competitive academic job market. It has also allowed me to publish as a creative writer in important Asian publications and to challenge myself as a concerned advocate of free elections and freedom of expression in a changing Hong Kong political context. This short reflective piece examines how one expat academic and writer who is committed to such practices must confront both the limitations of his own understanding of the local context as a non-fluent Cantonese speaker and the impossibility of ever being wholly accepted as 'in the know' in regard to how politics relates to local affairs in Hong Kong. One wears two masks; one is expected to be an 'expert' in the classroom on a certain subject but a *gweilo* in the street. Problems arise when you start to bring the street into the classroom!

My experience in a course called Literature and Politics that I taught in Hong Kong brought this conflict home to me. I was teaching the class during, and shortly after, the Umbrella Movement of 2014. The 79-day protests brought about a million people to the streets to demand universal suffrage. I had focused on the French Revolution and on political history in my other course on Romanticism. I therefore simply could not avoid the related issues raised by this protest movement in Hong Kong, especially when students would often return to my classes having spent nights on the streets. Some students would email me at the start of the week to say they would be spending the day or the week at a protest site, either attending lectures given by volunteer speakers or, in some cases, giving lectures themselves.

Many commentators have erroneously linked the protest movements to what they perceive as a disruptive influence from 'Western' ideas. There is also a strong movement against Western theory in universities in mainland China and, of course, this will eventually become a major concern for Hong Kong universities as we move closer to 2047 and the end of the 'one country, two systems' period. Chinese President Xi Jinping has made frequent calls for universities in China to be governed by, and grounded in, State Marxist-Leninist ideology. Teams from the Ministry of Education of the PRC conduct regular tours and inspections of universities on the mainland. Shantou University, a high-ranking Chinese university with a reputation for internationalisation, was recently publicly rebuked for allowing 'illegal religious' elements to be taught in its courses and for not sufficiently 'managing' its international staff and faculty. These kinds of controls appear alien to the practices and education policies academics have become used to if they have studied and worked, like myself, in such countries as Ireland, the United Kingdom and the United States. Should the universities in Hong Kong be made to pursue similar policies to those on the mainland, then foreign academics may well feel even more disconnected here.

The Literature and Politics course quickly became a forum in which students could voice their opinions on the Umbrella protests that were unfolding. I remember one particular debate between two brilliant young men in the class, one of whom has gone on to become a foreign correspondent with a leading international media company and the other who is climbing high in the legal profession in Hong Kong. The law student refused to condone the actions of the protesters, arguing that progress could only be achieved by making legal challenges on the basis of the Basic Law, the closest thing Hong Kong has to a constitutional document. The other student, an English major, then referred to numerous instances where the Basic Law has been overlooked or interpreted for political advantage by the legal teams from the PRC, even if their interpretations were challenged by legal scholars in Hong Kong. He argued that the Basic Law had become nothing more than a foil for political manoeuvring on the part of the PRC in Hong Kong. However, what I found difficult to keep up with in the class was not so much the detail of the different cases they were able to reel off, but the extent to which they appeared to have thought through the issues I was only touching on in the class.

In order to be better prepared for the class when I taught it the next year, after the protest movement had finished, I read all the recent articles I could find by Hong Kong academics on the Umbrella Movement. These writers examined how the movement revealed certain truths about Hong Kong society, how it differed from previous protest movements in Hong Kong, and the possibilities that remained for Hong Kong activists in the wake of the purported failures of the move-ment. I discussed the ideas with my class and I was a little annoyed by how unmoved they were by my industrious research, especially when I rather foolishly presumed I would be introducing them to debates they had not yet thought about. However, I was in for a shock. When I opened the class up for debate and discussion one student was quick to say, 'Professor, you are out of the loop!' This was, I knew, not aimed only at me but possibly at all Western professors who had good intentions and were eager to respond in some way in lectures to the recent protest movement. The student explained her point and she effectively told me that the *Apple Daily* and other online Hong Kong news sites, wholly in traditional Chinese, were way ahead of me and these Hong Kong aca-demics I was quoting from, who wrote in English.

I was, rather foolishly, taken aback by how well informed the students were and how incredibly passionate and well-organised they were about the kinds of ideas I had felt validated as a *gweilo* for being privy to.

I had more surprises in store. After I had licked my wounds over a coffee following the lecture, and had done some read-ing up on the kinds of sites she was talking about, I returned to my office to find an email from the student in my inbox. She had sent me a seven thousand-word email translating all the key ideas and important arguments being raised by these Chinese language sites. She had included links to all the sites she mentioned in her email. She had done all this in a matter of hours. Once again, I was, rather foolishly, taken aback by how well informed the students were and how in-credibly passionate and well-organised they were about the kinds of ideas I had felt validated as a *gweilo* for being privy to. Then it hit me. Wasn't the protest movement and the swirl of commentary surrounding it still chiefly an academic concern for me? No matter how I tried to make myself feel that it was my responsibility to read up on the topic in order to feel more integrated into the community I lived in, it could never be such an urgent issue for me. For the majority of the students in the class, the protest movement was dealing with life and death issues in terms of the only identity they had, namely a Hong Kong identity. Before their eyes, the nature of the environment that formed them and which they hoped to shape for themselves, their children and their families, was changing beyond recognition. They felt they were losing control of the only region and identity they could call their own. The very basis of their regional identity, a kind of belonging so many of us *gweilos* took for granted by embodying an expat identity with its presumption of a 'home' elsewhere, was slowly being taken from them. The basis of their identity was being reinterpreted from a distance by politicians in Beijing who could not even speak their language and who yet claimed to speak for their best interests in describing Hong Kong as part of a unified nation. The majority of these students had wrestled for so long with these questions of belonging in their mother tongue, Cantonese, before they had ever come to express their concerns in English.

> Before their eyes, the nature of the environment that formed them and which they hoped to shape for themselves, their children and their families, was changing beyond recognition.

However, the reaction also made me realise that it was not only my identity as a *gweilo* that was keeping me 'out of the loop' but also a slight distrust of academics that was often displayed by many of the localist groups who were at the forefront of the protest movement. Hadn't I seen the same coolness in the faces of these students when they spoke about the academic 'leaders' of the original Occupy Central, which later morphed into the Umbrella Movement? Hadn't the general public been quick to turn against the academic leaders of the Occupy Movement and hadn't I marvelled at how quick they were to get behind student 'leaders'? Sometimes the students were as young as seventeen. In fact, hadn't students and even the general public been very eager to see the movement as 'leaderless'? Had they already understood that the movement would need scapegoats? Had the academic leaders themselves seen this coming? Hadn't I been surprised when I saw one of the leaders, during the protests, sitting on a kerb in Admiralty looking less like a man leading a revolution than a man staring down his own slow political execution? Or was there something distinctly distasteful about being led by academics even if they were locals?

The student began her email to me as follows:

> *As mentioned during the break, I have recently become aware that people are virtually living in a parallel Hong Kong if they do not know Chinese/Cantonese. There are simply too few English media in the city. I do not expect that media can give an 'objective' portrait of what is happening; everyone has their agenda; however, if more information is available, the audience can at least make better choices and judgments. The emergence of* Hong Kong Free Press *[a recent English language news site] is a good sign, but we definitely need a lot more. Some localist media are also trying to publish English articles, but not all of them are that good.*

She then went on to describe in detail the nature of the different media groups in Hong Kong, the origins of the localist movement, and the nature of the different protests in Hong Kong since the 1960s and 1970s.

It became clear to me then that I was living in this 'parallel Hong Kong'—a Hong Kong of locals and *gweilos* where each group complements each other but can also feed off each other. Not only are fluent Cantonese and fluent English required to try to understand how the groups work to keep themselves separate, but one would also have to understand all the slang and idioms of local Cantonese. Many foreign academics in Hong Kong are doubly removed from the realities of Hong Kong life. They are non Cantonese-speaking *gweilos* and they are academics. They cannot interact meaningfully with locals and their research might also take them into highly specialised discourses with no obvious connection with the community they live in. Many foreign academics also live an on-campus expat existence where one is never really required to speak any Cantonese in daily life. Academics can very easily live in an English bubble in a minority group within campus boundaries, or within expat communities in the more expensive parts of Hong Kong. Discussing local issues with expat academics can also quickly become an exercise that brings out the implicit 'us and them' mentality between locals and *gweilos*. This is exacerbated when there is no interest in learning the local language or even getting to know locals as friends.

However, the distance is maintained on both sides. My wife is a Hong Konger and thanks to her I can often eavesdrop on the ways locals also use the lack of understanding to gain what advantage they can from expats. On one occasion in a local restaurant in Hong Kong, where the lunch menu is only written in traditional Chinese characters, my wife and I were sitting beside two local women. Both were landladies trying to rent property. At one point one of the women advised the other woman to get a *shui yu* (水魚), a local expression derived from the term for a Chinese soft shell turtle that means someone who is easy to rip off or fool. My wife understood that one woman was advising the other to get a *gweilo* or expat new to Hong Kong who knew nothing about the property market here and can therefore be asked to pay above the market value. Of course, expats working in the privileged English language business and university environments can also be regarded as taking advantage of their status in a highly stratified, unequal society with a lingering colonialist mindset. The 'parallel Hong Kong' has emerged over time so that both locals and *gweilos* can regard themselves as gaining an unspoken advantage from the other group; it is often perceived as an undeclared economic advantage, something that suits the general ethos of Hong Kong as a low-tax economy sustained by investment and gambling, pursuits that might be described in terms of hedging one's bets and getting one over on the other.

However, I feel my students have not yet settled in comfortably to accepting the divide between these groups; they are still finding their way in Hong Kong and have privileged access to a liberal arts education. They had perhaps recognised that I was trying to understand the local context. Despite the fact that I was taking up the role of 'expert' in the lecture theatre, they had acted out of a sense responsibility to their own society by alerting me to what was really being said by the local community about localism and local politics. In other words, they were trying to do their small part in bridging the divide between the two groups in Hong Kong. For me, as a teacher here, the Umbrella Movement was a social movement that briefly allowed the contrived nature of this division to make itself felt. There was a coming together both in the streets and in the classroom. There was an eagerness to get everyone on the same side in working towards shared ideals for society. Since the movement ended it has been difficult to capture the same willingness to listen in the classroom. Students have perhaps found it easier to accept that Western values are Western and Chinese values are Chinese. For this is what our discussions were really aimed at in the class; they were aimed at reviving an interest in how the Western values and indigenous Hong Kong and Chinese values that constitute Hong Kong society have always cohabited. These are values built on an openness to cross-cultural encounter and investigation, an East–West educational ethos, and a respect for the dignity of civic life. As we move closer to 2047 one feels that the 'parallel Hong Kong' my student drew my attention to acts as a kind of secretly-cherished known unknown. It is an often- unacknowledged marker of difference, but it is as important for maintaining the uniqueness of Hong Kong identity as is the mainland China identity it often rails against.

My Journey as a Student Activist

Joshua Wong

I 'm a twenty-year-old university student, born a year before the handover.

Having grown up under Chinese rule, I don't have any memory of colonial Hong Kong or feel any attachment to it. Instead, I was spoon-fed daily a hearty serving of self-evident truths: that Hong Kong is and always will be an 'inalienable part' of China; and that the Chinese Communist Party, or CCP, always has our best interests in mind under the 'one country, two systems' framework.

But twenty years after the transfer of sovereignty, I now know an altogether different set of facts: that Beijing continues to deny us the right to a free vote in breach of the Joint Declaration, an international treaty it signed with Britain in 1984; that, as a result, Hong Kong is stuck in a rut on its never-ending path to democracy; and that the CCP has launched an all-out attack on our civil liberties, from academic and press freedom to the freedom of expression and publication, and is using the red dollar to 'Sinofy' our entertainment and media industry.

The situation is dire. Many things that Hong Kong people have long taken for granted, such as an independent judiciary, due process and the separation of powers, are vanishing in front of our eyes. The most disconcerting example of that came in 2016, when five booksellers who published books critical of the Chinese leadership were abducted by undercover CCP operatives. Months later, two democratically-elected opposition lawmakers were disqualified for 'insulting China' when they took their oath of office. All that, and much more, is adding to our growing frustration and anxiety.

That was precisely the reason why a new crop of young activists like myself decided to go into politics with the hope of defending our core values and moving Hong Kong out of its existential rut.

Six years ago, under Beijing's directives, the Hong Kong Special Administrative Region (SAR) government announced a citywide plan to introduce a 'national education curriculum' in all primary and secondary schools. It was a thinly-veiled attempt to inculcate in our youth a sense of unquestioning patriotism and blind loyalty to the CCP. Perhaps because veteran politicians had been so far removed from the classroom, the news drew little interest from the opposition parties.

I was fourteen years old at the time, just starting secondary two. I knew I couldn't stand quietly by while a brainwashing curriculum poisoned our education. It was then that I founded a student organisation called Scholarism with a small group of secondary school students to defend free and independent thinking in the classroom through demonstrations and other means of grassroots resistance.

Our campaigns had little traction at first—our street rallies drew only a few dozen participants and our soapbox speeches didn't get much press coverage. Our efforts were met with a general sense of resignation, as many people thought it futile to try to push back against Beijing's agenda.

More critically, Hong Kong society had yet to fully embrace the idea of student activism. Our rote-based education system was—and still is—so focused on grades and public exams that anything else was considered a distraction. This was understandable. For generations of Hong Kongers, the only means of upward mobility and the only way to meaningfully contribute to society have been to obtain a respectable university degree (preferably in business administration) and a professional accreditation (in finance, accounting, law or medicine). Politics was so far off the beaten path for a teenager that it must be discouraged at any cost.

But the Bible has taught me well. St Paul told us not to 'let anyone look down on you because you are young' and I took that lesson to heart. The night before the national education curriculum was rolled out, not long after literature sponsored by the Department of Education described the CCP as a 'progressive, selfless and unifying ruling body', we finally succeeded in galvanizing the public to stand up against flagrant propaganda. More than 120,000 citizens showed up at 'Civic Square' outside the government headquarters in support of our movement, forcing the SAR government to withdraw the plan the following day. Months of street protests, social media campaigns and hunger strikes had not gone to waste.

But our movement did more than thwart a dangerous curriculum. It created a paradigm shift among young people whose political apathy had for too long been an enabler of our unpopular government. Encouraged by its early success, Scholarism quickly shifted its focus to engaging students in the fight for democracy and more specifically our constitutionally guaranteed right to freely elect our leader.

Our chief executive is chosen not by the city's 3.7 million registered voters, but by a small committee of 1,200 mostly pro-Beijing business people That means our leader is accountable not to the people but to a small circle of individuals who have handpicked him or her. Instead of protecting our interests, he or she takes direct orders from Beijing and has a vested interest in protecting the undemocratic electoral system by indefinitely delaying the promise of universal suffrage.

Since the handover, 'electoral reform' has been a pawn in the chess game between the government and the pan-democracy camp led by long-time political elites. The subject has been kicked around for nearly two decades and very little progress, if any, has been made. I believe elitism in politics is over, and a new path to achieving democracy should be charted by young people who have the most at stake in the future of our city. I also believe that real changes are brought about not by playing by the old rules but by civil disobedience and mass uprisings, and that young people, free from financial burdens and family demands, have the least to lose should they be arrested or convicted and therefore should take a more prominent role.

Those beliefs enabled us to embrace the Occupy Movement of 2014 by organising, in the lead-up to the actual street occupation, a citywide class boycott, various mass protests and a referendum on electoral reform in which over 800,000 citizens participated. In fact, it was our impromptu decision to retake the Civic Square on September 26th, two days before Occupy erupted, that led to the start of the 79-day struggle.

For the first time in our history, students—instead of politicians—were put in the driver's seat in the city's pro-democracy struggle and, more specifically, in expressing our collective indignation towards the so-called '8/31 Decision'—the framework of the Standing Committee of the National People's Congress on August 31st, 2014, that made clear that only a candidate pre-screened by Beijing can be elected chief executive. It was that decision that set in motion the largest political uprising on Chinese soil since the Tiananmen Square protests in 1989.

The Occupy Movement, dubbed the Umbrella Revolution by the foreign press, has rewritten Hong Kong's history. Hundreds of thousands of citizens braved tear gas and police violence and took over major thoroughfares across the city for two-and-a-half months, all the while adhering to the principles of a peaceful, nonviolent resistance. In the process, we not only made a compelling case for universal suffrage on the world stage, but we also demonstrated what it means to be a Hong Konger. Even so, the movement ended without achieving the political gains it had set out to achieve, and Beijing remained as uncompromising as ever towards our call for electoral reform.

Perhaps not surprisingly, the SAR government began to systematically go after leaders and participants as soon as the Occupy Movement ended in December 2014. Since then, countless students have been charged with unlawful assembly, public nuisance, obstruction of police and other crimes.

For many, prison terms seem inevitable. Likewise, Beijing has acted swiftly to extend its long arm to restrict our mobility in the region. To stay on China's good side, a number of Southeast Asian countries have refused entry to me and other Occupy leaders. In 2015, I was detained by the Thai authorities at the Bangkok airport without cause. Fortunately, these tactics have done little to slow down the pace of civil awakening and political engagement in Hong Kong; they only expose the CCP's insecurity and underscore the broken promise that is 'one country, two systems'.

For too long, Hong Kongers have subscribed to the belief that the Joint Declaration and the Basic Law, our mini-constitution, will protect the freedoms we enjoy, at least until 2047 when the 'one country, two systems' policy expires. Given China's tattered human rights record and the country's political regression under president Xi Jinping's iron fist, the notion that our semi-autonomy will remain intact is increasingly in doubt. On this twentieth anniversary of the handover, we can't help but wonder what will happen in the coming thirty years, as 'one country' continues to rear its ugly head, and indeed what will happen *after* 2047, when 'two systems' devolves into 'one system'.

In 2015, I founded a political party called Demosistō with my fellow Occupy student leaders Nathan Law Kwun-chung and Agnes Chow Ting. Our goal is twofold: first, to safeguard our constitutionally-enshrined rights through political participation and civil disobedience; and second, to initiate public discussions over Hong Kong's future after 2047 and advocate 'self-determination' by holding a referendum at that point to assert our political status.

We believe the Legislative Council, or LegCo, is a crucial platform to achieve our twin goals. Because I was too young to run in the LegCo elections in 2015, I threw my support behind Nathan's bid for an elected seat. Vowing to bring the spirit of nonviolent resistance from Occupy into LegCo, Nathan ran a successful campaign and, at the age of twenty-three, became the youngest lawmaker in Hong Kong's history. His win has not only given us a seat at the negotiation table with the SAR government and other political forces, but it has also cemented Demosistō's status as an opposition party.

Twenty years ago, the idea of a large-scale political uprising that would paralyse the city for months was simply unthinkable. Equally implausible was the notion that a university student could enter LegCo as an advocate for the city's self-determination. Twenty years after the handover, what was once unthinkable and implausible is part of a political reality, proving that Hong Kongers are not just economic beings and are much more than what meets the eye. We desire and thirst for freedom, democracy and the rule of law just like anyone else. And we are prepared to fight tooth and nail for all of those things.

From leading the resistance against a patriotic curriculum to leading a political party in support of self-determination, the past six years has left an indelible mark on my adolescence. The journey has been both educational and trying. I don't know what the future holds for me or for Hong Kong. What I do know is that the road ahead will continue to be fraught with challenges and setbacks. To stand up to the world's largest autocracy, it will take more resolve and conviction that we have known or shown.

By 2047, I will be fifty years old. I want to be able to tell my children that their father and many in his generation fought a beautiful battle for the city they love.

Translated from the Chinese by Jason Y. Ng.

POETRY

Four Poems

Eddie Tay

groundwork

there is power in granite
not of your choice,
earth-deposits of a history of money.

so today you are digging
out of the pavement a strength
you always possess,
a faith in stone.

i wonder what would happen
if you find a fish gasping in the dust,
or if a hundred-year-old turtle crawls out
to proclaim the good news.

i am waiting for a minotaur
to emerge to start a fresh flood.

we imagine ourselves to be trees
in the thick sulphur of this city
where no one needs to speak.

maybe you're waiting to tell a story
of an underground government
of broken bodies.

who are our leaders,
that they would stay quiet?

these are eruptions
too deep in the ground,
metaphors of stone,
groundwork of hands.

don't ask

don't ask me how it is

that someone who does the right thing
fixes a light bulb
thinks it is not enough

that a bed is not enough

it is nowhere
when one cannot name it

one is nowhere
until a phone chirps

until one could place himself
in an economy of a sensible skyline
overlooking the harbour

there is something
in yachts idle in marinas

something with a view advertised
that gives meaning

it isn't the birds
unless one remembers a scene from a film

unless there are appropriate flowers
romantic
like a billboard one has seen again and again

one can only be a tourist
constantly taking pictures

posing and making sense

negative capability

today i shall be a clueless tourist
in my own country of the self:

i tell my son i am a tree
though i am a tree trying to be a man

because it takes ten years to cultivate a tree,
a century for a human being;

sometimes i have to be a rock
though i am a rock trying to be a man

because jesus was a rock,
and peter was a rock;

on other days i tell my boss
i am a calculator

though i am a calculator trying to be a man
because a calculator is convenient;

am i a pencil that i must write,
or am i to be water?

i tell myself i am a camera
though i am a camera trying to be a man

because a camera captures everything
and is nothing in itself.

Hong Kong Village

At the next village house
there's a rooftop BBQ going on.
I could hear the clink of wineglasses,
smell the meat-scented smoke.

They call this *yan hey*—human breath,
and of course noise is always better
than silence, especially when someone sets off
firecrackers at midnight during Chinese New Year.

There are teenagers loitering about
and there is always a boy with a homemade
motorised skateboard cruising around.
The dogs here are big, and sometimes loud.

Someone has left a note on my car's windscreen.
The entire village's parking area is to be used
for a lion dance performance this Sunday,
and I'm to call to check where to park.

The Chinese New Year riot at Mong Kok
is on the news. People are still being arrested.
Noise is always better than silence.
They call this *yan hey*—human breath.

Where there's smoke, there's fire.
All those hellos, good mornings, BBQs, scuffles,
shots fired, blood. Neighbours, community,
we make it up as we go along.

Jungle

Gérard Henry

The small roof terrace of artist Ko Siu Lan, and later of poet Madeleine Marie Slavick, surrounded by high-rise buildings, in Wun Sha Street in the old district of Tai Hang.

Three Poems

Lui Wing Kai, Eric

Looking Down From a Footbridge

Late at night, warm breezes still blow through the street
Red lights are no longer red lights, no trams on the tramways
Sogo is no longer Sogo
You no longer look to the big clock on Times Square
Late at night, they've lost their words
Time seems to be drawn out
Streets seem able to stretch
We recover our faces and eyes
Late at night, we silently glide
walk down Lockhart Road, through Percival Street
up to the footbridge still lit
Waiting out the rain in silence
light a cigarette
a smidgen of loneliness
But we
feel weary

Hoardings hang in the air, their green lights flashing
We realise the city always has some places lit

while dark places darken still
We start bringing up what we've lost:
Once we wished to plant a cypress in Time Square
we thought snow would one day fall on Pak Sha Road
there would no longer be demonstrations at Victoria Park
no candles lit, or sad songs sung
that words painful to read would be shelved in the library
or the pier's debris might be found in the water
Sometimes we long for a dance in the road
Sometimes we're on a treetop, dreaming to reach the sky
and we come across a smiling eagle. The city has love
In the depth of a swimming pool is the dream of a seven-year-old boy
The bedside lamp will never be switched off
like the night's fireflies scatter light
on the white wall where secrets are scribbled
The self who lags far behind is right in front

since when is our courage only enough to ward off
the cold blades of one night
Even though no trucks are there blocking our way
still we will go to a warmer place
We don't need to search or think over every day
as if biting a rope to drag an ox
We only have a frail body and muddled senses
no more than the mannequins in the store windows
waiting for strangers to put their favoured clothes on us
for passersby to cast envious glances at us
that have nothing to do with us
At last our skins languish and wrinkle
just as memories cake and crumble

We light a cigarette and hide in this smidgen of loneliness
imagine many years later late at night

our eyes have aged, we will think of
the silhouettes shattered on the street
tonight. Let's make a promise—
We will pick them up, scrap by scrap
the cypress
half of the snow-laden street
the time of smoking this cigarette
the smidgen of loneliness
although we finally catch on to it—Their meanings
only lie in their having-been
or their never-have-been

Yes, never a moment not wordless
I seem to walk on the overhead wire
stretch out my hands to keep a parlous balance
Never a moment of courage to open my eyes
keep my mind on the deep cold and shiver beneath my feet
Sometimes I hear a voice that urges me to go on
Sometimes it asks me to pause
Sometimes I seem to hear the wish gently uttered
at the bottom of the swimming pool by the seven-year-old
Sometimes I seem to hear the family laugh
Sometimes I wish I were a loose kite
that knows freedom and knows not the fall
Sometimes I imagine I am a raven fully merged into night
Sometimes I long for the eyes of an eagle that smiles

Still we are on the lonesome footbridge
listening for quickening footsteps
The world won't stop spinning for anyone
Trams in the terminal are anxious about tomorrow
We wish to fall into the dawn's light
and find solace in the most tender blue

We wish a see-through flower would blossom tomorrow
knowing it will wither
We wish to carve unchanged inscriptions
on its petals thin like cicada wings—We are only too tired
looking down from this footbridge still lit
we choose to forget
sit here, numb
senses slip

Dark Night at Mong Kok

The boundless strangeness in the crowd is like particles dispersing
Stubborn thoughts perhaps clot into mighty black trees
Crows unwilling to fly become blades of leaves
in a roofless world wait for encounters and stare at everything

As if we should put up with polluted air
hope still surpasses hatred at moments when nothing translates
The city's dark corners have no caves that aren't escapes
only that we prefer to listen for the words we want to hear

We didn't know a number would be assigned to us at the
        time of birth
We catch breaths in and out of life, sickness, ageing and
        death, and we stroll
and cast away stability. Since when do we wish butterflies to
        carry rocks
through a still obscure world of red lights and iron rails?

When Mong Kok wraps black cloth over one's eyes

lost is the path itself, not the crowd. A city longing to burn
clears its throat. Carved on one's shoulder are another's stern
look and crushed name, hence the hatred

Spring Flowers Drop

A mass of moisture envelops the apartment
Beads of water seem to carry the sounds of dripping
The TV broadcast is endless
Father in bed, that brittle whiff of retiring
Carefully you walk along the slippery corridor
I watch the hill next to the apartment building merge into
        the boundless night
Silence sprouts. A gecko slips down from the damp wall

But let me be precise
This is not a sense of helplessness that comes from life
Five o'clock in the morning, many birds sing on the hills
I know a day's work starts
You stretch your body in the living room
I look at the scratched shoes, and in haste
I throw into the briefcase the key to home
I don't know, sometimes,
space splits bit by bit in half

I grow up and leave Tsing Yi Island
Now you and I return to our separate homes
Similar are the corridors, and their turnings and silences
The same strange apartments cut off by scissor gates

Everyone has to deal with his own distress
in the end like a stone cast down on the couch
grumbling about everyday trivia between rapid breaths
You and I return to our separate beds
stare at the ceilings for dramas of silhouettes
sound has lost its reference. This damp night
floods our rooms thousands of miles apart
Echoes reverberate and glide down a vast endless tunnel
Turns out the days would be cut back once they stay long enough
Too late to piece the past together
a great many scraps
so remote like myriad stars
So you say

Later we learn to read body language
Hints of smiles at dinner are like moonlight on spring nights
Meeting for a few hours every week allows us to have a new start
You slowly let down stones in the heart
while I can't help piling them up
You lock up the spring. In the damp
you hide the groans of joint pain
I'm weak and always feel at times
as if the road fogs up over one night
The white devours all the doors along the corridor
The moisture on the window can't be wiped away
Melancholy of damp tropical heat
when the humidity reaches one hundred per cent
I become afraid of slipping after all

Remember? When I was a kid, I often went into the hill
          near our house
and played hide-and-seek in the woods. Over the other side
I could see peaceful waters and a vast dock

hear ships' whistles from the sea
When the park was hewed out, it was no longer like an island
At the time father was wearing the uniform and patrolling buildings
You chased daylight while I walked slowly on a footbridge
When can we put these away
and listen to the sea's murmur?
The tides ebb and flow
from the eye of bleak moonlight
Mysterious was the dock's white fog
that foreshadowed our parting ways
Even if we fixed our eyes on it, unwilling to close them
we still couldn't deny the vastest land is but a floating island

A layer of white shade grows on your retina
and your world blurs ever since
The badminton racquets are tucked away
in the narrow gap on top of the closet
Is this an overture of separating? Is the world
real? Will you recognise me
when by chance we walk closer
and closer still towards each other on the street?
Can each find the other's whereabouts by
Sensing their voices, smells and blood ties?
Can we meet again in the world in the unknowable future?
Can we annotate our lives and measure out our memories?

Time is an art of folding. It follows the creases of being
and slowly puts on his shirt. Future comes unknowingly.
Weakens or strengthens, it soothes all trembles
A pair of clingy shadows in an alley
I watch your figure diminish
and enlarge again in the yellow lamplight
Spring fades into the mist and shines in the dampness

I grew up on Tsing Yi
not until I moved off this small island
did I realise its original name:
Spring Flowers Drop

All three poems translated from the Chinese by Chris Song.

Two Poems

Shirley Geok-lin Lim

Thursday's Child

Thursday's child is out again
in rain and shine, white in her hair,
home and homelessness still ahead,
unsure which is the dream.

She thinks the answer is
inevitable: no one chooses,
despite the ballot booth
and voices of authority

and power who promise the land
before her. She'd walked down the road,
stranded, travel-wrecked, past
shut gates behind which no one

appears. She'd never rung the bell
declaring, *Here I am in your
promised land.* Born in a caul
that stung, tongue blistered, she's

moving from elsewhere to elsewhere,
each homecoming a pilgrim's stay.

Packing

I am doing this everyday,
having learned from Mother,
who maybe packed before she disappeared
to a place I could not imagine:
our lives so estranged I did not know
Sorrow when she sat down beside me.
Or from Father who never left.
He grew smaller, crowded with new
babies he welcomed as if with fire-
crackers each year.
                              I had to leave
to find a room of my own. What did I
pack then, their harried daughter,
who carried no suitcase, no backpack,
baggage heavy in my head, stored
for life? I'm packing again for the room
not my own, the families not my own,
stuff no one needs, luggage in the head
still there, that cannot be tagged, lighter
than air, vacuum-sealed, trash turned
treasure the hoarder cannot live without.

Two Poems

Nicholas Wong

Mother Turns to Cantopop, and Waits for the Narrative to Turn to Her

Album: *Fable* (2000)
Artist: Faye Wong

Track Title	Time	Appropriate(d) Thoughts
The Cambrian Age	-0:01	a dagger stops me from ribboning myself
New Tenant	0:54	a lethal weapon with a sense of cleanliness
Chanel	1:02	smell delayed by the self-reflexive-ness of air
Flower on the Other Shore	1:28	hope is a reproduction of the odd search for predictable time

If You Were Fake	2:04	I would be fake like the centre in a cento
I Won't Love Anyone Who Doesn't Love Me	2:21	the trouble of nonsense isn't about nothingness
Farewell Firefly	2:58	no wonder a long dark night vomits illumination
Book of Laughter and Forgetting	3:19	this comes as no real surprise/language afraid of enosis
Firefly	3:47	so shamefully ask why it takes so long to save enough light for a week
Love Letters to Myself	4:44	lying to oneself isn't hard/what is is what to lie about

Re: work

Proof 4: Elvis Yip Kin Bon, *If You Miss Home* (2016, single-channel video)

This is your cultural capital speaking.
Shrouded in mosaics, timed
and spent by a video, what will

you do? *Think, I will, the future
of my son.* Your melancholy
is overbooked. We ask you to focus.

To practise: … *bridge is falling down.*
Downed ownership: What
will you do if you miss your family?

I will keep myself busy. Focus,
adjusted, falling down. But self:
Ah —This is cultural

capital speaking. Your self
is sublingual. *Kalau tidak bobo*:
If you are not sleeping, odd

your self out. Self in English only,
such as: *wood and clay
will wash away.* Such as R.I.P.

for self storage. *Ah, I will hard work,
boy bared.* It is human interest
to have verbs come first:

done work, bear this. *Ah*—.
Diaspora, prolific in bawling.
Infirm. Of it we don't speak

much here. Though sere,
severed, focus. *Even iron bars
will bend and break.* What will

you do if you break? *Photos,
wrinkles, blender.* Remember,
no one expects shoes

to clean themselves. *Ah* —.
Self: neither an ad
nor a calling. To box it, we ask

you, what is worse than falling:
a floor that cants and can't
refuse what falls.

Two Poems
Wawa

Sea Drawing I: Tung Lo Wan Road

light #eedd82 sunlight by 3 pm

early may's summer

29 C

misty 7-eleven

misty fairwood
misty fishball stall   misplaced royal poinciana
misty baby product store

no traffic
tung lo wan road

deep breath ten feet under

                                        when all lives are young
                                         bathing in the sun
                                        golden victoria park
                                        murmurs

sun seen through glass
suffering on ground floor
lives folded towards
        victoria harbour

        'Jesus loves you'

                                folded high-rises
                                folded central library
                                folded clouds
                                folded prairies   towards
                                        victoria harbour

        folded people
        stand up
        opening a hand
                towards
                    their mountains

                        words take off

                                        victoria harbour floods
                                        swallows take off

Sea Drawing II: Tsing Ma Bridge

humidity 92 per cent   slate gray
#9fb6cd
light steel blue #bcd2ee

unfocused overcast

skeleton of
tsing ma bridge   low pressure

cadet #536878 kai tap mun
south china sea

thick fog
of abandoned silhouettes

white dolphins coming

rusted bridge
covered in moths
longing to fall

lighthouse still giving light
those sitting on the sky's edge
    see home
      in the dark

                  I swim among dolphins
                  in doubled survival suits
                  listening to sprouts
                  budding on the shores

        between my feet
        and 3,000 feet under
        a sunken city floating
                underwater

Happy Return

Douglas Young

Two Poems

Louise Ho

On Borrowing

Some catchphrases
Have a way
With staying power.
This one, for instance,
Has been around
Since the 1950s.

Nuances remain
Grey and slippery,
Swimming or hiding,
Among murky waters.

There were uncertain times,
Some more volatile than others.
Whatever molecules or atoms,
Whizzing around,
In things unstable and in flux,
Became crystallised in 1997.

Nor was there borrowing or lending
During colonial rule or its aftermath.
Then, our fifty years were given, not lent.

By the thisness of the here and now,
The citizen of Hong Kong takes his stand.
'I live here,
This is my time,
This is my place.
The haecceity of this place, this moment
Makes this mine, mine, mine.'

Silly Notion...

silly notion: eight pieces of a pie
seem more than the whole one

ditto: cut-up muffin
arranged to fill a plate

divide place into spaces
the sectional becomes quasi whole
informs qualified identity
may even begin its own history

many moons ago
folks used to say
'Hong Kong Island people
are so

different from Kowloon people'
as for the New Territories
they were another world

more recently
we've been sectioned
into eighteen districts
if only for voting purposes

wonder if
in the next decade or so
more or less
these parts would flesh out
and give this place
something of a new tenor
a different amplitude
a new dispensation

Two Systems

Sarah Howe

Note to 'Two Systems':

The poem's title refers to 'one country, two systems', the principle that Hong Kong's capitalist way of life should remain unchanged for fifty years following its return to China on July 1st, 1997. The former British colony is currently more than one-third of the way through this limbo-like phase, in which it supposedly enjoys a 'high degree of autonomy' from China's socialist system, as the countdown ticks ever closer to 2047. In the early summer of 2014, just as I was working on this poem, Beijing released a white paper that aroused widespread concern in Hong Kong. Many there interpreted it as yet another sign of the mainland seeking to interfere in the Special Administrative Region's domestic affairs—including, for example, the suggestion that its judges should show fealty to Beijing.

During the 1980s, preparations for the handover in 1997 included London and Beijing negotiating the document that would become the Basic Law of the Hong Kong Special Administrative Region, the new Hong Kong's constitution. In reading through and about the Hong Kong Basic Law, I couldn't stop thinking about its nature as a sort of self-deconstructing text—self-*destructing* even, given that it enshrines within itself the date of its own undoing. It put me in mind of the 'erasure poem', a form that's been popular among Western *avant-garde* writers since the 1960s. One famous example is Ronald Johnson's *Radi Os* (1977), which erases most of the words in Milton's *Paradise Lost* to create a new, surprisingly affecting work out of the earlier poem's rubble.

It was satisfying, in a childlike-way, to set about these pages from the Basic Law with Photoshop's eraser tool. I imagined myself releasing their anarchic, subversive, gloriously vulgar undersongs. I was delighted to find, in amongst the nonsense, touches of sense emerging: allusions to the current unrest about Hong Kong's path to universal suffrage ('power to the People'), or, more subtly, to its colonial past. (I found myself writing about a hapless character called 'Reg', whose name is an irreverent nod to the *'Regina v. X'* formula of English law: a sort of cut-down Crown.) I chose the pages on either side of the Article 23 anti-subversion law, because in 2003 it caused huge protests in defence of freedom of speech and the press. By the poem's final page—which seeks to define a 'Hong Kong resident'—hardly anything is left, except that haunting date: 2047.

The courts of the Hong Kong Special Administrative Region shall have no jurisdiction over acts of state such as defence and foreign affairs. The courts of the Region shall obtain a certificate from the Chief Executive on questions of fact concerning acts of state such as defence and foreign affairs whenever such questions arise in the adjudication of cases. This certificate shall be binding on the courts. Before issuing such a certificate, the Chief Executive shall obtain a certifying document from the Central People's Government.

Article 20

The Hong Kong Special Administrative Region may enjoy other powers granted to it by the National People's Congress, the Standing Committee of the National People's Congress or the Central People's Government.

Article 21

Chinese citizens who are residents of the Hong Kong Special Administrative Region shall be entitled to participate in the management of state affairs according to law.

In accordance with the assigned number of seats and the selection method specified by the National People's Congress, the Chinese citizens among the residents of the Hong Kong Special Administrative Region shall locally elect deputies of the Region to the National People's Congress to participate in the work of the highest organ of state power.

Article 22

No department of the Central People's Government and no province, autonomous region, or municipality directly under the Central Government may interfere in the affairs which the Hong Kong Special Administrative Region administers on its own in accordance with this Law.

If there is a need for departments of the Central Government, or for provinces, autonomous regions, or municipalities directly under the Central Government to set up offices in the Hong Kong Special

The court of   Kong   is rat   hall
       diction over acts   such   fence and   reign affairs.
   our   Region shall obtain a   cat
       on quest

                                    the   cat   of
       cat   hall   Before
                   all

                                         eg   joy
power   to   the   People
       he   he

       zen
             shall   entitle   the   age
                 to

       dance   number   the
                                                    citizens
among the
           elect
                     work   the high   organ of

       men   over   and
over
   mini rat   mini   dance

   there is a need for   art

Administrative Region, they must obtain the consent of the government of the Region and the approval of the Central People's Government.

All offices set up in the Hong Kong Special Administrative Region by departments of the Central Government, or by provinces, autonomous regions, or municipalities directly under the Central Government, and the personnel of these offices shall abide by the laws of the Region.

*For entry into the Hong Kong Special Administrative Region, people from other parts of China must apply for approval. Among them, the number of persons who enter the Region for the purpose of settlement shall be determined by the competent authorities of the Central People's Government after consulting the government of the Region.

The Hong Kong Special Administrative Region may establish an office in Beijing.

Article 23

The Hong Kong Special Administrative Region shall enact laws on its own to prohibit any act of treason, secession, sedition, subversion against the Central People's Government, or theft of state secrets, to prohibit foreign political organizations or bodies from conducting political activities in the Region, and to prohibit political organizations or bodies of the Region from establishing ties with foreign political organizations or bodies.

Note:
* See The Interpretation by the Standing Committee of the National People's Congress of Articles 22(4) and 24(2)(3) of the Basic Law of the Hong Kong Special Administrative Region of the People's Republic of China (Adopted at the Tenth Session of the Standing Committee of the Ninth National People's Congress on 26 June 1999) (see **Instrument 17**)

Reg   must obtain
the approval of   People

by   art   or by
autonomous   ions,   ire   under the
Government

                                   Among
them, the numb   who enter   the   pose of
settlement shall be   the competent author

Reg

                       may establish an
off   Beijing.

                     Reg   shall enact
any act of treason,   sedition
                or theft of
                         ducting
        he   bit it
bodies   reign
organ   or bodies.

Chapter III: Fundamental Rights and Duties of the Residents

Article 24

Residents of the Hong Kong Special Administrative Region ("Hong Kong residents") shall include permanent residents and non-permanent residents.

The permanent residents of the Hong Kong Special Administrative Region shall be:

(1) Chinese citizens born in Hong Kong before or after the establishment of the Hong Kong Special Administrative Region;

(2) Chinese citizens who have ordinarily resided in Hong Kong for a continuous period of not less than seven years before or after the establishment of the Hong Kong Special Administrative Region;

*(3) Persons of Chinese nationality born outside Hong Kong of those residents listed in categories (1) and (2);

(4) Persons not of Chinese nationality who have entered Hong Kong with valid travel documents, have ordinarily resided in Hong Kong for a continuous period of not less than seven years and have taken Hong Kong as their place of permanent residence before or after the establishment of the Hong Kong Special Administrative Region;

(5) Persons under 21 years of age born in Hong Kong of those residents listed in category (4) before or after the establishment of the Hong Kong Special Administrative Region; and

---

Note:
* See The Interpretation by the Standing Committee of the National People's Congress of Articles 22(4) and 24(2)(3) of the Basic Law of the Hong Kong Special Administrative Region of the People's Republic of China (Adopted at the Tenth Session of the Standing Committee of the Ninth National People's Congress on 26 June 1999) (see **Instrument 17**)

:

("
")   .("

.

:

()   ;

()   ;

*()   ()   ();

()

;

()   ()

;

7

Umbrella Poetics

Jennifer S. Cheng

In making for ourselves a place to live, we first spread a parasol to throw a shadow on the earth, and in the pale light of the shadow we put together a house.
—*Tanizaki Junichiro*

1/

We might only begin mid-sentence. After my family returned to the States, I only ever thought of Hong Kong as a place of shadows: a loose daydream, a small hour, a vague and lingering homesickness. Or: After the island was given away, and then again and again; after its people were not let out after dark, told to carry papers and lamps to light their faces, after they were relegated to live apart in disease and poverty; after it was ruled over, conceded, occupied, after it was returned but only to another history—

First: *And isn't liminality a longing for voice?* Then: *What is the poetics of longing?*

2/

From Ackbar Abbas, *Hong Kong: Culture and the Politics of Disappearance*:

'Post-coloniality... means finding ways of operating under a set of difficult conditions that threatens to appropriate us as subjects...for example, thinking about emigration in a certain way, emigration not in the diasporic sense of finding another space...with all the pathos of departure, but in the sense of remaking a given space that for whatever reason one cannot leave, of dislocating.'

3/

4/

For many immigrants and children of immigrants in America, our belonging is a kind of longing. It is not as simple as saying that we belong nowhere or we belong everywhere but only that it is somehow precarious, that there is a quiet yearning for, an understanding of, some undefined space ever in the periphery of one's eye. When I began travelling back to Hong Kong as an adult, I found I could still only know it as it belonged in my heart: deep green hills that cradled my body, moistened tile platforms and pedestrian walkways that rose and twined and ended at the ocean, passageways and alleys I could know and not know, bus rides up and down unkempt mountains, toward and away from the sea. What I mean is: I have never been able to know what Hong Kong means to other people, whether they are outsiders or my own father, and when I think of the city, I think of it as an aberration, a tiny crescent yearning in the midst of a large starry sky.

What I mean is: As much as home is an anchor in the body, a protected space no one else can ever know, we have always known how identity is yet also fluid, murky: how we have had to construct it and claim it with twigs we collected and terrains we named, here and there: how its boundaries shifted and burned with memories uncovered, histories re-learned, linguistics transformed, distances and shadows narrowing and growing and looming.

5/

6/
'[Hyphenation] points precisely to the city's attempts to go beyond such historical determinations by developing a tendency toward time-lessness…and placelessness…a tendency to live its own version of the 'floating world'…' (Abbas).

8/

After the protests began, my friends in the States asked me to explain what was happening. I listed for them the history of Hong Kong, 1841, 1997, 2047, the handover, the Basic Law, the 'white paper' debates, the yearly protests. But it is not merely the pursuit of universal suffrage, as large as that is. It is not even merely the shadow of an oppressive hand. How does one describe the meaning of *home* or *selfhood*? How does one list a familial history of fear and survival and separation—and yet love for one's culture, rooted and unrooted as it is? How my mother and father are bound, not to China or a nation or any government, but to something else unpinned—like the rough weave of my grandmother's voice mixing Shanghainese, Mandarin, English and Cantonese, a blur-ring that intensifies without awareness as she ages. How the texture of freshly fried *youtiao* softens as it is dipped into soy milk on Sunday mornings after a cooling ferry ride, how the overhead clicking of walk-way traffic signs fills the air with footsteps underhand, how rain rushes down outdoor stairwells into a maze of drainage networks during typhoon season, how the air *smells* green in the quieter parts of the island. How does one say, even to oneself, how an immigrant's longing for legitimacy is like this too, the loneliness of the moon, a bright eye turned toward the unbounded sea?

9/

'...not as a neither-nor space that is nowhere; not even as a mixed or in-between space, if by that we understand that the various elements that make it up are separable...' (Abbas).

10/

When the police began to clear Mong Kok, I could barely read the news stories. As closely as I had scoured and searched the internet for every word and syllable at the beginning of the protests, now I almost had to force myself to read the headlines, take in their literal meanings. I do this sometimes with my relationships: distance myself when I sense a distance already threatening to swell. The facts and the news media would never tell me what I needed to know: What shape did the shadows cast on their bodies when they raised instruments meant to keep the weather out, in protection against a governmental force that was coming down on them? When they lifted those shields as a symbol alongside structures they built in order to shelter themselves in the city streets?

My friend who was there on the ground asked what is the difference anyway between a shelter and a shield. *One protects inward and the other outward*, I thought to myself, but I knew this was not what he meant. What my friend meant, maybe, was that a shelter and a shield are structures of desperation, and that's all that matters. Those assemblages of tents, barricades, first-aid stations, mobile libraries, study centres, shrines and umbrella monuments—the people struggled together for days, weeks, months, to articulate their voice, and perhaps what matters is exactly this, that the desperation to erect a home is a fundamental human instinct, even, or especially, if what we are protecting, or protecting against, is something clouded, imprecise, ambiguously large.

11/

12/
'Above all, hyphenation refers not to the conjunctures of 'East' and 'West', but to the disjunctures of colonialism and globalism… a very specific set of historical circumstances that has produced a historically anomalous space that I have called a space of disappearance' (Abbas).

13/

14/

During the years between my family's departure and my return as an adult, what changed was the protests. This is not entirely true. The July 1st marches were of course a new occurrence after 1997, but I later learned that the June 4th candlelight vigils had always happened. It began with 1989, one-sixth of Hong Kong's population emerging in support of the students across the waters, and in the years after the handover, pro-democracy protests swelled. This history of public demonstration is yet another mark of disjuncture from 'Chineseness' in a city already anxious about identity. When you are one in thousands, a body among bodies, sitting and lighting flames one by one, neighbour to neighbour, you cannot help but ask, *Why are all these bodies here? What heat do they feel inside?* When you are one in a night on the street, sleeping side by side. Hong Kong is a city that has always protested, and these bodies emerge *en masse* again and again not necessarily because they think it will bring about real change, though perhaps more and more they are believing it can. Perhaps the city protests because that is a freedom afforded to it:

an avenue for voicing itself: Hong Kong protests because it can.

At some point, the instinct to protect inward became a need to protect outward. It is the difference between keeping oneself dry despite the weather, and wielding fiercely, if vaguely, in the face of such weather. What is a city's identity after hundreds of thousands of bodies have made a home in the streets for more than seventy days?

15/

From Rey Chow, *Between Colonizers: Hong Kong's Postcolonial Self-Writing in the 1990s*:

> 'Hong Kong's postcoloniality means both a kind of freedom (from the restrictions of 'national' culture) and a kind of danger (anything is possible).'

> 'To write itself, Hong Kong must move beyond...the simplicity of the paradigm of 'foreign colonizer versus native colonized'.'

> 'What is unique to Hong Kong, however, is precisely...an awareness of impure origins, of origins *as* impure.' *[emphasis mine]*

16/

17/

18/

In the year that I returned to live in Hong Kong as an adult, I spent much of my time walking along the water on Lantau Island. Beyond my usual path by the pier, every so often I would take a rickety bus through the mountains, and I knew that I was close when the bus lurched upward between two green hills and reached a point where the ocean suddenly appeared, brazen and silver under the midday sun. I am by nature an anxious person who relies on precision and plans, but I never needed to know where the bus stops were located, I only waited to see the beaches appear through the trees. Hong Kong is the one place in the world where I can feel both familiar and lost in the best of both senses, where a sense of wildness and safety intersect.

I have never developed a language beyond this to describe Hong Kong, deep inside my bones.

Growing up, my parents taught me that the most important measures for a good life were safety, security and stability. *Do not go to Hong Kong,* my father cautioned me when the protests broke out, even though he believes in the freedoms that come with democracy. Safety was what we were all taught, so what does it mean that so many of this next generation are still longing, desperate, for some unnamed shape, a wilderness to shield them in the night?

19/

'Hong Kong's postcoloniality is marked by a double impossibility—it will be as impossible to submit to Chinese nationalist/nativist repossession as it has been impossible to submit to British colonialism.'

'What would it mean for Hong Kong to write itself in its own language?' (Chow).

Notes:

This essay appears in *Drunken Boat* #21 and expands on the author's blog post on *Kundiman Fireside* on October 16th, 2014.

Original blog post: *http://kundimanfireside.tumblr.com/ post/100146252324/umbrella-shield-poetics-part-ii.*

Related blog posts by Henry Leung: *http://kundimanfireside.tumblr.com/post/99988319454/um-*

brella-shield-poetics-part-i, http://kundimanfireside.tumblr.com/
post/100310503189/umbrella-shield-poetics-part-iii

First photo by Vivian Yan. Final photo by David William Hill. All other photos by the author.

Abbas, Ackbar, *Hong Kong: Culture and the Politics of Disappearance*. University of Minnesota Press, 1997.

Chow, Rey, *Between Colonizers: Hong Kong's Postcolonial Self-Writing in the 1990s*. *Diaspora* 2(2). 1992.

Peculiar Orchid

Arthur Leung

Yellow stars flying away, better hold the pole
tight – and the petals, soon you see they swing
on your left. You raise the flag, fasten the halyard,
salute, read the whiteness of your uniform, whiteness
as dove and peace. Soon you stop to fight back,
these boys pull your necktie and their parents

come to grab milk powder, sickbeds and shelters
while you grasp the word for love. Soon you learn
their language as they give up, say *xie xie*, forgetting
how there are two thank-you's in Cantonese,
how Jolly Crispy gratifies your *bun bun*
on her Sunday mat in Statue Square. *Salamat.*

Walang anuman – her sleep in your bathtub,
a space more precious than dream. Soon you tell
land is everything: welcome to Hong Kong.
Doors open, *huanying guanglin*, big spenders
across the river. Gucci wallets, diamond bracelets,
promiscuous cosmetics, insurance of risks

unknown, flats looking at the Victoria, proudly
in *renminbi*. Shopping bags in piazzas, landmarks
in Wan Chai, the giant bauhinia with golden petals.
Soon you know this city by watching people in the street,
jobless kids, cubicle dwellers, difference makers,
fire in their strides and clamours. In rain

they never bow their heads, each move of the queue
ploughs a grain of freedom; each addition to the chronicle
counts – May Day, birth of Buddha, one country,
four pandas in a decade, minimum wage at thirty, a pier
of eighty-two summers, clearance on the seventy-ninth.
All this you have lived in replaced dignity,

and soon you ignite the longings of your grandfather
and great-grandfather as you heighten the petals,
lightening the sky in red, red as your blood and China.
In any aspect the wind blows, you move on and start
to believe this is home, your purgatory, paradise, garden, whatever you
call it, let the flower grow.

Umbrella

Harry Harrison

Two Poems

Law Lok Man, Louise

Chair

Each with its own cause, chairs
Moved one by one to island seclusion
All-purpose plastic chairs
Youthful lounging beach chairs
Loosened soft cushion tavern chairs
Crook-backed slanting office chairs
From the State for resting bench chairs
From the salt wind rusting and corroding chairs
Grown in moss and vines wooden chairs
Some facing seas alone, some gathered in three or five
Some facing long unpeopled roads, corners poorly lit
Insensate, seeming unaggrieved
Some moved out of place by people
To re-talk yesterday's talk.
By the pier each day old grandmas
Idly talking idly silent see skies rise and fall
Till time brings the next grandma, sitting,
Talking, seeming to have talked this through before—
Then another—the chair

Still the little chair
The island these days
Facing by chance a direction
Dusk throwing down along the day's shifts
The depths of a moment's floating
Like a flagpole without a flag.

Journey of Plating

Pier unloaded, a page of history
resting, this trip of minor waves and wave tips
bursting into ten thousand arms to dissolve
in a wink and bear the rising sun's
branching golden yellow shards of minutiae.
Heaven too unloaded, all along biding a time
to shroud the world, declare an end
to it and itself and all that is—
Splendid.

No, the ship arrives, time and again this
awkward mother's body cutting faceless throngs of waves
amassing a few day-to-day anticipations,
it's time to arrive, come ashore, soul cleansed once
and at once swept up, aspersed with the past's sealed past
and the past ten thousand punctual and slightly lagged ships,
and even if there's grief or joy or terror or there's
unseen trees rising up or withering,

all of it becomes
a statement.

I am narrated, stepping on the 9:28 pm
return trip—

charge into a black belly, three days and nights
in a far place tongued with fire with people waving from the mountains:
All that you've hoped for will come to be. A far place
with all the fine and fair freedoms you long for,
where you can unfold your home, run through prairies,
work to build and share, receive and contain, to be made new, a gift to
your cherished people,
a far place that can burn forever,
with an ever burning jail of fire and the fire jail's children.
But the far place—
its end is postponed by the absurdly endless,
a shadow and a shadow's shadow as far as the eye can see
the whole desolate city aside
it's time to pierce the tents of sparse stars
the ships gone at dark, the mountain cries
like broken static from an old radio, irregular,
a stretch of unending songs turning to sea

—returning to my island, I gather up
dry skirts gowns and flags, cook a dish of
dim star trails scavenged the night before, only to find
night and fire's colours
already plating my shoulders.
I see myself tomorrow
incarnating inside infinite waves,
resisting what remains of a fiery sun blown over the world in vain,

with a whole body of waves hauling the hull
to shatter anew, submerge in that sea
that roiling sea, ruminating.

Both poems translated from the Chinese by Henry Wei Leung. Translator's note: the second poem alludes to the 2014 Umbrella Movement.

Three Poems

Marco Yan

Rain as

a mother's persistence   unsteady   tested
over the hours   when she sits beside her son
at a dinner table   shoulders taut   her hand
tight around his   guiding a pencil through
lines of graphite   wild curves   limp thistles
an eraser lets loose   to the thirteen strokes
their family name in Chinese

                                    the foolscap
blackens the way their joint fists blacken
until   when the boy closes his eyes   he sees
the word   black upon black   then his given name
the first character is *think*   the second means
the expanse of many seas   more strokes and effort

rain of April 1990   began on a morning like this
lucid   so light   and went on for days

What Word

Of course it is *death*, the five letters
arranged before the twelfth century
now strewn cursive across the page,

a sound to capsulate
finality, a leaked pass—
word, never obsolete.

     *

And it is the Chinese character
set in the copybook I had
when I was six,
                  when I wrote
words that stood for the primordial
like fire, wind, life,

and if death wasn't the last on the list, what came after?

How old was I when I first spoke
that word? And—how strange—
in my mother tongue, it rhymes
with *say*
            as if it demands to be heard.

     *

It's also the deepening of night
where a lamppost is resilient as a million stars
unchained at once
above the bed I mute myself,

only imagining a vacuum where I'll discard
my shirt, skin and warmth to move
past the physics of things, the people
I learned to love, some galaxy unreachable—

right before I close my eyes, I see
less light, breathing in less air,
muscles relaxed, a sinking motion
propelled by a need to hold someone's arm—

no longer aware of the sheets,
the ancient script that my body is.

Days of November 2014

The girl grabbed an umbrella—a colour
she learned to prize—and left for school, knowing
this subtropical island had become so red,
so warm, there'd be downpours in early winter.

Should the sky stay clear, she'd block
the sun;
              if not the sun, then pepper spray,
tear gas, rubber bullets, whatever
the police in the dark would use.

She returned, at dusk, to the makeshift study
erected on one lane of Harcourt Road to revise
for her history test
                           and tried to conclude
what was missing, what had gone wrong, not minding

the onlookers, their voices, or being reduced by the cold
lens of a camera—
                 she was present, part of the past
that would glint as a yellow pixel
on the next day's front page.

Foundations

Shahilla Shariff

I arrived in Hong Kong in 1993 as a newlywed. Homesick in Happy Valley, I befriended an old Shanghainese lady I met one day on the tram. Much later, she presented me with a lacquered wooden gourd and wished me sons. My first son was born two months before the handover; my second one two years after. I live in a different neighbourhood now, but the hills around my rented flat are still heaving with bamboo scaffolding as well as many different species of bamboo.

Twenty years ago I framed
the future, seed by seed,
the way bamboo incubates
concrete on these hillsides.

Night ajar,
a frontier to the moon,
but where are all the stars?
Spring arriving soon,
trees whose names
I cannot pronounce
petal a flamboyant

trail—palanquin red—
just in time to mark
your birth, return,
the festival of Ching Ming.

Cape Collinson, the cemetery
rounding into Shek O.
Celadon sea,
the abandon of sand,
drift of ash,
weight of bones.
Try numbing memory
by burning mugwort
on my wrinkling skin.

Or testing it
by summoning familiar ghosts.
One day your children
will call me in a foreign tongue.
Can you decipher these characters?
Count how many Muslim tombs
are engraved with Chinese names?

Tell me about stone.
How I manicure weeds,
cover cracks, brush dirt,
contain this family.
In every echo, read
your father's blessing,
the residue of rain,
a reminder—

nothing remains,
nothing belongs.
Especially here.
But please don't force me
to exhume these bones,
sacrifice their mystery,
reduce dust to air.

Soon nothing will be visible
but the shape of our absence,
the contours of aloneness.

Soon nothing will be left
but a window looking
into another window
past vertical darkness,
laboured sleep,
laddered slopes.

Will you listen then
for my creak?

This Is How You Go Back

Mary-Jean Chan

for H.K.

just leave knowing   *far* is a time   a place
    you can be blank there once more
turning the years over   in your palm   forget the zodiac
    the stars are not there

to haunt you   the flat: *returnable?*   go back, anyway
    try a few days   a week
months   try a year   i mean three meals a day
    with familiar eyes   and lips

hold someone close   to stop the trembling
    run around in circles   if you must
but try staying   for a bowl of rice   chopsticks
    Iron-Buddha   ask *how are*

you today   dim the screen   shut the laptop
    sit next to the one   you've called
every single day   from the US   the UK
    abroad for seven years   stay awhile

listen to local weather   that once soothed you
     into dreams   serenade the dark
don't leave just yet   let torrential rain   tame your
     riot of black spikes   kiss

mom & dad goodnight   dear heart   travel far enough
     you'll no longer expect
different skies   those windows   sweet honeycomb
     at night everything glows

Hong Kong:
99 Days and Counting

Larry Feign

Three Poems

Tammy Ho Lai-Ming

TWO ZERO FOUR SEVEN

In Hong Kong, an art installation is taken down when the
artists explain what it really means.

Stop all the clocks, Hong Kong people.
That which we hold dear about this city

is likely to end in 2047.
But if we do not recognise the objective

passing of time, might we stay
in the present? Might we conjugate

still on the street and believe in the policy
of one country, two systems?

Might we forget 2047 as a momentous date,
but consider it a random four-digit

number, signifying the money
a recent university graduate has in her bank

or the miles between two estranged
lovers working in separate cities?

But perhaps it is better to collectively
count down the year, the month,

the day, the minute. Let 2047 be displayed
on tall buildings and spoken of often,

before our shared euphemism
becomes another censored year.

**How the Narratives of Hong Kong Are written With
China in Sight**

1. Call me One Country, Two Systems.

2. It is a truth universally acknowledged that the democracy
    fighters in Hong Kong must be genomically modified by
    the West.

3. Hong Kong and democracy—it was love at first sight.

4. An order from the PRC comes and never leaves.

5. Many years later, as the Hong Kong people remembered the 'generosity' of the Chinese government for not shooting them or overrunning them with tanks, they would be forced to cry in gratitude.

6. China, non-light of my life, non-fire of my loins.

7. Happy cities are all alike; every unhappy city is unhappy in its own way. Hong Kong is unhappy because it wants happiness too much. It believes that the right to vote for its own leader would contribute to its happiness. It believes.

8. democracyriverrun, past Mong Kok, Causeway Bay, Admiralty and Central...

9. Hot days in September. Some rainy nights in October. Tick-tock tick-tock tick-tock the clocks were striking and Big Brother was watching. Let him watch. Let the whole world watch.

10. It was the best of times. It was the age of wisdom. It was the epoch of belief. It was the season of Light. It was the spring of hope. We had everything before us—in short, the period was so far like the present period, that some of its noisiest Chinese authorities insisted on its being received, for good or for evil, in the superlative degree of comparison only.

11. You are about to begin reading the story of Hong Kong, 'One Country, Two Systems', when you realise that such a story doesn't exist. Keep the 'country', remove the plural marker in 'systems' and replace 'two' by 'one', then you are truly beginning to read the story of Hong Kong. (One and one is always one.)

12. Someone must have slandered Joshua Wong... for one evening, without having done anything outrageously wrong, he was arrested.

13. Whether Hong Kong shall turn out to be the hero of the international fight for democracy, or whether it will be utterly defeated, the pages of history must show.

14. It was a broken promise that started it. The students returned to the streets day after day. And the voice on the other side of the border responded with contempt, scorn.

15. Through the facial masks, between the crooked handles of umbrellas, people could be seen fighting, in their own way, which is the best way.

16. 689 was spiteful.

17. In the beginning there was the Party and the Party was with the Country and the Party was the Country.

18. There is a spectre haunting China—the spectre of Umbrellaism.

19. The Hong Kong people said they would fight for the city's future themselves and they would bring umbrellas.

20. They say the past is a foreign country and people do things differently there. We say the past is always upon us.

21. Hong Kong was born many times: first, as a fishing village; and then, as a British colony. After that, it became a Special Administrative Region. And then one summer, it became very special indeed.

22. Where now? Who now? When now? Hong Kong now. We now. Now now.

MAYBE

Maybe when three sparrows
line up neatly on a swing in Yuen Long,
whoever looks on patiently enough
will win the Mark Six.

Maybe goldfish bought in Mong Kok
are telepathic and share the secrets
of their new owners. 'She is lonely.'
'This one is lonely too.'
'Nobody in the family talks.'

Maybe in the small hours
the letters on Lan Kwai Fong street signs
rearrange themselves to thwart
drunk English professors.

Maybe the stray dogs in Tin Shui Wai
are soldiers who died heroically
in the Battle of Hong Kong
reincarnated.

Maybe in the many nearby ghost towns,
ghosts do roam
and send old-fashioned good wishes
to abstract relatives in distant homes.

Five Poems

Chow Hon Fai

No Bigger Time Than

At Heng On Estate in Ma On Shan

'Such a time of impediments; such a moment
of looking into the time future.' Future comes
through his own collective face, before Fong Man
jumps off the building in Episode Twenty-eight.
They're still confused about fate, like their
families can't tear off the news clippings
pasted up in corridors, words glued to obscenity—
The rerun only reaches Episode Six
so far in early hours. Heng On Estate
takes in the Fongs. Three sisters and Sister Ling
sit pressed next to each other, biting into
their noodles and wontons, veggies with oil
and having a conversation about starting a family business.
(It was all shot at the Chun Chun Diner.)
The sun rifts a certain noon apart many years later.
I open my eyes but my eyelids can't hold up the night.
You're right next to me, not any more sober, whispering
words of regret, Fong Fong and Fong Ting

fallen dead, and Sister Ling shot dead on the day
of the big stock market miracle, like lights and shadows
drawn on the person sitting across the table. The more he eats,
his old face blurs, and the younger he looks. Luck
might have it that the shooting team comes by—I
leave my seat, make a detour to
the Fongs' table when other neighbours pay
their bills. Take a seat and look across the cups and plates
and leftovers towards the lens. You take a snapshot
with your cell phone; I knock over a cup of lemon tea
that spills into the shape of Fong Man's stretched-out
body pressed on the ground. We look down
towards that spot, pay our respects, and up
towards Hang Yuet Building. I want to get in there,
intrude upon a young lovers' tryst at the entrance.
The scissor gate clatters up. We reach the hall
and enter the lift. Eleventh floor. Fourteenth floor
and then take the stairs down two floors. A vent looking out
over Ma On Shan. A full hill of jade green looks out
at the rising buildings. The residents of the estate live in and out
and run into scenes of TV dramas that attract
our stealthy visit and chance views of the hill's
colours and elegance—Room 1206, near the end
of the corridor, is the Fongs. Light wells in
through windows and excavates large folds
of shadows over the hallways and apartment doors,
unlike stage lights that do not allow fuzzy details.
We walk back and forth through the drift
of cooking smells from someone's home. A frugal girl
is cooking for her wealthy stockbroker neighbour. Meeting up
and parting ways we must be hungry—
Sitting next to me at the table we share, the young
lovers take out a selfie-god's pop stick, unaware of our

curious watch. They eat and drink. We get out
to walk those roads we find, like leading a mass
to a theme park where an array of wooden posts
bolster a platform where we can climb the stairs
up to the arch and slide down the steel chute.
Selfies uploaded lead our way. Pick up a tune
and get back. 'People say you're leaving the country.'
Dark night presses down and buries 2015 alive.
The frugal girl and the stockbroker's smiles
and tears are carved between wood and metal.
'Suppose you go. Pains follow.' The piano
doesn't seem to stop. The subdivided flat
inside a factory building lacks a window that
opens to the sky, so we switch on the TV,
still too early to binge-watch the 1992 programme.

A Curious Encounter
In Tin Shui Wai North

Two footbridges across intersections are locked in
a tug-of-war. Think of an old friend. Climb up there.
Forget him. Pause. Pray for a string of hints.
The last car streams past beneath. The air up here

chokes and rings in the ears—A football cuts through the air and drops
on the empty road. Several kids are chasing it. The one in the front
stumbles. You help him up and ask him the way. Mind drifts.
Still can't hear. He waves hands and you follow him

down the bridge. One or two cargo trucks. Soles tremble and itch.
Hearing's back. And his first words—
Your Cantonese sucks. Where the hell are you from?
Cycle tracks carry footsteps and the white shines past the afternoon's

floral patterns, cartoon characters, solid colours, cotton quilts
that have bathed in sunlight, paralysed like one national flag ironed
upon the other. Walk past these countries. Take a turn. Go inside
a housing estate, into the cool shelter forked out by Link REIT.

People mass on the benches. You fear losing yourself among them.
He's back licking an ice-cream and can't recognise you for a moment—
Who's just old enough to be you?—One cabbage after another,
one oyster after another, are drying in the sun at a nearby estate.

He devours stirred MSG noodles and knocks back a Coke.
        You pay the bill
just like his parents take him on a crowded bus to Lok Ma Chau
across the border to Shenzhen, and eat and drink through the weekend.
He wishes for a longer holiday when the whole family can move north

and never come back, just like you asked him the way to a place
that did not exist. Now stuffed full he leads you past a crossroad
where you could turn back to look at the footbridges at the
                intersections.
You ask him if we're lost. *You idiot. I live in the neighbourhood.*

Then on a traffic island, you see all directions turn
their backs on you. You can't go any further. You forget him.
He doesn't know how to retrace your path here—only you
remember to make a sign of the cross and say 'Amen'.

Trousers wet, just like among buildings of ten thousand homes
a gap of the only sky that leads down to earth.
He loses you in a hurry and crosses the road. Trams come and go.
On the way of escape rolls over a football. On that he treads.

Up and Down the Slope
For Tuen Mun Tsing Yeung Circuit Cooked Food Market

Up and down Tsing Yeung Circuit,
a little truck picks you up
before and after school.
Back to the workshop is more like a homecoming.

Out of our separate homes, we come
together for work
and meet again outside of work.
You hold my hand in the rain. We climb

a low hill. The workshop
takes up only one corner of the food market.
You stare at the fishballs bobbing—
every sunrise squeezed out of Dad's purlicue.

An umbrella like an upturned-boat
carries us upstream—dodging industrial buildings
losing workers on a daily basis. No other weight
but the lone island with stove-fire left on the stream.

Wind sounds like fire. Forks and spoons clatter all day
like growing up. What waiters and diners chat about is like
Dad holding your hand, showing you the purlicue of your hand,
which is also the purlicue of your sons' and grandsons' hands.

Our hands pull apart. Sheltering from rain
we realise how deep silence can be. You lower your head
towards what used to be the workshop, then to cold lemon Cokes
fizzing, recalling the hubbub of the place's past.

Naturally I wasn't here. The same stall at
this food market. People came back on time
for afternoon snacks. You and Dad's daily
coffee-tea mix and toast, both with condensed milk.

Slacking off is more like working. When I was there
the stall was closed and customers were turned away. Puddles all
along the street reflect the changing clouds and the family affairs
that you told me about. Up and down Tsing Yeung Circuit.

Visiting Flying Horse Restaurant in Kowloon City

Walking down the tunnel, pile-drivers
drill through the city above my head. Our footsteps
slacken and resound along the walls like a holiday
put off day after day until I find myself again in the crack.
The tunnel rolls forward. More than one stairway
reaches down. Kids in school uniform rush in

merrily. You meet me in the crowd and we
clumsily smile, as if we too are
young again just like the kids—Time slips away.
Now we stare at each other. We each try to catch up
with the other. We blindly run around. Life
is still in its strange original place. Ask
an old couple for direction. Climb up the stairs,
not forgetting to glance back at the emptiness.
Surrounded by cars big and small, a street corner
becomes a traffic island. Past a church
and its shackled gate. Many flowerbeds
cramped at the tip of the island. Thick leaves
breathe in car exhaust, like outside the restaurant
the table's grey glass tabletop. Pressed beneath are
yesterday's papers. Ants crawl between
the lines, from Politics to Entertainment
waiting for our crumbs to fall—
Peanut butter toast tastes burnt and bitter.
You fetch my condensed milk tea which is
improbably sweet and thick. The grey-haired
owner sneaks back from the storeroom
and makes food sizzle. The scent of oil
wafts across a pendulum, bird cages,
arcade games. We look at each other. You ask
whether we have come to the wrong place—
The owner smiles as he finishes his sandwich and
comes out to give people more change than I
can remember. He ignores me, and the cups
and plates left on the table next to ours.
Back to his seat. Makes himself a coffee
when the pile drivers from across the island take a break.

Flow of People

Blackbirds flying beneath dawn's light, you hold up your head
to look, and clouds wipe clear the sky. The ditch water
carrying graveyard shadows; are they arcing towards you
like the line of ants up the edge of this ditch?
You step in a puddle, blue sky spills out and
ants detour, blue rolling up the blackbirds
stranded in another slab of sky—on the hill path ahead
you see figures of people, faces drooping when you pass,
hear the far-off river washing down the hill,
the afternoon buildings and the streets: make way! make way!
like you never put on a police uniform, yet still wade into the river
as if you still had long hair, still raised a fist
inheriting the wave, crashing, onto you—to hold on
or to let go of your best friend's arm, guarding the intersection
make way! make way! the building wall moves
is it not a tree? yielding the path under your careless watch,
gravestones on the slope, each posthumous portrait
looking into the distance, like a thousand windows living in the past—
after lunch the family takes a walk in the park, cooling in the shade.
you like to walk at the edge of the shadow, between darkness and light,
circumventing childhood, realising you're mature
only when you're passed the metal jug. Descending you
      realise there's no return
and push your family into a circle, but the branch
is always time's axis, revolving night and day.
the flow of people under streetlights streams further towards
      the shadows,

cast into the city's depths—everyone faces away from the light,
sinking and floating, holding back tears, backs turned to you facing
the fireworks that consume all the lights of the city
and fall to the ground, where bone ash had been glimmering.
noon's light still piercing through the leaves, the elderly look back
and call you out of the shade, up the lift
to search among the numbers along a wall of ancestral tablets,
past so many dead and their worldly positions
like walking in a leaf, up through its veins towards the tip—
on the stelae no one looks sick, just bemused
that day you smiled and pressed the shutter. Click!
a cross on a small vase, accompanying the stele.
you say we should have picked a flower
when you notice an ant climbing out of the vase
towards another stele, the subject shifted to
what's outside the window, and looking down the hill,
a row of trees more or less separates the graveyard and the public
          housing block,
its residents so tiny, marching with the ants.
the tablets are brand new, with only names
and dates of birth and death, and you find someone
born the same day as you, and can only stare into the blankness
traversed by that lone ant, how at the end of a flow of people
there is no one, as you change into civilian clothes and head back
to the square. Your family reminds you that
you're on duty later, and you turn away from the stelae
to see it's dark outside, then look down at the square
where there's one ant, holding up his head and gazing at you.

*First four poems translated from the Chinese by Chris Song; last poem trans-
lated from the Chinese by Chris Song and Lucas Klein.*

Three Poems

Leung Ping-Kwan

An Old Colonial Building

I.

Through sunlight and shadow dust swirls,
through the scaffolding raised-up around
the colonial edifice, over the wooden planks
men live on to tear it brick by brick, the imperial
image of it persisting right down, sometimes,
to the bitter soil in the foundation, sometimes finding too
the noble height of a rotunda, the wide, hollow corridors
leading sometimes to blocked places, which, sometimes,
knocked open, are stairs down to ordinary streets.

II.

Down familiar alcoves sometimes brimming
with blooms sometimes barren I go to Xerox
glancing at the images caught in the circular pond,
now showing the round window in the cupola as the duck weed drifting,
day and night caught in the surface, no longer textbook
clean, but murky, the naïve goldfish searching
mindlessly around in it, shaking the pliant lotus stems

and the roots feeling for earth, swirling orange and white,
gills opening and leeching, in and out of the high window bars.

III.
Might all the pieces of ruins put together present
yet another architecture? Ridiculous the great heads on money,
laughable the straight faces of running things. We pass in this corridor
in the changing surface of the pond by chance
our reflections ripping a little. We'd rather not bend;
neither of us is in love with flags or fireworks.
So what's left are these fragmentary, unrepresentative words,
not uttered amidst the buildings of chrome and glass, but beside
a circular pond riddled with patterns of moving signs.

Translated from the Chinese by Gordon T. Osing and Leung Ping-Kwan.

Postcards of Old Hong Kong

The pictures we sent off had been touched up
images of scenes we never experienced
                                        On the back,
I'll send greetings, in that space
were I to tell my deepest anxieties and worries
would they among endless strangers circulate, before
curious or indifferent eyes, bleaching the sepia
lighter and fainter, until those old-style tea-houses in Happy Valley,
flower stalls along Lyndhurst Terrace, hawkers of all sorts,
like the old woman spinning threads at branches of trees,

gradually fade

From mass-produced pictures
I pick and choose, wondering how to convey news of me
I don't want to sensationalise the huge fire at the racecourse, or
the typhoon
that sank the cruiser in the harbour, I'm not the tourist
scribbling at the margins of a disaster scene:
'We are off to Shanghai for a jaunt!' I'm no
smart broker or colonial official, engrossed in sending home
exotica: opium smoking, long-plaited
gamblers, songstresses, kung fu masters, rickshaw pullers,
I flip them over, disgusted. True,
they exist, but I rather not use them to
represent us

At the picture border I wrote
hasty words straying sometimes into Kennedy Town side streets,
the first Chinese school in Morrison Hill, the reservoir where
China-bound ambassador-laden horses stopped and drank
I've always wanted to ask how history was made
Lots of people tinted the pictures, lots of people
named the streets after themselves, statues were
put up and taken down. Amidst overflowing clichés
I wrote you a few words, crossing set
boundaries

How do we, on gaudy pictures of the past
write words of the moment? Stuck in their midst, how we
paint ourselves?

Translated from the Chinese by Martha Cheung.

Images of Hong Kong

I need a new angle
for strictly visual matters.
Here's an old portrait shot originally
In Guangguang studio in Nathan Road;
They don't paint on them like this any more.
For no reason of mine, Mid-Levels scenes are on the television.
She'd come from unforgettable Shanghai, from glamorous
Jaffe Road, with its White Russian coffee shops, violins
playing into the night. How does it add up?
A bottle of lotion, Two Sisters, smashed forever on the floor.
Imagine the old vendors throwing olives up into a
        postmodern tower.
Even the lady who knows only we're all different has a point.
Here's a man who studied anarchism in France and came home
to work for *Playboy*, then *Capital*.
The tiniest angles divide our views of the moon
when we look up. The Star Ferry clock tower;
sunsets in Aberdeen: too familiar. Only now somebody plans to redo
        everything. Queen's Café. China Club
One has only to push buttons to change pictures
to get in on so many trends one can't even think,
too much trivia and so many places and stories
one can't switch identities fast enough. When can we—?
And here's the Beijing journalist who became
an expert on pets and pornography under capitalism.
When can we just sit down and talk?
Our attentions get lost in factories of images and songs;
appetites are whetted in the hungers of the tiny screen.
Reach out and touch—what?
History too is a montage of images,
of papers, collectibles, plastic, fibres,

laser discs, buttons. We find ourselves looking up
at the distant moon; tonight's moon—
does it come at the beginning or the end of time?
Here's another from Taiwan, who thinks
she's Eileen Chang writing Hong Kong romances, with neon
dancing in the back-churning waters of the Star Ferry, on
      the old depot,
with Repulse Bay Hotel rendezvous produced on cue.
All this exotic stuff, of course, is for export.
We need a fresh angle,
nothing added, nothing taken away,
always at the edge of things and between places.
Write with a different colour for each voice;
Ok, but how trivial can you get?
Could a whole history have been concocted like this?
Why are there so many good Oriental spy novels?
Why are there so many things that can't be said?
So now, once again, they say it's time to remodel
and each of us finds himself look around for—what?

Translated from the Chinese by Gordon T. Osing and Leung Ping-Kwan

FICTION

Twenty Years

So Mei Chi

1997

April 27th—Former British Prime Minister Margaret Thatcher officiates at the launch ceremony of the Tsing Yi-Lantau Highway during her visit to Hong Kong. To the amazement of one fledgling reporter, she is chosen by her editor to cover the event. It is only her first year on the job. What luck! Petrified, she arrives early and gazes in awe from her vantage point on the viewing platform. World's longest two-deck suspension bridge to carry both road and rail traffic, a main span of 1,377 metres, a suspension of 2,160 metres. She did background research and learnt these scattered facts, but having the actual sight of it is yet another thing. She is overwhelmed. The day slowly darkens before her eyes. First, gold sprinkles all over the sea, then skies suffuse with shades of red and orange, last of all, night comes to engulf all in its way. After nature completes her daily witching sequence, the performance of the material world is staged. Fireworks in gold flow down from the bridge, like a magnificent waterfall, like a torrent of blindingly white rain.

The spectacle is rendered at a judicious pitch, without brashness. She is dumbfounded.

She rushes back to the office afterwards and buries herself in an A3-sized lined paper, as big as half the table. The assignment editor is right next to her, waiting for each and every completed page, snatching it up from her for editing. Rulers, glue and scripts of various sizes are all piled up on the desk. For the first time, the fledgling reporter experiences an amusing blend of excitement, as if the pen in her hand was bleeding not only news for the next day, but also history which will belong to the future. The former British Prime Minister stands between 'soon-to-be-former' Governor and Chief Secretary for Administration, showcasing the final glory of the colonial government.

The next day, the assignment editor walks over to the fledgling reporter's desk and brings along the newspaper. It turns out that Margaret Thatcher, who was described as wearing red in the text, wears blue on the film photo. There is discrepancy between Text and Visuals, a totally avoidable mistake. But her brain has created another reality for her.

After that, she witnesses more and more news for tomorrow or history for the future. But every time she feels a concealed, nameless anxiety. The glory beneath the five-star flag, the rousing national anthem, the leaders' poker faces, the solemn transfer of power, as well as her fellow citizens who celebrated the return to China with heartfelt excitement—'Discrepancy between Text and Visuals'.

2007

In order to understand the matter of one's own roots, a departure is required. She leaves the city in which she was born and stays away from it for two years. She lives in the land of the red clothes/blue clothes lady, her home under the Union Jack. It is a place with grasslands and rabbits, where she can tilt her head to a sky un-fragmented by skyscrapers. She likes the tranquillity and thinks that maybe she could stay for good. Until an emergency summons her back to Hong Kong. From the aeroplane, she sees the bridge opening she had watched. Her restless soul finds comfort, and then bursts a thought: 'It's good to be home'. She realises that she has been wrong. Her roots have always been coiled inside this island. For her, a calm and peaceful life was all well and good, but home should be a little bit noisy, a little bit crowded.

For her, a calm and peaceful life was all well and good, but home should be a little bit noisy, a little bit crowded.

March 25th—The fledgling reporter is still a journalist, but the nature of her job has taken a step away from history for the future. She works as features editor of a magazine and is now also a fledgling mother; for the sake of a new life, burying small roots into this slice of land.

Her one-year-old son as usual pours out his toys from boxes and drawers; the television, as usual, is tuned to the news channel. It is a live broadcast, showing 800 members of an election committee, emerging from goodness knows where, voting for the new chief executive, on behalf of all Hong Kong's more than six million citizens. Everyone knows who will win the election, but the staff counting the tickets appear to be quite serious, as if it hasn't been a done deal all along.

'Discrepancy between Text and Visuals'—the characters resound in her head like a curse.

On behalf of Hong Kong people, around 600 out of the 800 members selected Mr Tsang who loves wearing a bow tie. Mr Bow Tie is winning the election for the second time. The television plays the promotional video of his campaign, in which he is standing on an open-top double-decker bus, yelling into the microphone his campaign slogan—'I. Will. Get. The. Job. Done!' The crowds by the bus cheer enthusiastically in response. The little one in front of the television raises his head from piles of toys and tries to respond too. He shouts himself hoarse, with all the vocabulary in his grasp—'Cars! Flowers! Ducks!' Fledgling Mama vigorously shakes her head to banish the weird slogans in her mind, including 'I will get the breastfeeding done!' and 'I will get the diaper-changing done!'—not without difficulty.

People say that Mr Bow Tie represents an aspirational 'Hong Kong Story'. Born and educated locally, he worked hard to gain a ticket to university, only to find out that he had to give it up due to his family's tight financial straits. It was a long way from pharmaceutical salesman to the head of the government. No one would have thought that this 'Hong Kong Story' would later be described in court as 'a story about greed'. A chief executive turned prisoner.

In the couple of years following the election, a tide of 'China Stories' rushes in. The Olympic flame was ignited at the Beijing National Stadium, which 'completes the century-old dream of the Chinese people'. The day the Olympic torch arrives in Hong Kong, the kindergarten requests its students to dress up in red. Fledgling Mama's son also wears red and brings along a home-made Olympic torch. It causes a commotion at school, the little one is carrying high the 'Olympic torch' and running back-and-forth hysterically in front of the school gate. His action invites a group of equally fanatical tiny followers. Together they swim, like a collective school of red tropical fish, to the right, the left, and then the right again—blindingly yet enthusiastically.

Among the Hong Kong representatives who are carrying the Olympic torch, there is a Mr Leung. He is responsible for running the section on Tsing Ma Bridge. At first it is the bridge that catches the fledgling Mama's attention to the broadcast, but then it is Mr Leung himself. The man wears a stiff smile and runs in intriguing postures. Lifting his knees up high, it looks as if he is running on the spot, giving this optical illusion of a stop-motion animation. This is a man displayed in a series of photos.

Nobody expects Mr Leung to soon run into Government House, receive the baton passed by Mr Tsang and bring forth a lasting mystery for Hong Kong people: whether or not there is an actual person underneath the smiley face of the chief executive.

2017

March 26th—Her son and daughter are both primary school students now, but fledgling Mama feels as inexperienced as before. Several years ago, Hong Kongers experienced crushing sorrow in a protest named after, curiously enough, umbrellas. People casually split into factions and tormented one another. Eventually, everything returned to its respective former status, except the one thing everyone refused to mention—the great white elephant in the room.

Another Sunday, early evening—the television at home has been turned on since noon, broadcasting waves of cheers and boos. A group of 1,194 representing eight million Hong Kong citizens are selecting the new chief executive. The election is a little bit different this time because around 300 people out of the 1,194 have fought their way into the committee, wanting to bring hope. But the rest of the committee belongs to an entirely different species. They are allergic to the expression 'Free Will' and will sneeze at those two words.

On Facebook, there are various strange kinds of live-streaming. Someone is live-streaming the process of making breakfast. Someone is live-streaming being on the bus. Someone is live-streaming a stuffed toy sitting quietly at home. All are captioned with the same line—'When 1,194 members of the Election Committee are choosing the Hong Kong chief executive, 99.97 per cent of Hong Kong citizens are excluded from the election. What are the rest of us doing? This is the REAL Hong Kong during election.'

Fledgling Mama ducks into the kitchen to do the dishes, but keeps an ear open to the live television broadcast of the 1,194 people. A scene from ten years ago resurfaces—the Olympic torch held high above a school of tropical fish in red, blindingly moving in a uniform manner.

Her son enters the kitchen. The little tropical fish has now grown into an adolescent. 'Will I ever have the chance to witness true universal suffrage?' he asks.

'Of course you will! Keep your hopes up!' Fledgling Mama, who was gloomy moments ago, suddenly straightens her back and pulls her spirits together.

'How about China?' The son pursues.

'I have no idea …' Fledgling Mama hesitates.

'If there isn't any universal suffrage in China, can Hong Kong have it?' He asks again.

The question pierces straight to the heart of the matter. Fledgling Mama surrenders, she will only be frank: 'Your questions are really hard to answer. I can only tell you that there will be nothing if you stop hoping.'

Inside the giant wheel of social progress, where could the takers be, if there were no givers?

After you are crushed, you rebuild your hope. When you are beaten again, you rebuild your hope once again. It is hard, to struggle to stay afloat, the chaotic wielding of rods is back …

Someone once told fledgling Mama that the path to democracy is very long, that pain and setbacks come with the package. Take South Korea, maybe twenty years of fighting is a reasonable deal. After all, look around four corners of the world, do any democratic systems come about just by spitting on your hands? On hearing that, Fledgling Mama feels a sense of urgency and cries embarrassingly hard. Inside the giant wheel of social progress, where could the takers be, if there were no givers? She understands this logic rationally. But this insight does not lessen her reluctance to witness her two children put in the position of givers and grow up exhausting the best time of their lives in a distorted social context.

But people must live like cockroaches. There is no other choice than to drill ourselves into staunch willpower.

The day following the election, the soon-to-be-former chief executive shakes hands with chief executive-designate in front of the camera. They share the same smile.

'It (the chief executive election yesterday) demonstrated once again the successful implementation of the principle of 'one country, two systems', 'Hong Kong people administering Hong Kong with a high degree of autonomy', says he, with the stiff smile.

… 'Discrepancy between Text and Visuals'.

Translated from the Chinese by Suzanne Lai.

Going Up in Smoke

Larry Feign

Key Strokes by Loong Hei

Xu Xi 許素細

N ote by the author: These post-1997 op-eds are by a bi-
lingual (Cantonese-English) native of Hong Kong. 'In-
ternational' writers, who do not embrace either the language or
ambivalence of the majority, opine and emote on developments in
this city till their keyboards are worn, certain their words define a
superior moral stance. Loong Hei, whose pen name means 'Drag-
on's Breath', has never been entirely sure that words, or rather
'keystrokes', should ever carry such weight. Likewise, Loong Hei
is uncertain whether pen names, however pseudonymous, do in
fact conceal an author's identity.

The Chinese-ness of You
October 2005

Because it is 'National Day', the imperative this Saturday
morning which upsets digestion of the *dim sum* with my *jo
cha* is this: 'Identify Yourself'! It is almost enough to make
you cancel your subscription to the *South China Morning
Post* in favour of resurrecting the *Eastern Express,* an English
daily that was evanescent even before its demise.

Several surveys, it appears, have tried to measure what is described as the '*shifts* in Hong Kong's sense of identity'. So surprise, surprise, despite the fact of our 'national' day, a day when patriotism should swell our hearts full of Chinese blood, we learn that the majority of survey respondents consider themselves more 'Hongkongese' than Chinese. The pundits have much to say about this. Earlier this year, the same local rag reassured us that our city does indeed have its 'place' in China, because we are 'one nationality, two identities'. Everything deflates to politics. If you want universal suffrage, then you are excessively individualistic (read: Westernised) and prefer to call yourself 'Hongkongese'. If however you put the nation first, as any 'real' Chinese would, then you will identify yourself as Chinese. Notably, one academic quoted in today's report cites a former Xinhua director who observed of Hong Kong that 'while the territory has returned (to China), people's hearts haven't'.

How hypocritical, this nationalised concern over identity! There is an archaic definition of the word to mean an 'individual or real existence'. How refreshing to think that identity could be linked instead to the idea of existence. I exist in this space called Hong Kong from which I consequently derive an identity. Of course, if I happen to be Cantonese or Shanghainese or some other kind of Chinese, or perhaps, not even ethnically Chinese at all, but if I happen to exist here, this space will certainly lay some claim on me. To limit identity to a political or national construct, or to demand that it be a choice certifying loyalty to the nation seems unbearably sad. Identity emerges from who we feel we are, who we have evolved to become over time, and is larger than mere nationality or political bias.

As one friend often used to say: *Ask me no questions and I'll tell you no lies.*

All this pontificating over survey results, of polls that ask unanswerable questions in the first place, simply masks the absence of critical thought. A more meaningful consideration on this, our national day, would be to reflect on why this day must be celebrated and what bearing that has on us as a people. After all, in the years before the handover, it was not October 1st, but October 10th, which many Hong Kong people called 'national' day. Did that make us traitors because the Nationalist flag flew, because a different way of being Chinese asserted itself among some of the citizenry? Rather than pontificating, shouldn't we examine, honestly, the contradictions of existence, of being human?

For inspiration, let us turn to the Chairman, because he was the man responsible for the Motherland's current form of existence. Among his many thoughts was this treatise: 'On the Correct Handling of Contradictions Among People' dated February 27th, 1957, published approximately a lucky eight years after the founding of the People's Republic in 1949. That is roughly the same span of time since we abandoned our British colonial identity to this present moment for a specially administrative Chinese one. As we all know, Mao was a mass of contradictions, and you can only pay attention to his thoughts with measured tablespoons of salt. Nonetheless, this little grain on the handling of contradictions is worthy of attention:

'The only way', he said, 'to settle questions of an ideological nature or controversial issues among the people is by the democratic method, *the method of discussion, of criticism, of persuasion and education,* and not by the method of coercion or repression.' (*italics, mine*)

What does it really mean to be an ethnically Chinese person in a special administrative region? Must I wear my Chinese-ness on my sleeve, wave a sunny red flag, and sing an anthem in a dialect that is not my mother tongue?

Now isn't that interesting? His own actions in later years repudiated that notion, but his words remain to taunt us with possibilities. Of course, Mao is out of fashion these days, especially in 'Chinese' Hong Kong, so the local editorial tries instead to convince us that this commemorative day has a 'wider significance' for Chinese people to 'take pride in being Chinese'. In bold type, the polite command is—and as well mannered as the tone may be it is a command rather than a discussion—that this is the day to 'celebrate a common bond'.

What does it really mean to be an ethnically Chinese person in a special administrative region? Must I wear my Chinese-ness on my sleeve, elevate the connection of blood and ethnicity to the highest level, wave a sunny red flag, sing an anthem in a dialect that is not my mother tongue, exemplify the 'healthy development', as one pundit defines it, of a 'more balanced attitude towards the mainland'? We are privileged to be an educated people in a stable, global economy where peace has long prevailed. The fundamental paradox of our state of being has less to do with identity and more to do with what that privilege affords. Call me irresponsible, perhaps, but I believe we would be more responsible in examining the poll result of the 72 per cent who said that 'some affairs happening in China make me feel ashamed'. If history is any guide, Hongkongese have voted with our feet on many occasions in the past and will again, if strong enough feelings overcome us. Identity is simply not just a national issue.

Grant us, if you will, the right to speak our mind and criticise without fear of imprisonment. Grant us, if you will, the right to say that universal suffrage is something we want and desire for our piece of China. Our Chinese-ness has to do, in part, with the physical proximity of our space. But the emotional proximity, the 'identity' that binds us to China, will ultimately arise from being able to see ourselves reflected in the face of the country, in both its mind and heart, and most of all, in a moral conscience of which we are truly proud.

Ai guo, love the nation. We hear this imperative sounded over and over again, as if who we know ourselves to be is not good enough for the nation, that we must deny who we are to become 'real' Chinese. This is insufferable nonsense. 'Chinese' is an enormous enough concept—historically, culturally, philosophically—to embrace a multitude of voices and ways of being. Anything less would be an insult to the Chinese-ness of us. And no, we need not always agree.

If Chinese-ness were a love song, then consider these lyrics from 'The Nearness of You,' one of the sweetest love ballads ever composed in the opinion of this 'Chinese' person:

When you're in my arms
And I feel you so close to me
All my wildest dreams come true.
I need no soft lights to enchant me if you'll only grant me the right
To hold you ever so tight, and to feel in the night
The nearness of you.
—Lyrics Ned Washington, Music Hoagy Carmichael (1937)

Or if such Western influence is too much foreign mud, then, lest we forget, there is always Mao and his little red thoughts.

On a Dreamless Isle
March 2007

I watch the fadeout of my city-village as I knew it—long before the sheen of meta-globalism and wealth became its second skin—with a mix of nostalgic longing, despair and a tenuous hope. China's gentle giant hand on democracy in Hong Kong ensures that we will eventually be swallowed up and digested by our sovereign ruler, the way the Motherland always intended, despite whatever protest we and the world might register.

> China's gentle giant hand on democracy in Hong Kong ensures that we will eventually be swallowed up and digested by our sovereign ruler.

The Basic Law that Britain promulgated with China prior to the 1997 'handover' is a blip in yet another of the 'unequal treaties' that litter China's history with the West. This time, though, the unequal tips in favour of the People's Republic. Perhaps this is redress, revenge of the nerds of short stature and glasses who kept their heads down in the world's universities and colleges for years, waiting for their moment in the sun. Mao came, saw, conquered and died early enough for US-style free trade economics to drive the country forward into the twenty-first century. In that respect, the Chairman's lusts gave life to China with his passing, the way Fidel's Spartan longevity did not for Cuba.

In Hong Kong, we sneeze and wheeze, our sinuses infected beyond repair. Pollutants drift downwind from up north because China industrialises, manufactures, synchronises with the world to become the mother of all superpowers. Yet even our 'freedoms of speech' absolve the Motherland; a recent government study confirms that the city's own carbon emissions are to blame for the state of our air ways.

Who knew? The one-time sleeping giant across the border already has gargantuan dams and shining highways to bolster and link the exploding urban centres. Maytag is replaced by Haier, Hollywood by Bamboo-Go-Lightly, freedom fries by naughty noodles. Steel mills will rise in Eastern hinterlands while American steel workers 'retrain' for absent jobs. Britney Spears is welcome as long as she doesn't undress but Hillary Clinton must choose her words for entry. And the 2008 Olympics logo blazes across Tiananmen Square, a proud symbol and photo op for the masses. It is Free World *dim sum*, and China has an appetite for more, picking off from whichever carts suits her fancy.

Gently but firmly, as befits a responsible parent-state, China will strip this little city of our unnatural resources to aid in this endeavour. Canto-pop? Infotainment? Shop-till-you-flop? Sure. Rumblings of democracy? Reminders of Tiananmen? No way. Many in Hong Kong offer themselves up willingly, since those who protest are not the governing elite, not those who engage the world's ears and eyes with the promise of shiny lucre. They will negotiate and implement Beijing's diplomacy, as swiftly and with as little fuss as they can, so that the world will barely register protests for longer than a second in the global information gush.

But these are the political musings that befit the citizen of a nation state! Hong Kong is now a Chinese city, post-colonial perhaps, but hardly liberated. It once was, in the words of the journalist Richard Hughes, a 'borrowed place' living on its 'borrowed time'. We've been self-funding for a long time now, with our regulated and transparent stock exchange, a laissez-faire capitalist economy and a gambling appetite that fills the coffers of the Jockey Club, which in turn funds hospitals, schools and other socially necessary infrastructure. In fact, we've even recorded our history, and schoolchildren today are brought on field trips to a proud new museum where exhibits prove that yes, the Chinese roamed these shores long before the British arrived and will continue to do so now that they're finally gone.

If the gods are smiling on our people, as they did on Monkey, *laissez-faire* mothering will *laissez* us alone.

I am not a Chinese citizen, although ethnicity allows me to be. What I am is a Hong Kong *yan*, my gaze fixed on an evanescent home, trusting it will find form and footing somehow as a Chinese city. All I have to be is a writer from within, who can and must record this transit. Sic transit gloria mundi. May the pearl's lustre not fade too soon.

Walking through Hong Kong

Mishi Saran

I t is never good news when your landline—if you still
have one—rings in the middle of the night. Specially
not when the voice at the other end belongs to an old lover
you haven't seen in twenty years, a lover who asks, hesitant
and desperate, if you could buy him a set of clothes including
underwear; who instructs you to bring the package to him in
a Wan Chai hotel. You know the place—Christ, you realise
you even know his collar size. You have time to notice: he
didn't need to tell you who he was.

'I left China with only my passport, I'm sorry … I … didn't
know who else to ask. I can't leave the hotel. I have to hang
up now.'

'Anton—'

A dial tone can taunt.

I sat up, felt for my iPhone charging on the bedside table. It
wasn't midnight. It was 5 am. I was freezing, goose-pimpled.
The air-conditioner thermostat was set too high, as always.

Beside me, S. slept.

I stretched my toes, felt for my clothes bunched at the bottom of the bed. Panties kicked off, tank-top yanked off in last night's raucous reunion. The sheets had pulled away from me, and swirled in a lump over S.; he was an iceberg adrift in a sea of sleep, remote, unknowable.

Lucky bastard could sleep through anything.

Anton was in trouble and every cell in my body leaned towards him, like a plant towards sunlight: who said humans don't suffer from phototropism? My thoughts were unruly racehorses on an undefined course.

Why doesn't Anton have clothes? What happened in China?

The shops are not open. Does he still have that ponytail?

Where's the instruction manual for this situation?

There isn't one.

I swung my legs off the bed, clothes balled in one hand. In the jangling tangle of my mind, I recognised worry and confusion, but even twenty years later could not name the dip that Anton produced in my centre, somewhere between gliding and falling, a misstep in a dream, or when you've been seen for who you really are.

A twinge at my left temple and a lurch in the pit of my stomach made me wince. These days too much wine in an evening hurt hard the next day. Under the shower's hot water, I tilted my head back to rinse off shampoo.

Twenty years ago was the night of Hong Kong's handover—or return—to China.

The difference is more important than you'd think.

For us foreigners in Hong Kong, it was not yet clear if we were implicated. We had bought tickets to the local movie, along with buckets of our own private histories, but the Exit sign was clearly visible.

Anton was a boarding-school brat, half-English, a quarter Chinese, part Indian. Hong Kong was a gap-year turned gap-decade.

My own diplomatic parents had been reassigned long ago. Detached from my distant German father, my assiduous Malaysian mother, I was tired of being yanked around the globe with no place to call home. I remembered a satisfactory affinity to Hong Kong from my childhood, moved back and declared a moratorium on the search for roots.

Anton and I were reporters at the same news agency, assigned together to an outpost in the New Territories, the spot where the People's Liberation Army was to cross the border from China into Hong Kong.

It was 5 am that day too, and rain slashed our faces. Hunched inside a flimsy rain poncho, I checked the batteries on my flip-top Nokia phone, clutched pen and pad closer to my body. I was ragged from being up the whole night, watching on massive screens at the Wan Chai Convention and Exhibition Centre the British flag waft down, the Chinese flag swim up. Jiang Zemin's wax smile, his tight elbows, his held-in clapping, those big square glasses.

Prince Charles looked nervous; he was gate-crashing a party he did not even want to be at. Certainly, the Party did not want him.

Senior, more seasoned journalists—many had flown in from headquarters—were handling the trunk of the story. They ranked so high in the seniority ladder and were deemed so capable, that younger reporters like me had plenty of time to lounge, drink cups of bitter coffee from a dispenser. Anton and I took turns to go out onto the balcony and smoke.

Anton had been employed longer at the news agency. He and I had quickly developed a kind of bantering kinship, based on music and bad puns.

'How is the steel industry?' he said, glancing up from his computer as I walked back in from a press conference. It was my first week at the news agency. Something about an increase in China's manufacturing of steel products.

'Riveting.' He bent to hide a smile. I made a face at him.

He was laconic and savage all at the same time. It hypnotised me. Is that a form of love? Not being able to look away? Or did I just enjoy the frisson when he walked by.

The word 'frolleague' had thankfully not been invented yet. It would not have sufficed, for whatever electricity connected us.

This much is certain: We recognised in each other a liminal existence, both straddled too many cultures, stood at too many thresholds and perhaps that's why living in Hong Kong was a relief. Everyone here was first from somewhere else—if you went back far enough in time. Here, among the hills, our collective pasts could fade in the glare of Hong Kong neon, become hollow footfalls behind locked doors. In Hong Kong, it was possible to exist in a daily state of wonder, nose and palms pressed up against windows, permanently transfixed at the drama.

It was Anton who first asked me the question I hadn't yet answered:

'Of all those who arrived in Hong Kong like so many washed-up pebbles, do you belong in the pile that was running away from something? Or towards something?'

Landing with a backpack and a letter, or a friend's phone number, each of us crossed a *Hu Du Men*, a Tiger Line between backstage and stage and we became somebody else.

Or perhaps we became more ourselves.

In Hong Kong, it was possible to exist in a daily state of wonder, nose and palms pressed up against windows, permanently transfixed at the drama.

Around midnight, that long ago night in 1997, Anton spotted Jeremy Irons lounging alone in a folding chair at the Convention and Exhibition Centre. The actor's legs were crossed, one elbow rested on the back of the chair so that his wrist dangled by his right breast pocket. His expression was distracted, but mostly, he looked commonplace, and unperturbed at how history in the South China Sea had stolen his spotlight. Anton walked over and Jeremy Irons agreed to being interviewed. Later, Anton told me that 'Jez' is smaller than you'd imagine, given his screen presence.

Around 2 am, the bureau chief decided to send us to the China border. We'd have to grab a taxi, wherever we could find one. It took an hour and a half to reach the designated spot from Wan Chai. Our agency cameraman, Kenny, came along. He sat in the front seat, his camera in his lap. He was a silent, always busy man given to gentle Cantonese curses. His bony face occasionally broke into a smile as sweet and bright as tangerines.

A smattering of other reporters from various newspapers and news agencies had also collected. Anton sauntered over to talk to someone he knew.

I was tired, but taut with expectation and flying on adrenaline: an insignificant witness, doing her job, but I knew that I stood on the doorjamb of history.

When the rain began that dawn, Kenny bundled the expensive TV camera into its plastic shield and built a makeshift network of three umbrellas fastened together. The exercise was laced with mutters of yao mo gao cho ah, but he still had time to light and smoke a whole cigarette that he ditched and crushed underfoot, as the first trucks rolled in.

'Here comes the new era,' muttered Anton, who had returned to stand beside me.

When the camouflage green army vehicles splashed through across the border, the open trucks seemed small, oddly innocuous. At the back, the soldiers in three rows had no shelter from the rain and they were sodden. Raindrops leaked down their smart caps, behind their ears. Their uniform shirts and pants were drenched. Good thing they were not marching, their shoes would have squelched and overflowed.

Not a single soldier gave any indication he was aware of his own sopping condition. Not one looked around to take in this new land, the lush hills that surrounded us, the steel-hatch fencing topped with rolls of barbed wire, the language of boundaries.

The tires of the army trucks passing by threw up mud that streaked our faces.

Then, suddenly, it was over.

Just like that, the People's Liberation Army had entered Hong Kong, dragging ancient treaties and old wars in their wake.

The desk editor called on an intermittent cell phone connection to say that the wire service would just go with the photos and a caption, could Kenny please return to the office, they needed him elsewhere. The two of us were instructed to return to town and phone in any *vox pop* we found. That was journo-speak for accosting passing innocents and extracting their thoughts on any matter at hand.

I hated *vox pop*. It seemed arrogant to demand a reaction. Maybe there wasn't one. Or was a private thing.

It turned out, Anton sort of agreed. At the corner of Luard and Hennessy Road, he said with immense gravity:

'Actually, I don't give a fuck about the popular voice.'

Giddy with fatigue, the weeks—years—of build-up to this dismembered night, I found myself laughing.

'Neither do Britain or China,' I gasped. We stood outside a deserted, locked, neon-lit 7-Eleven. The giggles spread to my belly. I wiped my eyes, snorting-gulping, I bent over, clutching my stomach. He stood still, facing me, his grey eyes amazed. When I stopped, breathless, he reached up and picked dried mud off my cheek. The way he did it told me he'd been wanting to for a while.

My feet ached. The entire city ached. Even the sky ached.

That must be why when he stepped forward and kissed me and I slipped in my vertiginous dream, the moment was stamped with an undertone of loss and failed experiments.

Later, in that dishwater light, we wandered through empty Wan Chai streets, found a still-open bar called Chinatown. Seated in a fug of old beer and faint vomit, we ordered coffee and eggs from a barely-smiling Filipina.

Your grey eyes are hard and haunted. How can they be both?

The Giordano in Causeway Bay opens at 9:30 am, but I'd been standing in front of it for half an hour, shifting from one foot to the other, biting my lip, trying to avoid being crushed by the morning office rush, the flood of people stampeding past, leaning slightly forward.

Work is Hong Kong's religion.

It happens more than we realise: wrapped in work, people neglect to love, they forget to get married, they put off children. Should some negligent soul fall into such matters, the exigencies created are obstacles to getting to the workplace, and frankly, they are ridiculous detours from a sturdy, necessary path.

The question everybody in Hong Kong asks is not 'Where are you from,' or 'How are the kids?' but 'What do you do?'

For the first time in years, in front of that Giordano, I wanted a cigarette.

The question everybody in Hong Kong asks is not 'Where are you from,' or 'How are the kids?' but 'What do you do?'

After a staff member bent to unlock the glass doors I hurried in to choose khaki pants, a teal-blue T-shirt, a light rain jacket. Underwear. The strange, accidental intimacy of holding garments that would lie against Anton's skin; it was faintly arousing and also repellent, like sitting on a bus seat still warm from its previous occupant.

My cell phone buzzed.

I saw that it was S., but I didn't answer.

I hid my confusion behind the small acts of collecting clothes, paying with cash, stashing the purchases into a backpack.

Twenty years collapsed into a dust heap. Anton summoned me, and I could not refuse. Nobody refused Anton, it turned out. I had said 'no,' just once and we had not spoken since.

I shoved the packet of underwear into the bag.

Anton wore boxers, I learnt during our short, heated entanglement.

'Men,' he said, 'are divided into those who wear briefs and those who wear boxers. That choice says a lot about a man.' I told him then that his mongrel genes made him obsess over categories.

'I'd like to put my category into yours and make a sub-set,' he said, pulling me towards him. 'Do you care that I only have one testicle?'

We were in sun-soaked Goa, in the old part of town, in a back-packers' haven that served Goan shrimp curry but also banana milkshakes and pancakes, because you may be trying to leave home behind, but there were limits to compromising on breakfast.

The bed in the room on the top floor was hard and the printed cotton bedspread smelled of sun and starch. The dhurrie on the floor had faded. But the place was clean, and walking distance from St Francis Xavier's tomb. At the back of a cool vast church, the displayed relics were a jumble of small bones, arranged inside an elaborate sarcophagus. Anton said the Jesuit wanderer was the patron saint of exiles and of those who died far from home.

Outside, a kite circled the plunging blue sky.

India had a way of slowing our feet, even our lovemaking ebbed from its usual hectic pace.

It was bloody hot.

'Did we have to do this pilgrimage in July?' I lay atop sheets and sweat trickled down the sides of my forehead, into my hair.

Anton sat on the edge of the bed, with his back to me. He lit a cigarette, crossed skinny legs, propped his right elbow onto a knee to smoke more comfortably, and stared outside the window. A large black ant crawled along the windowsill. We could hear the bleat of a vendor's voice pitched to carry, then the ring of his bicycle bell. The shouts of children, the hollow echoing bounce of a ball against a wall.

My body sank into a blissful enjoyment.

I turned on my side, lifted an arm and ran a fingertip along his bare shoulder blades. He shivered, despite the heat.

'I never knew my Chinese grandfather,' he said to the window. 'I don't even know if there's an equivalent term in Chinese for 'quadroon'.'

That was our deal.

He'd give me time to think, I'd travel with him on his family quest. Goa was his first stop; he had Goan ancestors. We were following a ghost ship, adrift on old seas.

In Macau, visiting his aunt's home, I felt uneasy.

The room we slept in at the back of her house seemed to press in on me.

Anton did not notice. He was cheerful, looking at maps, asking his aunt questions, which she answered in Cantonese, slowly, so Anton could follow. He looked at family photos for a long time.

His aunt lived alone and she followed us around silent, with a gaze made malevolent by its intensity. She wore a man's shirt buttoned down the front, and an open sweater over it, despite the weather.

I'd turn around and find she had been staring at me for some time. She spoke little English, but there was no mistaking her lunacy. To my jumpy nerves, it felt as though she gave off an energy that was sticky and evil with neglect.

When we finally left Macau, and returned to Hong Kong, I told Anton 'no.'

I didn't say that being with him was like living on the outer curl of a typhoon's tail, flying through empty sky, lashing around the Earth's poles. I didn't say it was too much, too soon, that I did not know the secret to embracing the wind.

I understood dimly that I wanted a life like a Japanese room, tidy, spare, with one low table holding a creamy ceramic vase;

a hint of a flush at its flank.

I rested my hand along Anton's jaw line, my fingertips on his Chinese cheekbones, I looked into the grey eyes gifted by his English father.

Anton was crying, the way men cry; there is an element of surprise.

He said that all the histories and geographies swirling inside him were driving him mad. He said he had chosen his paternal grandfather to follow.

'Since I can't have you.'

I wiped my own, sudden tears.

'Yet. You can't have me yet. I'm just saying I need time. Leaving doesn't solve—'

'I keep feeling for home like a tongue feels for an absence in a gum.'

'So maybe home is here, in this moment, in this conversation, I—'

A few months later, Anton left Hong Kong and moved to Beijing. We never spoke again.

Over the years, I got snippets of news about him, from journalist friends passing through Hong Kong, friends who knew us both.

He'd studied Mandarin and spoke it like a local.

He'd married a Beijing woman, someone well connected in government circles. They said it made things easier.

He was writing a book on China—not a mighty, political tome on the rise of Deng Xiaoping, but about ordinary people living in Beijing *hutongs*. He had spent months interviewing people about their lives.

I pictured Anton blending in easily, with his Chinese bones, his dark hair. But if he looked up, those Atlantic-grey eyes would startle.

Occasionally, if a news item on TV panned across Beijing streets, I imagined I saw him bicycling through blue-suit streets in the early days. Later, I pictured him on a motor-cycle, dodging the cars, and still later, I put him in a car, as the money grew and the lines between ideologies blurred.

The truth was I'd lost him.

As for myself, I did not leave Hong Kong after the handover. There was no obvious place to go, and no immediate reason to leave. I found a comfortable editing position at the research wing of a boutique investment firm. The pay was excellent, and I liked the CEO, Mr Wong, a well-heeled Hong Kong man with a penchant for collecting fine jade.

He had bought out his British partner who had retired to Bedfordshire a few years after 1997. His final task had been to help Mr Wong's son gain entrance to Eton.

If Hong Kong was now a part of China, in the beginning, it hardly seemed to ripple the rhythm of our days. Sure, the postboxes were different, though every now and again, we still spotted one in an island market, a post-box that carried the old raised letters E.R. topped with a dotted crown, whispering Empire amid the smell of dried fish.

Our congenial firm's office started out at the Lucky Building in Wellington Street, then shifted progressively as the rents grew higher. Soon after I met S, we drifted into a gentle love. When we merged our paths, and found a small flat together in Wan Chai, I saw that I had rebelled my way straight into a system.

> It turned out that my life had became a Chinese antique shop on Holly-wood Road, crammed with unrelated dusty items of porcelain and rosewood, the detritus of somebody else's decorated days.

Still, that it all took place in Hong Kong gave my hours a spiced edge, as though I required this rigorous backdrop to counterbalance the terrible banality of the years unspooling, of growing old. In Hong Kong, even commonplace days became a story, with tension and sparkle.

It turned out that my life had became a Chinese antique shop on Hollywood Road, crammed with unrelated dusty items of porcelain and rosewood, the detritus of somebody else's decorated days.

I found I quite liked it.

The first thing I noticed about Anton was the dried blood.

He was covered in great rusted patches. His T-shirt was torn at the neck. A trench coat dropped over a hotel chair and a baseball hat that now lay on the floor had probably covered most of the damage and allowed him to travel this far.

'Anton! We have to get you to a hospital!' I dropped the package of clothes at the door and ran to him.

'Don't I get a hello? After twenty years?' His smile was wry, but he winced when he tried to stand. A brutal cut ran across the bone-side of his forearm. A defence wound.

I was panting, with panic, digging for my phone. He reached out a hand and stopped me.

'It's a long story.'

I didn't press him. We sat in silence in the taxi. On Stubbs Road, he turned his face to the window and his eyes drank in the green hills. When his fingers reached across the seat and felt for mine, I held them.

The doctor at the Adventist Hospital lifted the X-ray to the light. He was a young Hong Kong Chinese man, who had shaved his head bald and spoke English with a Manchester slant. A mask covered the lower half of his face.

He said that that the ligaments binding the right leg's tibia and fibula were badly damaged and Anton would need surgery to insert a screw to keep the bones together while the ligament healed. It required general anaesthesia, when had the patient last eaten?

It turned out to have been about thirty-six hours since Anton's last meal. The doctor asked how such an enormous impact to his leg had happened. Anton replied that he'd fallen.

The doctor's eyes above the mask were hard to read. He said nothing. He put down the X-ray and left the room to make enquiries about admission, beds, operating schedules.

I stood up behind Anton, to push his wheelchair to the narrow corridor of the waiting area. He felt as light as a sparrow. Looking down at the top of his head, the scalp under his dark hair showed bone-pale. From here, the silver strands interspersed between the black were clear.

'I suppose you'll eventually—'

'Yes, of course I'll explain,' Anton said.

He sipped lukewarm water from a conical cup that I handed him. I sat on a bench beside him.

It took a few seconds to realise that Anton was speaking. His voice was low, pressing.

'I had a long-haired dictionary,' he said.

'What?'

'It's a term. Your lover teaches you the language.'

I didn't interrupt. Was he starting in the middle?

'That's how my Mandarin became so good. She was with me night and day, so helpful, so solicitous. I felt I had been handed some sort of extraordinary key to the city, to the whole of China. The key to myself, even. She seemed to understand instinctively what I was looking for, she came with me to my grandfather's village. I felt whole, for the first time in my life.'

Neither of us looked up when a nurse walked out. She took Anton's temperature, scribbled a few notes, fastened a cloth flap around his arm for a blood pressure read. It took a few tries, the machine wasn't working very well.

Anton was silent till the nurse left. Then he spoke again, in that low, urgent manner.

'Of course I fell in love. The operative being 'I.' I stepped into a ready-made world, a language, a culture, a woman who wanted me—'

He glanced at me sideways.

I raised my eyebrows at him.

Seriously? You're going to bring that up now?

Anton conceded, but his smile was sad.

'Remember Goa?' he said.

'Every moment.'

'Still, I remember so much more about you than you remember about me.'

'What is that supposed to mean?'

'It's a measure of something.'

We were ushered to the reception desk. Anton had to fill out multiple forms, answer questions about insurance; it was tricky, because he lived in China and did not have any of his documents except for his passport. He pulled out a wad of yuan, but the hospital staff said they would accept only Hong Kong dollars. I dug out my credit card.

Then I wheeled him into the lift, following another nurse, up to the operating theatre area.

The previous patient's surgery was taking longer than anticipated, the nurse explained. She was very sorry, Anton had to wait a little longer.

He nodded.

The automatic doors closed silently behind her. We were in a small enclosure, along with stored wheelchairs, other unidentifiable machines. It was disconcerting, a sudden reduction to an item that needed fixing in the warehouse.

'If anything happens to me—' Anton said.

'Nothing will happen, you'll be fine,' I interrupted.

'You don't understand. Something strange is going on. Everything collapsed in China, after I tried to go to Fujian. This guy I'd being interviewing about his life turned out to know something. He let slip a few details about the top leadership, even Xi Dada; something that he did while he was the governor of Fujian.

'This man, he just said, "Go to Fujian." He gave me a name, a phone number. It was really weird, when I went back to see him, and ask him more questions, he wouldn't see me. He wouldn't even open the door. He just kept saying, "I'm sorry, it's not safe. Please go away."'

I turned to face Anton.

'Please don't tell me you went to—'

'I had just bought a ticket to Fujian, and was ready to board the train, when I realised that my bag had been slit open, my bag with my computer, my clothes, my money. Only my work stuff was missing, the notes, my computer. Everything else was intact. Luckily, I'm a fanatic about backing up and had everything on a hard drive.'

I stood up.

'I thought it was a fluke, but then, my train ticket was stolen. I tried again. I had a friend buy me a ticket. I got on the train, but then it stopped half-way there. It just stopped. They said the train had broken down. I didn't believe it. That's how China is, nobody will tell you anything and you get more and more paranoid.

'I thought I was going crazy, I had to try one last time. Finally, I was boarding a plane, to Fujian, when three men with low hats and dark clothes escorted me off the aeroplane. They took me to a black sedan car and blindfolded me. It seemed like hours, but I knew from the bumpy road and the smell of trees and grass that we were not in the city.

And then they beat me up. Expertly. Eventually, I passed out from the pain. The next thing I knew, they had dumped me outside my house. It must have been about 3 am. I don't know. All I could think was—I have to leave. I grabbed a bottle of Aspirin, my passport, a hat, my coat, all the cash in the safe, and I took a taxi to the airport.'

Anton spoke with a strange detachment. Maybe it was the pain.

My own landscape was shifting, however. I understood at that moment that we were all trapped in the same dark cinema. The Exit sign had wavered and then had blinked off.

It was too late to leave.

After the long operation, Anton was hazy with the drugs.

'My leg hurts,' he whispered. 'I'm cold.'

His leg was encased in a gunmetal armature filled with ice to keep it cold and insensate, so the pain would not hit too hard when the narcotics wore off.

His lips trembled. Under the blanket, he was shivering. I fetched the nurse, who installed a kind of hot-air blower that heated his body under the blanket. The force of the air lifted the blanket, and slowly, his shivering subsided.

The nurse flipped through pages on his chart.

Standing at her elbow, I glimpsed photos of the operation; the screw through the bone, the glistening flesh sliced bloodless, an X-ray that showed the inserted screw. It looked ordinary, floating in its shadowy bank of bone.

In the curtained-off enclosure around Anton's bed, I stood next to him.

'What am I going to do?' he said. I had to bend to hear him. I straightened up.

'You could always come back.'

Wasn't Hong Kong the haven we all returned to? The place that always accepted us back, no matter how many times we'd broken up with it and left.

'You should have married me,' said Anton, pale under his

brown skin. His mouth was dry.

'But then, who would come save you?' I whispered.

'I still don't know where I belong.'

I couldn't deny that Anton's search was futile. I wanted to tell him that he wasn't alone. Everybody thinks you belong somewhere—or to someone. Nobody realises that you are the Nowhere Ghost, and have fallen through the many cracks in the cosmos.

That night, back at home, perturbed by Anton's story, his failed quest, I slept badly.

In my dream, yellow dust choked the air, it was a dream so stinking and putrid that it woke me up in a sweat of fear. The darkness was in me, I was the murderer, with the potential for disappearing. I could hide in a sink half-full of water, gleeful, my dark hair swirling as I slid down the drain and they could not stop me, they couldn't see me and then I was streaking through the air, ready to kill again.

I lay awake, petrified and could not sleep again. I shifted closer to S. and thought, his goodness will shelter me, but I was too afraid to even get up and get a glass of water until the sky lightened and then I fumbled the curtains open, moved a chair to the side, pushed the window open to check on the rain and made enough noise that deep-sleeping S. stirred.

He mumbled, 'Tell me when you've finished redecorating.'

It felt good to laugh.

Anton has always said that Hong Kong's jungle soul waits.

There is nothing to do but wait; teaspoons of waiting. Waiting to get to work, waiting to get rich, waiting for dusk, for a good dream.

If humans did nothing for six months, if we just sat and breathed, the jungle would inch forward and obliterate our buildings, India rubber tree roots would drop through our windows, hedges grow across apartment parquets, great camphor trees would burst out of bathtubs and bougainvillea spray over kitchen counters.

In my mind grows the idea—Hong Kong's landscape, in all its heaves and swells, its drooling seas, its hairy hills, its raw-scraped rocks for knuckles and knees; a landscape lying on its back, submerged in water, listening.

There is nothing to do but wait; teaspoons of waiting. Waiting to get to work, waiting to get rich, waiting for dusk, for a good dream.

Waiting to see if the jungle takes over.

With thanks to Sholeh Wolpé for permission to reference her poem Sanctuary: *Home is a missing tooth. / The tongue reaches / for hardness / but falls / into absence. In* Keeping Time with Blue Hyacinths *(University of Arkansas Press, 2013).*

City of Darkness

Michael Braga

H ong Kong is already tense in the days before China is to take it back and now the city wakes to a new fear; a killer with particular, sadistic tastes has struck. Journalist Lewis Tang needs a scoop to save his job, and if he can track down the killer, the resulting story might just do the needful. Only after a priest convinces Lewis to use his informal contacts to find a lost orphan does Lewis begin to understand there is a connection between the butcher, the lost child and the change in sovereignty. Just then, the killer takes a personal interest in Lewis's throat, strangling him with all the power of his bull-like shoulders and arms like buttress roots. Having cheated death by luck alone, Lewis wakes in hospital, each breath burning his throat and no wiser about the killer's identity. He is powerless to dam a fresh flood of guilt and self-loathing, held in check for twenty years by liberal applications of single malt Scotch; guilt for the part he played in the death of his daughter, Millie—the result of many risks he took during his muckraking days. His wife Helen lays the blame for Millie's death wholly at his feet. Lewis leaves the Tung Wah Hospital wrapped in a dark, friable mood. In one of Hong Kong's wettest summers, the rain starts again, but a source who won't divulge his name might just have some helpful information.

A taxi dropped Lewis off by Wan Chai MTR station. The downpour drew a heavy curtain across Johnston Road. He could just make out the Lung Moon and Stone Nullah Lane on the other side.

In the tiny foyer of his building, Nose-Picker was settled behind his battered desk, his eyebrows pressed together, forehead creased, focused on the contents of his extended pinkie-nail when Lewis stepped in from the downpour. On seeing Lewis he shifted on his haemorrhoids, readdressed his scowl and grunted. He drew the digital tool across his belly, leaving a smear. Then, he used the offending hand to brandish an envelope at Lewis. The white square bore the precise Edwardian copperplate of 'A Friend'. No stamp, like the first letter.

The single page revealed a change in plan. Lewis ducked back into the rain and grabbed another taxi to the airport.

From behind his rain-speckled glasses the lights of Kai Tak Airport sparkled. An escalator took him up to the new place, Windows-on-the-World. Tonight, it ought to be sued for false advertising; the rain was impenetrable. On a sunny day those lucky enough to grab a table by the windows could see down the runway, on to Lei Yue Mun and into the wide blue yonder. Tonight, the only thing wide, blue or yonder Lewis was able to see was blue-tinted glass with a hint of the apron lights like a distant orange haze, on one side frost from frigid air-conditioning and on the other side rain. Maybe there were aeroplanes there, and if there were maybe they would be jetting off, but you couldn't see to tell.

Lewis's man was sitting at a corner table right at the back, near the bar, in a freshly-pressed shirt, Oxford collar, tie and jacket, twill Herringbone no less. The threads were old, worn but well kept. The lights from the ceiling bounced off his shoes like starbursts, buffed as much with spit and polish as by long habit. He would have registered the creases along the front of his trousers as a representation of otherwise concealed dangerous weapons. All that, and his short, no-nonsense haircut, screamed out, 'cop', even if Lewis hadn't already known. His clothes, his bearing, they also shouted to Lewis, 'bachelor for life'.

He stood. They shook; firm grip. They sat.

It took Lewis a few seconds to place him.

'You were a few steps below our good friend from Glasgow, nudging a shrub.'

A Friend nodded. Lewis noticed flecks of grey in his regulation cut.

'Again, I am sorry,' he said, 'for the way in which the inspector spoke to you.' He spoke in Cantonese and that was fine with Lewis.

'Forget it. You don't speak for the police force, and certainly not for the Glaswegian. But you do speak for yourself, and that's what I'm interested in hearing.'

Knife-Trousers nodded, then said:

'Shall we have a pot of tea?'

The tea had long since gone cold. Frigid air did that. But Lewis bet it was nowhere as cold as he was, chilled to his heart by what he'd just heard.

'Go on,' he urged A Friend.

'The man was broad and thick, shoulders set like a bull. Squat, I think would be accurate, and powerful. You could tell even all those years ago.' In defiance of the cold, sweat beaded the man's forehead. His eyes began to twitch from side to side, scanning the restaurant behind Lewis.

'How long?'

'1967.'

'How can you be sure it's the same man? It's been a while.'

'Who else could do the things to the boy we found in Hong Kong Park?'

'The world's made some impressive leaps since the '60s and I'm sorry to say lust for distinctive murder is amongst those. Besides, it has been a long time between drinks for him, hasn't it?'

'What,' A Friend said, 'makes you believe he hasn't been exercising his particular predilections all this time?'

Lewis didn't hear himself say anything, but he did hear distant laughter, a glass settle tic-tap on a table, a set of those jet engines rumble through the rain and ultra-thick glazing … maybe a coin drop …

Then he heard his own hushed voice mutter, 'Shit'.

He sat back in the chair, and let that all percolate. He looked the man straight in the eye and as far as he could tell was greeted by not an iota of deceit. He gave a gingerly rub to his right temple, reached for thinking sticks, lit one and drew in right down to his toes. No one bothered to enforce the anti-smoking regulation.

'So,' he said, exhaling a plume, 'why've you waited to speak?'

'My mother had not been well for many years, especially since the death of my father. I took care of her, and was afraid that were I to speak out she would become the target of some horrible campaign. Now, I have no ties I am free to speak.'

'Campaign?'

'You will see.'

'So, what about this monster? What had, or have you to do with him?'

He followed the plume of smoke to where it bounced off the ceiling and wafted slowly purple.

'Nothing!' The retort was angry. 'I am, I was, an officer of the law. I resigned yesterday, effective immediately. I gave all my professional life to the force, thirty years. I never rose above senior constable, though my ambition was to be commissioner. I was naïve. A commissioner of police must be a politician; being a good policeman with a desire to serve and protect the public is not enough.'

Lewis detected a note of bitterness.

'You sound like the recruitment brochure.'

'Mr Tang, I know what you do for a living and I respect you. I know that you must try to establish my honesty, truthfulness, so I expect that kind of statement and I do not take offence. In fact, I agree. When I joined, I thought nothing was more honourable than being a police officer. Shall we …?'

He waved at the bartender and indicated at Lewis and himself. A tall bottle and two glasses filled with a golden liquid appeared. He must have arranged it earlier. It never just rained, did it? The man A Friend took a healthy swig of his Scotch. Lewis poked a finger at his glass.

'You of anyone will appreciate how the force has changed since I joined. You can't imagine how disillusioned I was to learn that it was a place of great temptation, and because of that, corruption.'

'The police and everyone else.'

'That did not make it right or excusable.'

'What, and you thought you made the difference by staying?'

'My fault, one of many, Mr Tang, was to think I could contribute to making the force a better one.'

'Why not dream big?'

A Friend chose to finish his drink and refill his glass rather than address the obvious.

'So what happened to the commissioner's chair? Long time to brandish just the one stripe.'

A Friend reached forward for his shot glass, thought about it and left it there. He leant on his knees and said:

'During the leftist trouble the Governor ordered raids on leftist strongholds. Sir David Trench was shrewd, strong and when the sun set each day he knew that the curfew was doing only so much. The force was stretched and so fresh recruits had to step up. He was correct, of course. You can remember what police raids on Kiu Kwan Mansion found: bombs, weapons and a hospital with a dispensary and operating theatre. These people were prepared for war. Newspaper editors who were inciting violence, we also had to arrest.'

'Some good people amongst them. Excitable, sure, passionate, without doubt, but were they wrong?'

'For the sake of stability and safety, they had to be controlled.'

'However you rationalise it,' Lewis said, 'your boys did a pretty number on a couple of them. You beat one of them to death.'

This time A Friend picked up his glass. He replaced it empty. He kept one elbow on one knee and aimed a thick forefinger right at Lewis, centre-mass.

'You of anyone should understand how we operate. You of anyone! Many of your newspaper reports, they showed a deep understanding of police operations, of our need to show strength, of our need to—'

'Quit defending. The blue line's one man thinner tonight.'

A Friend pulled himself back. He nodded, saying:

'… catch up, our need to catch up. We were so often playing catch-up. But that wasn't it. You know, I know, everyone who was playing the game at the time knows.'

Lewis nodded.

'Tea money,' A Friend said.

'And boy, what a cup of tea it was.'

'Yes. When the very people you're expecting help from are involved with the people you're fighting against, it makes progress difficult.' A Friend was finding it difficult to hide deep disappointment. 'Damn tea money!'

Tea money, fragrant grease, hand-offs, call it what you will, the machine needed its parts slicked.

'But your boys had very good information—Kiu Kwan Mansion was a crack raid, you and the Welsh Guards. But you wouldn't have known to look for a false wall, and it was a very good one.'

'Another news story of yours. I've often wondered how your paper was able to run such vivid pictures and such good detail of our raids during that time.'

Lewis poked his glass, avoiding the man's eyes.

'Sources,' he said.

A Friend nodded. He said:

'Tea money.'

Lewis met his eyes; both men managed a weak laugh. Lewis dipped a finger in his glass and licked it.

Tea money, fragrant grease, hand-offs, call it what you will, the machine needed its parts slicked. From storekeepers to thugs for protection, from thugs to triads for leverage, from triads to the man on the beat and from him to one of the Four Great Sergeants, who made redistributions to ensure the right cogs were kept quiet, were encouraged to close their eyes, shut their mouths and sit on their hands except when action was necessary for the working order of the great machine. Tip-offs before raids, compensation for temporary loss of business, tacit understanding when brothels re-opened that monies would pass between operator and messenger, messenger and one of the Four Great Sergeants, who controlled everything and because they were integral to ensuring the smooth running of the colony, took an appropriate share of the fragrant grease. They controlled promotions within the force, they made sure senior expatriate officers who were of the same mind were kept in touch.

'The day of the incursion and gun battle at Sha Tau Kok police outpost Commissioner Sutcliffe cancelled all leave, the Auxiliaries too. Many of us believed the People's Liberation Army was going to invade. Sir David gave permission for military support, that's why the Gurkhas came. But by that time five of our officers were dead, Chinese and Pakistani. As a young constable I was deeply moved by their heroism. The following day was Sunday, and I was assigned to join a special squad to strike at the Kowloon Walled City.'

'Nothing like forcing a hot poker up an angry dragon's backside.'

'I was only vaguely aware of the stir that your article three days earlier was causing in the Commissioner's office, with Special Branch, and Government House, the one in which you predicted an invasion by the PLA. My head was full of anguish, feelings that I must act to avenge the killing of our fallen brothers in the force.'

'The PLA never officially invaded.'

'But the People's Militia did.'

'Did a pretty reasonable job of it.' Lewis sent the golden fluid in his glass into an eddy with an index finger, removed the evidence. Then he said: 'That was a nasty job to send you on, as inexperienced as you were then. Potential to blow up—in your faces; the whole of Hong Kong.'

'The politics of who had jurisdiction in the Walled City, I believe, had long before been decided—tacitly. But that still did not make me feel any less anxious. I had heard the many stories of the Walled City being the Devil's own sanctuary, *Hak Nam*, and so was succour to criminals of all shades. But I knew it was also somewhere that many refugees from China ended up, legally or not, because rents were much less than elsewhere in Hong Kong, and it was the only place where government qualifications and hygienic standards were not properly overseen.'

'I see you've developed the civil servant's gift for understatement.'

Lewis stirred his Scotch again; A Friend emptied his.

'Years of writing reports,' he said. 'A few of my colleagues, some who came through training with me, told me I was brave to accept the assignment; they offered their hands and we shook. But it was like that throughout the ranks then.'

Lewis agreed. The boys in blue—khaki back then—were a close unit. But they were trained to take commands and instructions without question, to respect senior officers. Gossip, undermining, questioning got men killed. So when ordered, they went in, and went in with both boots, heavy.

'It was early, still dark. Some might say that was a poor time, especially because the Walled City was unmapped, its buildings thrown up with hand-mixed concrete and no blueprints or care for safety standards, nothing uniform. But it all knitted together somehow in a sheer dense mass built solid from outside right to its dark heart. But then, the place was in perpetual twilight anyway ... *Hak Nam*.'

Hak Nam ... The City of Darkness. Lewis sensed a deeper silence settle around them.

'But what,' Lewis whispered, 'were you supposed to do in there?'

'You know, to this day I am not sure. It was never spelt out in either briefing. If there was a target, or targets, I never heard about them—we were just to follow orders. I imagined then that it was very secret, very sensitive and need-to-know.'

'Jesus. You went in there and had no idea why? No idea how to get around in there, or get out?'

A Friend's nod gave the impression of embarrassment. You can take following orders too far. He sighed, then said:

'I suppose I made up the numbers. But I got separated and lost from the squad.'

Lewis reached for his glass and sipped a half-inch of the rich fluid. It slipped down hot and cooling. The perfume of the Scotch hung about his nostrils, and he was glad for it. It was that or smell the dank rottenness of the world within the Walled City that for all intents and purposes was sub-terranean: the heat of butchers' hack-shops thick with blood that clotted the drains, saturated with the stench of death. He said: 'Christ.'

'I thought he was just one of the many illegal dentists. His shoulders were huge, hunched over a patient. They twitched, and there was some small movement—then an ugly scream. I stopped. Dull lights in the shop glanced off his head, bald and sweating. I thought, 'No laughing gas. You get what you pay for,' but I knew. Something wasn't right, and the scream had nothing to do with a cheap dentist from China.'

A Friend reached for his Scotch. His hand trembled.

'Then,' he whispered, 'I saw the others.'

The Scotch disappeared. The shot glass clanked empty on the table-top. Lewis refilled it.

'One at the head had some kind of strap under the man's chin and pulled back under tension. Others held down the man in the chair, torso, arms, legs. They had him tight. The huge man's shoulders moved again, so very slightly. Another scream, a shriek, really. I drew my service revolver and iden-tified myself—'

'Oh, sweet Jesus.'

'I commanded they stop. Identify themselves. Only two things happened. First, the men restraining did nothing.

Second, the huge shoulders turned, and with them came a hand with a scalpel and the face. It was a smiling mouth and eyes so black that I could see no whites. Then he turned fully square to me. The yellow from the light bulbs glinted a rosy colour off the blade. He began to nod. It was a slow, frightening nod. It was full of knowing—he had seen me. He knew what I represented. It meant nothing to him and he knew that I knew it.'

He reached again for the Scotch, drained the glass and gripped the arms of his chair.

'I called out again. 'Stop! Police!' The man in the chair made rasping sounds with his breathing. And then he stopped. The gang relaxed—yes, they relaxed, stood up. They all walked towards me. The cutter made to throw something at me. I stood my ground. Then he did. It struck me on the shoulder and fell away. They filed past me, like I was on inspection. Each eyed me. Three of them actually bumped my revolver as they strolled past. The last was the cutter. He stood before me. He raised his left hand and draped a heavy fabric over my revolver. I looked into his black eyes. He did not blink; bottomless … he nodded the slow nod again and walked away. I realised only then how much I was shaking. I knew he could have killed me, but that would have been no challenge. So, he let me live. And I let him go. And then I saw the poor man in the chair and he had no face … because his face was hanging on the end on my gun.'

A Friend covered his face with his hands. When he looked up finally it was circled with fingernail impressions.

'There was nothing I could do for him: my radio did not work in that labyrinth. I could not call for assistance. He was still, very still. I tried to replace the skin over his face, his horror of a face. His eyeballs … more white than brown. His mouth … it had fallen open without the strap. And I realised … because I turned and saw where it had fallen … what the cutter had thrown at me. I tried to fit his tongue back in his mouth. Then, he blinked. I'm not ashamed to say I fell backwards on my *pat-pat*. I heard one more sound—a heavy sigh. So, his pain was over. Then I saw his blood, on my shoulder, on my hands, and I threw up.'

They'd paid the good senior constable to shut up about the whole thing. Every week since he made it out of *Hak Nam*. First, a brown bag appeared in his locker at the station, stuffed with banknotes. There was no accompanying message, but he knew why it had been left and where, ultimately, it came from. The Four Great Sergeants were at work, quietly ensuring the well-greased operation of law and order in Hong Kong. When untouched brown bags came to dominate the locker, they disappeared and a birthday card replaced them with nothing written inside but a series of numbers. It wasn't his birthday.

A Friend said he had no idea how much money there was or which bank held it, and Lewis believed him. He believed him without being told, that he'd struggled financially to take care of his parents and then after his father died, his mother, even though there was a mandarin's ransom at his disposal, though he'd no idea how to get to it even if desperate and even then Lewis knew A Friend chose to struggle to provide for his mum rather than touch the bloody stuff. He sacrificed his career for her, for his self-respect. His fiancée left him as a no-hoper. He never looked or hoped for anyone else … he had attained perfect knowledge. The sergeants would have seen to it that he wasn't promoted, and ensured that he was never to be promoted.

That he got to add a stripe to his sleeve was a testament to how deeply the ICAC had cleaned shop. But back before that, before they slipped away, the Four Great Sergeants held men's careers in their hands, in thousand-dollar bills, in notes jotted in official files, in quiet whispers. Just as they traded in promotions within the force, so they traded everywhere in people's lives and others' death.

Lewis held his glass at the tips of his fingers and turned it slowly to catch what light there might still be on the third-floor joint. Back in the old days he used to take Millie out onto the observation deck, a real deck outside and in the open, and she would wrinkle her nose at the smell of used air and aviation fuel, but she'd be first to spot jets as they approached over Kowloon and then dip sharply at Checkerboard Hill, the scream of the engines shrill and sharp. Helen wasn't a fan and remained in air-conditioning sipping tea or doing what she did. In those days there wasn't Windows-on-the World … and he couldn't remember what was there, but …

Lewis shook off the memory.

A Friend … there was a man who needed a great deal of help with a lot of pain, and he'd taken his solace and was swirling.

'My mother is free and that has released me, and it is just in time.' He spoke with remarkable clarity given the volume of malt enriching his blood. 'I don't care what this Basic Law, this invention of London and Beijing, says, I don't care what Beijing has promised. Once the chance presents itself, those people will kill Hong Kong, my Hong Kong, the place where I was born, where my mother raised me, whose people I served and protected, maybe not as commissioner, but honourably, and I do not want to be here to experience it die too; I have already watched my mother die slowly. Because they will strangle it. Yes they will play the game, they will let the money-makers make money, because that is what it is good at, and they will

I will think of you, Mr Tang, here under the new flag, the new masters, and I hope you will still be writing your news reports.

horde their cut. These people, they inhabit the same shadows as the likes of Godber, Hunt and the others who pledged to uphold the law but soiled it for their own gains. But you and I know that making money is not what makes a city. When the British leave and the PLA comes, I will be far away. But I will think of you, Mr Tang, here under the new flag, the new masters, and I hope you will still be writing your news reports. I will look for your by-line.'

His story told, A Friend walked out Scotch-shaky on his feet but it was okay, he wouldn't need them. Just as the malt soothed his pain, a big bird was going to take A Friend under its big silver wings and ease it further with distance. The man's mother was dead, he had no more ties, his career was over, his dreams lay in innumerable splinters—the only spirit left in him was in the morning going to make him feel like he'd spent the night—maybe his whole life—head-butting a double-decker bus. So, what then? When he did wake up, it was going to be in a new country, new skies, new hope—and a whole lot of new bullshit no doubt, but still it would be new.

But for Lewis, no.

Perhaps that was why, in spite of A Friend's confidence in him, Lewis felt bitterness. There was a deeper corruption coming, he knew it, and it unnerved him. He wondered if the ex-cop realised but chose not to talk about it because his sense of loss just now was too great. Whatever the case, the bastards on the way were serious. They'd make local dirty-play look freshly laundered. He'd written about it; Toyneville chose spite and the spike. This incoming ruthless breed was plotting its domination of the soon-to-be special administrative region, its eye on the prize, yes, but also on executing the elimination of whatever identity Hong Kong had grafted for itself in the confusion between 1839 and 1984, when it was so publicly dumped on by Britain, and then 1989, when, already so very vulnerable, people panicked on seeing what the party thought about ideas contrary to its line.

...when the silent clock timed out June 30th, 2047, and Hong Kong and its people were just another indistinguishable patch in the enormous Chinese padded quilt.

Along with all that there was going to be a new count-down clock, one not as public as the one at Tiananmen Square tick-tick-ticking away until the great celebrations on the return of the child snatched at birth, but kept secret in the hearts and minds of the party's exalted, quiet men and it would begin at one second past midnight on July the first— for masters of the long game, fifty years was a tickle. Patten, democracy, Article 45 paragraph two, the whole Provisional Legislative Council thing—and if that wasn't United Front work at its best, he didn't know what was—all that was going to be dust in the skulls of a buried generation, his included, when the silent clock timed out June 30th, 2047, and Hong Kong and its people were just another indistinguishable patch in the enormous Chinese padded quilt.

A Friend ... Lewis might have liked his steadiness, crew-cut earnestness, naiveté, maybe needed it to counteract his own madness. But then again, maybe it would have driven him crazy, maybe Lewis would have corrupted the choirboy too. He could think of it from a thousand different angles, and Helen would still have gone. What happened to Millie was just too much to forgive ...

... For the final rumble through the glass tonight, the rain had cleared and Lewis watched the blinking wing-lights blink and the blipping tail-light blip and then blink and blip, blink and blip along the lines of blue and green specks straight and true on the runway into darkness and beyond, taking with them A Friend. And the rumble lingered just a moment. Then it too evaporated into nothingness.

A killer still stalked the voodoo half-light of Hong Kong's back streets, though maybe now for Lewis a little less anonymously: he knew where and with whom to start digging for answers. And the thought of a fresh encounter with the bastard's suffocating personality thrilled him no end.

Lewis tipped the contents of his glass down his throat.

The Peak

Kate Whitehead

Emma knew the path that wove up the Peak intimately, beginning on Conduit Road and going straight up the side of the mountain through dense forest. She had walked it enough times that her body adjusted automatically to the zigzagging route and the steep sections.

It was called the Morning Trail. When the early morning light cut through the trees, it looked quite beautiful. But dusk had its own charm. If she timed it right she could get to the top and run the four-kilometre circuit in time to catch the sun as it set behind Lantau Island.

No music, no podcasts, no distractions—this was her thinking time. She could march a problem up the Peak and by the time she reached the top she would have worked out what to do. Mostly the problems were mundane: what to cook for dinner or something about work and her overzealous boss. But recently she had been stewing over her marriage and hadn't come up with a solution. Perhaps it was the sort of problem that was best not faced head on. It needed to be left to bubble away in the background. The solution would present itself when she least expected it, glimpsed out of the corner of her eye.

The firemen were in the station courtyard, shirts off and torsos sweaty It must be nice to have a job that paid you to keep fit. It didn't matter whether Emma had a BMI of eighteen or thirty-eight so long as she could keep coming up with ideas for ads and writing the copy. Exercise for her was more about maintaining her sanity than muscle mass.

She struck up the steep path, past the public toilets and the concrete pagoda. Mr Kwan was rattling down the hill with his beagle, looking like they were strung together with chicken wire. She checked her watch—5:30 pm—he was bang on time. There was comfort in seeing the regulars. The world might be in chaos, but you could always count on the dog walkers to show up like clockwork. Now that she was on a nodding basis with many of them and had chitchatted with a few, she felt she belonged and was part of this community.

'*Gamyaht hou leng wor,*' she complimented Mr Kwan's pet, Bagel, before stooping to pat her.

'*Ngoh nam gam man ger yahtlohk wui zung leng ah,*' he said, predicting a beautiful sunset. They always chatted about the weather or the sky. It was a very British exchange.

'*Ho lah, joi geen,*' she wrapped up the brief exchange and waved goodbye.

The first time they talked, several years back, she spoke in Cantonese and he replied in English. That wasn't uncommon. Perhaps it was a hangover from the colonial days and the conviction that foreigners couldn't manage Cantonese, even when they did. Still, she persevered, and now their conversations were always in Cantonese. It was a minor victory. It was acceptance.

From some way off came a wistful tune—the flute player was back. The music carried on the breeze, audible one minute and lost the next. The regulars knew the arrival of the flute player marked the start of spring. That cheered her up.

Lihua heard the flute player from afar. Hong Kong was full of surprises, she though to herself. She stopped, head cocked to one side, and listened. The music snatched at something deep inside. It reminded her of her father, and the two of them walking the hills outside Beijing. That was some twenty years ago, back when she could see for miles. The memory came so fast and with such force that her eyes prickled. She hadn't expected to hear a flute player in Hong Kong and for a moment she wasn't in an alien city. She was in a softer, faraway place.

These days the air in Beijing got so thick sometimes she couldn't even see across the street. Pollution got Ba too. He had always looked after his health—he never smoked a cigarette in his life—and yet lung cancer had taken him away from her. Hong Kong people liked to complain about air quality, but what did they know about pollution? They didn't know how good they had it here.

Then the wind changed direction and the music was gone. But Lihua was still lost in her thoughts, as she often was since moving to Hong Kong six months ago. Moving here was supposed to feel like a victory—landing a job in a multinational and getting a fat paycheque—but it didn't always feel like it. Hong Kong was hard work, like a high maintenance *taitai*, pretty on the outside but cold on the inside. This was not a city that welcomed you with open arms.

The path up the Peak was steeper than what the *gweilos* in the office had her believe. That didn't surprise her. There was so much one-upmanship on the trading floor that it was often hard to make out what was what. There were only two topics of conversation: fitness and women. And the guys talked about the two incessantly and interchangeably—how they had scored, what they had scored and when they would score next. She made an effort to act nonchalant when they bragged about their seedy Wan Chai escapades like victories, when all they had done was to get blind drunk and ripped off by hookers. These white guys had no morals; nothing was too low for them. Were they like this in their home countries or did Hong Kong make them like this?

> Hong Kong was hard work, like a high maintenance *taitai*, pretty on the outside but cold on the inside.

She knew when to laugh along with them and when to act invisible—that's what you had to do when you were one of the few women on a testosterone-fuelled trading floor. Play along or get ostracised like D.D.—Doreen the Dyke. Doreen wasn't gay—they wouldn't have dared call her that if she was. She just didn't laugh at their jokes and play along. Even if she did, she still had an American bum, the sort that even a wrap dress couldn't disguise. Lihua knew instinctively that striking up a workplace friendship with D.D., or just being civil to her, would be office suicide.

The path turned sharply. The trees gave way and she got her first clear view of the city and the ICC. Hong Kong's tallest building jumped out of the scene not just because she worked there, but because it stole the show. Almost as tall as the Peak, it mirrored the IFC on the opposite side of the harbour. Every night an LED show lit it up like a giant glow stick—it was beautiful. If only Ba was around to see this. When they watched the handover ceremony on live TV in 1997, she told him she was going to work in that big shiny city. Her mum had laughed, 'You are only ten years old, too young to know what you want.' But Ba didn't doubt her; he had always believed in her. The ICC wasn't even built back then. If she could point it out to him and tell him that's where she worked, he would have been very proud. Suddenly bitter, she turned away and picked up the pace, ignoring the burn in the back of her legs.

Emma passed the gap in the trees and saw the ICC pulsing like a giant illuminated dildo. What a phenomenal waste of electricity! The flashy and wasteful light show symbolised much that was wrong with Hong Kong. And there was a lot that was wrong. It wasn't the same place she had grown up in. Her mother had given birth to her in Matilda hospital on the Peak. It had been the expat hospital of choice and still was, but little else about Hong Kong had stayed the same. There were pockets that remained unchanged—some of the private clubs, a few expat neighbourhoods—but almost everything else had either pivoted through a series of small changes until it was unrecognisable or been flattened in one fell swoop.

The physical changes could be catalogued—there were photographs and videos to do that—but changes to the spirit of the city were much harder to pin down. She wondered whether Hong Kong had lost its magic, and thinking that made her feel old. Didn't old people always say things had been better before?

Maybe it was her who had lost her touch. There was no doubting her mojo twenty years ago. She had just come back on a massive high from three years at Edinburgh University—Dad's alma mater.. She had got her degree and returned to the city she loved just in time for the historic handover. Better still, she had dragged her new beau with her. Rob was a Londoner and had barely travelled—Edinburgh was already a big deal for him—and she did everything she could to make sure he took to Hong Kong. She taught him to use chopsticks, showed him her favourite haunts and, most importantly, got him a job. Well, Dad did that. He made the introductions at the bank, put in a not-so-subtle word or two and, bingo, Rob was on the payroll and calling Hong Kong home.

This was a city that embraced expats. People were always coming and going and it was easy to make friends. During those heady days, they had money and buckets of energy. They would work all week, party late on Friday night and still make the junk trip the next morning. They lived by the mantra: 'you can sleep when you're dead'.

Newbie expats—Rob included—had a pet phrase they rolled out when asked about Hong Kong's prospects: 'China won't kill the goose that lays the golden egg.' It had seemed like worldly wisdom at the time. The pre-handover jitters had been for nothing, just as a few years later the Y2K fears would seem a joke. The handover came and went and nothing changed. It was business as usual. Not a peep out of the People's Liberation Army that was bunkered down at camps around Hong Kong.

So when did the change set in? She couldn't even remember the cracks appearing. It seemed she had gone from feeling so secure and confident in her world to suddenly being all at sea, no longer sure of what she had or where she was going. There must have been warning signs. There were always warning signs.

The sweat was running down her back, pooling around the waistband of her shorts. Summer was still a couple of months away and already she was dreading it. After almost forty Hong Kong summers she still wasn't used to the humidity that wrapped around her like a wet tea towel.

One of her socks slipped down her foot and worked its way under her heel. Her ankle was rubbing against her trainer, the sting of a blister forming. But she wasn't about to stop to fix it. Stand still for thirty seconds and the mosquitoes would launch a full assault. Dusk was their feeding time.

She kept on up the hill, the mild discomfort distracting from her personal angst. Isn't that what the meditation teacher said: focus on your environment and be in the moment? To her left the city was obscured by a jungle, but she could hear it, the shrill call of the cicadas. As soon as she noticed them she could hear little else. They were really screeching tonight. It was funny to think that there were thousands of those bugs in the trees and yet she never saw them. They had freaked Rob out in the beginning. He had never been able to pronounce the word 'cicadas' and so he just called them locusts.

That was it—locusts! That was when things changed, the watershed moment. It was Chinese New Year five years ago when a group of Hong Kongers took out a full-page advertisement in the *Apple Daily* to vent their rage at the mainland Chinese. The ad showed a giant locust looming menacingly over Hong Kong and sucking the city dry. It was a metaphor for mainlanders who overwhelmed the maternity wards in public hospitals, took all the kindergarten spots and pushed up property prices. That's why there was so much open hostility towards the mainland Chinese on the streets. She had tried to explain it to Rob, but he hadn't got it. He always saw things purely in terms of economics. Of course people are angry if property prices are going up and if they can't get their kids into school, he would say. But she knew it was more than that.

The boundaries between her two bugbears—her marriage and her vanishing city—were beginning to blur. Had things been unravelling between them for years? It was five years ago when she and Rob started trying for a baby. Well, there was a half-hearted attempt a couple of years before that, with the lackadaisical 'I'll go off the pill and see what happens' strategy. It wasn't until 2012 that they launched Project Baby in earnest. It was fun at first, and Rob loved her newfound enthusiasm for sex. They made special weekends of it with trips to Boracay and Bali. 'If the baby is conceived on holiday, we'll call him Boracay.' 'But is Boracay a boy's name? What if it's a girl?' Silly, meandering conversations of a couple that was happy—or at least content.

After a while it all started to get like hard work. There was nothing romantic about in vitro fertilisation: the nauseating daily hormone injections, the not drinking, and the pressure of it all. Weekend trips were now to Bangkok and it was no longer about getting frisky but about going to the fertility clinic. Rob didn't help. He took IVF as a slight on his manhood and didn't want anyone to know. She couldn't even tell her parents for fear that her dad might let it slip at the bank. IVF became their secret, although the longer it went on the longer it wouldn't work.

'What do you need me for? You've got enough of my frozen little fellas for ten kids,' he spat one night. He was right. Technically she didn't need him anymore to make this baby. But what was the point of having a baby without him? Something had to give and so she took the easy option: she stopped talking about it.

Having a baby was the last thing on Lihua's mind. So was marriage or any sort of long-term relationship. She had to make her first million—US$ million—before she would even think about any of those things. Hong Kong had seemed the obvious place to achieve her dream, but already she was beginning to have doubts. Maybe she should have taken a bigger jump, like going to New York or somewhere further away. Or perhaps she should have stayed in China. She could be working her way up the ladder in Shanghai, which might end up counting for more than Hong Kong.

She was a first-year student at Tsinghua University when Hong Kongers started calling mainlanders 'locusts'. No one could believe it, not at first. Hong Kong was a glamorous place with great shops and restaurants. Why would the people be so horrible? But it got worse. Those people went out of their way to make mainlanders look bad. Someone took a video of a mother helping her kid pee in the street and posted it online, making out that mainland Chinese always urinate in public. She should have known then that Hong Kong people weren't going to make it easy for her people.

Still, she hadn't expected it to be this hard. As soon as they heard her accent, their faces would change—some of them would even flinch. Hong Kong people liked to think that they were cultured and well-mannered and that mainlanders were uncivilised. But that's not the real reason they didn't like them and called them names, was it? The real reason was that these 'uncivilised' people were now making more money than them. It was always about the money.

She had seen it at the bank. She was earning more than others in her team because of her mainland experience. If Hong Kong people were so snobbish and didn't want to go to China to get the experience, then they had to put up with earning less. Making out that they were more cultured and better-mannered was laughable. They felt superior just because they had been under British rule for 156 years. Guess what: Hong Kong was part of China now—it had always been. So they should suck it up or get out.

The flute player started up again. This time she recognised the tune—'Flowing Water of Paradise'. The song interrupted her angry rant. She shouldn't let herself think like that. So what if Hong Kong people were petty and mean-spirited? They would get what was coming to them and in the meantime she should focus on what she had come here to do. It shouldn't matter that they looked down on her. The feelings were mutual.

Ping.

The markets were already closed. What could the office possibly want? And what could be so urgent that they had to send an email with a WhatsApp chaser? But even as she felt annoyed at being disturbed, there was the comfort of being needed. She clicked open the email, and it was about the Shanghai Stock Exchange. Of course they needed her—this was her patch. She skimmed the figures and the Morning Trail disappeared along with the flute player and the cicadas. Her sole focus was the email. She would need to call her old boss for help.

Emma was coming up the hill at a good clip. She saw the woman in the middle of the path, head bowed over her smartphone. By then it was dark enough and the screen illuminated her face—she was young and quite pretty despite the frown. That's one good reason for turning off her phone on hikes: she wouldn't want to get pulled into work in her down time.

Work was likely the problem between her and Rob. He had been so distracted the last few months—it was as though he wasn't even seeing her. After the failure of Project Baby, sex seemed pointless. She had been relieved when he stopped pestering her for a shag. But it couldn't go on like that. She would make a real effort when she got home tonight. Instead of getting straight into her pyjamas after her shower, she would put on something a little more inviting. She smiled at the prospect of it. It had been a while since she had dug out the negligee—it could be fun. Maybe she would cook. Yes, she would tell Rob not to pick up takeaway and that she would prepare a proper meal from scratch. They used to take time over dinner, have a glass of wine and talk. But recently—well, for some time—they had let that slide. They were in a rut, that was all it was, and she was going to dig both of them out of it.

Perhaps it was the endorphins kicking in, but she was beginning to feel more upbeat than she had been in a long time. She thought she had heard some people coming up the hill and she moved to the side to let them pass. But it was just one woman and she was speaking loudly into her phone. It was sometimes hard to tell when people spoke Putonghua if they were angry or just chatting. She slowed for the woman to pass, but rather than overtaking her she fell into pace with her. This was not conducive to a quiet meditation on how to fix a marriage. She slowed even more to let the woman pass. Bizarrely, the woman, who was still speaking at full pelt, slowed as well.

Emma turned to her, 'Excuse me?'

Clearly her implied message to 'bugger off and leave me in peace' was lost on the woman. She just gawped at her, not letting up on her phone conversation.

Emma walked faster in order to pass her, and the woman picked up her pace too. She slowed down and the woman did the same, now almost shouting into her phone. This was getting ridiculous.

'Can you take your call somewhere else?' snapped Emma.

The woman turned: 'Why should I? It's a public space.'

'Go ahead of me or behind me, but don't shout in the phone right next to me.'

The woman pulled the phone aside. Her face was black; she didn't look so pretty now. 'Go back to your own country!' she said.

'What?'

'You heard me. Foreigner, go back to your own country!'

'This is my country. This is my home!'

'No, it's not. You *are* a foreigner.'

'It's more my home than yours.' Even as she said it she realised how insanely childish this was.

'Foreigner go home!' the woman shouted.

With the benefit of at least ten years more wisdom, Emma did what seemed the only sensible thing, 'Oooooh,' she said mockingly and smiled a fat, fake smile.

That did it. The woman turned away. But it didn't resolve the immediate problem. Since they were both storming up the hill, there was only one thing for it—Emma would have to go faster. She steamed ahead, her heart pounding. She had never gone this fast up the Peak, but then again she had never been fuelled by such rage. Who was this woman to tell her to go home? Aside from university she had never lived anywhere else. And if Hong Kong wasn't home, then what was?

She gained a five-metre lead and worked hard to keep it. The woman was younger and looked fitter than her, but she was still speaking on the phone. That had to be slowing her down.

Lihua's old boss in Shanghai was in stitches. 'You tell those white-skinned pigs where to go,' he said and she heard him light a cigarette. He must be enjoying this. Getting help with her stock exchange query from him would be easy now that he knew she was giving them hell in Hong Kong. He would send over the stats, no problem, and he started talking about an ex-colleague who had moved to New York.

Lihua let him ramble on—she was on an adrenaline high. She didn't know if she was extremely happy or desperately sad, but she felt more alive than she had felt in a while. Her old boss was right: the foreigners needed to know that things had changed. They didn't run the show any more and they had better get used to it. That woman was a real bitch, acting like she owned the trail. White people were like that—

> She didn't know if she was extremely happy or desperately sad, but she felt more alive than she had felt in a while.

they thought they were smarter and deserved better. It was the same at work. Those white guys were always so arrogant. Most of them wanted her and they didn't even try to hide it. And when a guy's dick was involved it was easy to get one over him—that was her trump card. Next time that guy in the office who kept hitting on her asked her out she would go for it. Why not take him for a ride?

She thanked her old boss and rang off. The path split and opened out into a park. The white woman was there waiting for her, hands on hips and breathing hard. Opposite her, sitting on a rock, was the flute player. He put the flute to his lips and played a slow, mournful note.

'You know how I know you're a mainlander? Because you have mainland manners!' the *gweipo* barked.

Lihua was seething. How could this bitchy woman even know if she was from Hong Kong or not? Didn't foreigners think all Chinese people looked the same? And did they really think they had perfect manners? Who did they think they were, royalty? She had seen the way they ran after taxis and got drunk in bars.

The music stopped. The flute player looked from one woman to the other. Lihua knew how ridiculous it must seem to him for two total strangers to get into a fight on a hike. Then she caught his eye and looked away, suddenly self-conscious. It was as though he were in on it too. These Hong Kongers and foreigners all looked down on us mainland Chinese, the *real* Chinese. Right at that moment, her phone rang. She looked at the caller ID and answered it on the first ring.

'Hello, Rob?' she said, still staring at the woman. 'I'm hiking that trail you told me about.'

The woman's face fell. How strange—she was probably jealous, probably didn't have a man of her own. Who would go near her? Or perhaps she was surprised that she had Western friends. She decided to lay it on thick.

'So what are you up to tonight, Rob?' Lihua said, not taking her eyes off the woman. 'Want to meet up?'

Emma felt like she had been punched in the gut. Rob? She turned and started running away. The blister was beginning to swell. It couldn't be *her* Rob—that was ridiculous. She mustn't be thinking straight because of the row with that mainland bitch. But still, just to reassure herself and put an end to these crazy thoughts, she would call his mobile. That should put her mind at rest.

She slowed down and fished her phone out of her pocket. Her hand was shaking as she hit the first name on speed dial.

It was engaged.

Atelier Wong Yan-kwai

Gérard Henry

The former studio of Hong Kong painter Wong Yan-kwai, and his self-made musical instruments, in Wan Chai, near the Blue House

Lantau Island

Ilaria Maria Sala

B ear in mind that he was the descendant of Zulu princes. That's what he said. And it is not the kind of thing you'd forget.

I do not promise to be accurate, but the first time we met was the first time I had come to the island: which is a funny way of saying it, really, since Hong Kong Island is obviously an island too. But you get on the ferry to Lantau, and you get a text from someone who wants to know what you are up to and you say, 'I'm going to the island.' Meaning Lantau Island. At 147 square kilometres, it is the largest of the islands that make up the Hong Kong Special Administrative Region.

It is the largest, but it had been partially forgotten until 1991, when the colonial authorities started building the new airport, beginning with a 9.38 square kilometre land reclamation project that connected the small islands of Chek Lap Kok and Lam Chau to the northern shore of Lantau. The airport opened in 1998, thus starting its life under Beijing's sovereignty. In the fitful months before the handover, even the airport had been a source of controversy and quarrelling between the outgoing British authorities and the incoming

Chinese ones: the airport is too expensive, they cried from Beijing. Maybe they feared that a lavish airport would mean a Hong Kong handed back to them with depleted coffers. Or maybe they were afraid the grandness of the international airport here would dwarf that of the others in the Pearl River Delta. Nobody really could tell in the cacophony of constant bickering that lasted until midnight, June 30th.

Whatever unhappiness Beijing felt about the airport, though, the project's completion marked the beginning of a development frenzy in one of Hong Kong's green lungs that is not over yet and that is on the cusp of becoming a disaster. I'm going to get to this shortly, but as I try to tell you his story, the descendant of princes I mean, there are so many threads that call for attention that it is hard to stick to just one narrative.

Anyway. Back then, it must be close to fifteen years ago, I got off the ferry in Mui Wo, and was walking along the winding paths, trying to figure out if there were landmarks I could pin my eyes to. They all say it for a reason: in Hong Kong, you are never more than half an hour away from greenery. Leung Chun-ying, the divisive Chief Executive we have had since 2012 (scheduled to step down in June 2017) has done all he could to make this less of a reality, and the damage he has unleashed on the territory is heartbreaking—or infuriating, depending what mood you are in at the moment.

In spite of his pro-Communist Party left-wing credentials, the former surveyor has embraced the real estate developers with reckless abandon. Should I have written 'in spite of?' Is 'because of' more apt? When people complain that Hong Kong might turn into 'just another Chinese city' surely this is part of what they mean: the vicious destruction of memories that weave themselves in and out of the landscape; the pulverisation of complex local communities whose grounds are turned into cookie-cutter condos for real estate speculators—too often coming from the mainland, yes, no point in being cute about it—even as they live god knows where, leaving the flats empty.

I'm getting ahead of myself again.

We were still at the very beginning of all this when I first saw him, and I couldn't figure him out. The descendant of Zulu princes, he said. Some intense British imperial wandering meant he also was more than one part Indian, I believe, and so much else.

> When people complain that Hong Kong might turn into 'just another Chinese city' surely this is part of what they mean: the vicious destruction of memories that weave themselves in and out of the landscape.

So there I was, in Mui Wo for the first time, and I was wondering which direction I had taken and where it was going to lead as I looked at the densely green hills, the bend in the river that goes to the beach, and the neatly farmed fields with old CDs and weather-beaten stuffed toys hanging from poles stuck in the dirt like postmodern scarecrows. And as I hesitated, he was standing there, a cup of coffee in his hands, perfectly aware of my presence, a stranger to discretion.

'This is what we do all day!' he bellowed, in greeting. 'We stare at the leaves. All day long! So *greeeeeeen*', he said, half moaning and half laughing. Was he being sarcastic? Was I meant to answer? Who was he, anyway?

You don't need to answer every greeting in Hong Kong. It is okay to be warm and it is okay to be rough. What has not changed in twenty years? This: it's a fast city, business is business, whatever goes wrong you can say you had no time, you were just too busy.

So I didn't reply. I sent some kind of a smile in his direction, looked at my companion who was similarly perplexed, and we walked onwards. Or maybe backwards—that leafy path, so familiar today, looked like a riddle then.

Shortly after, I left behind the constant construction noise of my former neighbourhood in Sheung Wan, and moved here, to 'the island'.

As it always happens, as one becomes slowly accustomed to a new place, unexpected landmarks popped up everywhere from the indiscernible mass. The eye suddenly recognises a flaming tree just before the bend in the small path; a java apple jam-like mess on the ground that signals the arrival of summer, just before a small bifurcation; or farmers' fences made on the cheap with old doors, pipes, construction leftovers, random plastic and wooden planks that appear once you have cycled nearly all the way home.

The prince's house, though, was a lot more than just a feature on the way home It was hardly a proper house, with its leaky tin roof and shaky walls. Everybody knew about it even if only a few had ever stepped inside. He was always standing or sitting outside, by the main path. He had adorned a large tree and a few shrubs with painted knick-knacks and managed to turn discarded junk into a decorating statement—at times tongue in cheek, but by and large, unexpectedly tasteful. The decorations changed with the seasons: silver and white ribbons and dried plants emerged for Christmas. Painted eggs popped up at Easter. And all red hell broke loose for Lunar New Year.

As time went by, though, I noticed it was usually not coffee in the mug, but beer, and that most of his visitors were of the heavy drinking sort.

I'm not telling you the whole story: some details are missing, some you really do not need to know, and others were always pure invention. But his presence, and now, his absence, carved what seemed to be an indelible impression.

His name was Mark.

He would say hello, or *jou san*, or any greeting to that effect, to everybody who passed by— in a handful of languages. He spoke with a British accent, and eventually I saw photos of him looking dapper in London. At one point he had followed a boyfriend here. Things had headed south abruptly and he was still scarred from that. But I was not his confidante.

He wore large designer glasses and kept his hair short. If people cycled past him in a hurry, late for the ferry, he would just call to them, 'Ding-ding!!'

Me, he called Maria Callas because my first name can be a mouthful, and because I like large sunglasses. One Christmas day he seemed upset as I walked past. I wore a *salwar kameez* that seemed perfect for the weather, but he disapproved, scoffing loudly behind me, 'That is a Muslim dress!'

Once, I walked past him while I was upset and he took my hand and asked what was wrong and I was not going to talk but I frowned so painfully that he said, 'Whatever happens, always keep your dignity. And walk away. Like this!' He let go of my hand and sashayed for a few steps in one direction and then the other, and afterwards, someone told me Mark had been a model and a dancer, and now I know that, as I was looking at him then, he had not forgotten any of his former aspirations. And everyday, he was being fabulous, looking at the leaves and the birds and exchanging a short sentence, a whole conversation or just a sound with anyone who walked by, in spite of the drinking.

That is how he knew that the plan for Lantau, where he had lived longer than anybody I know who was not born here, was simply awful and that there was no way of stopping it, do what anyone may.

I cannot explain, even at this point of the story, why the destruction of the island and his death seem connected, but somehow they are. Maybe because of the care he took in keeping his surroundings so chic, as if he wasn't doomed, as if the island could count on somebody to defend it?

Listen, this I'm not making up. In 2016, there were about 105,000 people living on the mountainous island of Lantau, mostly concentrated in the Tung Chung area, which is near the airport, Discovery Bay, which is near Disneyland, and the little dots on the map that are Mui Wo, Pui O, Tung Fuk, Cheung Sha, Tai O. Not a lot more.

Mark was already terminally ill when Leung Chun-ying created the Lantau Development Plan and the Lantau Development Advisory Committee, in 2014. We never really talked about it—but the exploratory digging, right in front of his house, had already started, and then was temporarily suspended. This was as it always happens. They dig up a small area, damaging trees and plants as they crack the concrete open and cut apart the roots underneath, then they close everything up again, leaving everyone hoping that a miracle might have occurred and it was a false alarm, in spite of the damage done. But shortly afterwards, they chop down the injured trees, that they can now classify as 'dead' and maybe even 'dangerous', and they start digging all over again, drilling the concrete open once more, right where they just did, and a bit further too.

The villages on the side of the river where both Mark and I lived were the last in line for the installing of the pipes that the authorities have assured the residents are to upgrade the water treatment facilities. This has meant mayhem in the whole Mui Wo area for close to ten years so far, but the 'necessary improvement works' have been the perfect excuse for other initiatives too—by the authorities, and by enterprising male villagers. The latter have been given small parcels of land on which to build 'village houses', as promised to them in 1972 by colonial authorities keen on earning their support as they spearheaded the development of the New Territories. It turned out to be quite a grand deal for the villagers, who were rarely displaced, but simply had to accept some roads, and a few real estate developments on lands they were not actually using. In exchange, they obtained unprecedented political clout, and free land for construction in housing-hungry Hong Kong. This environmentally unsustainable and discriminatory policy (women are excluded from the largesse) has meant that the villagers are strongly supportive of the government—as long as the 'Small House Policy' system remains firmly in place. Nor does it matter, in this corrupt equilibrium, that these 'villagers' now live in what are, for all intents and purposes, urbanised areas. The number of farmers and fishermen in Hong Kong is dwindling, yet they are still considered strategic interest groups.

Do not be overly surprised: this is an arrangement that truly embodies the rot of Hong Kong's political system. The rural interest group called Heung Yee Kuk, a statutory advisory body headed by a dynasty of billionaire landowners belonging to the Lau family, commands a vote in the local parliament and in the committee that selects the chief executive. Given how many favours they have received from the government, in terms of the Small House Policy and other shows of benevolence, this vote is guaranteed to be pro-government. The same loyalty comes from the Agriculture and Fisheries 'functional constituency', which once again comprises villagers with land entitlements and a few fishermen never punished for illegal trawling fishing methods. In exchange, even if not in quite so many words, these two groups can count on the government's generosity during policy making. Should that not be feasible for whatever reason, they can be assured the government will look away when it comes to illegal dumping of construction waste or industrial material, building or fishing infractions, or illegal driving. I'm putting down just a partial list of the most common offences. One thing you learn in Lantau is that there are things nobody will ever tell you, no matter whether you ask to know, or demand it.

One thing you learn in Lantau is that there are things nobody will ever tell you, no matter whether you ask to know, or demand it.

So, the Plan (let's call it that) is promoted by the LanDAC, the short name of the ill-advised committee, and it is sheer folly. Here everything happens between the chief executive and his friends, there is no referendum, nor even a credible consultation on the project. The LanDAC, by the way, is just twenty people, and most of them do not live on Lantau. I told you, I'm not making any of this up. And there is more. These twenty luminaries are from a cross-section of pro-government types: some are from the largest pro-Beijing party, the Democratic Alliance for the Betterment and Progress of Hong Kong (DAB), and the rest are businesspeople connected to the airport or Disneyland, both on the island, and real estate developers. I am going to spell out the plan for you now, and I hope you are holding your hat tightly, because you know you should worry when the government says that it is going to build a 'kaleidoscopic recreation and tourism destination' and a new shopping hub where visitors will be able to 'splurge and indulge'. Where the last few pink dolphins swim, the government plans to build an artificial island—near Mui Wo—to house one million people (yes, the Hong Kong birthrate is very low, so the happy million would be from elsewhere, the north presumably). Add to that a bridge that connects it all.

Once you build new roads there is no stopping, and a whole network is planned. In comparison, the enlargement of Disneyland, which is already underway, is but a little blight on the landscape. Finally, there is the 'uplifting of Mui Wo', for which I went to a consultation meeting in the spring of 2017.

As I cycled to the newly refurbished Rural Committee Road's Assembly Hall, I wished Mark were still there, as I would have loved to comment on the outcome of the meeting with him. But he probably would have been too sarcastic about it. There we were—a number of round tables filled with residents in front of a panel of government officials (all men, and not residents either) who had been told to renounce their Saturday off to go talk to Mui Wo people. The last time a consultation like this had taken place had been in 2008, and it had concluded with not very much. At the beginning of this new consultation, one person walked up before the debate officially started in order to stuff a wad of papers under the nose of the officers saying: These are all the letters we have written since 2008. These, here, are our comments to the previous plan and the previous Mui Wo consultation. You never replied. You haven't taken anything into account.

The meeting went on for about three hours. All of us said the same thing, countless times. We want as little development as possible. All we really need is more parking places for bicycles.

One of the officers approached me, hoping I would be happy about the idea of building 'a plaza' just outside the ferry pier. I said it seemed a terrible idea, and he was taken aback. 'You mean you like it rural?' he asked, and when I said, 'yes', he had no further words for me. He smiled nervously and went back to the table with the other panellists.

It was very interesting: a full-blown exercise in futility.

On the way out, I looked at the new towers going up that will house about ten thousand people. More may come: on the north of the island, just next to the airport, is one of the most controversial projects of all, again one for which no Hong Kong citizen (outside of a few billionaires close to the government), let alone a Lantau resident, was asked for an opinion: the Hong Kong–Zhuhai–Macau Bridge. It will link, by road, Lantau Island to the mainland. Once, I spoke with Eddie Tse, of the Save Lantau Alliance, about all this. He said that most people in Hong Kong, on the rare occasion when they are asked, support preserving Lantau as a green space. 'They come here to hike, children come for school trips, teenagers for camping trips. They like having the possibility of Lantau when the rest of Hong Kong is getting more polluted and congested all the time,' he said. And then he added, 'But it's a crime without victims. The plants, the mountains, the animals and the rivers, they cannot complain. They cannot oppose the government. But it remains a crime.'

I cycled home. The house that belonged to Mark, the descendant of Zulu princes, is now bricked in, and is now under heavy renovation—I think in order to turn it into a regular village house, but I cannot say yet. I was away when he was last taken to hospital, and after I came back, he never returned. Friends left pictures and notes on the table in front of his house, and they remained under the rain and the sun and the wind, discolouring slowly until they were carried away by the wind.

It Was All Wasted

Shen Jian

The lights don't come on at Southorn anymore. There was a time when Mo and I couldn't hear ourselves out here on a floodlit Sunday night. The whistles and chants for the Filipino league games on one court, the boomboxes, balls clanging off the other five rims, double-decker buses loading and unloading on Hennessy Road, taxi horns unhinged, uncles swearing at each other on the football pitch. I couldn't just call for the ball; I had to wave my arms, and even then, Mo was never really a pass-first guy.

Now Sunday nights at Southorn are dark, to discourage public gatherings. A couple kids shooting around in Adidas sneakers—like how Mo and I used to, even in the rain—pull their hoods over and scurry away when they see me, knowing they're breaking the under-sixteen curfew, probably scared I could be a witness. Across the wall they run past, someone has spray-painted, 'NOTHING WE DID COULD HAVE SAVED HONG KONG IT WAS ALL WASTED'.

There is no one else. My eyes have adjusted and the white backboard reflects just enough of the moonlight so that I'm not aiming blind, but I still miss my first shot badly, and the sound of the ball striking the back of the rim and bouncing off the asphalt rattles a cavernous echo off the once-occupied office towers and apartments that surround the playground. I am deep in the canyon of Wan Chai, and there is no life down here.

Growing up, Mo and I were equals on the basketball court, but nowhere else. I'm two years older, have always been a couple inches taller, and got much better grades. Mo has more hair, never needed glasses or braces, and has this silky, enveloping voice. He's generally better with girls, mostly because they wither when he sings, and he knows it, he cradles them with his vocal chords until they relent. I can hold my own at karaoke too, but damn can my brother sing.

We used to sing K every week. We would have these marathon karaoke sessions, going six or seven hours at Neway, emptying buckets of Blue Girl and bottles of Chivas mixed with green tea. I was a willing accomplice, always happy to load up Eason and Jay hits all night because Mo would just kill it. I wasn't some dutiful, selfless brother; these were good times, tipsy with friends, pretty girls for company, my little brother in his element, and, every time, front row seats to a virtuoso performance.

We were already hours into one of these sessions when dusk fell on September 28th, 2014, that Sunday almost half a year ago now. Mo, who basically failed high school but still crooned himself into the Academy for Performing Arts, was beginning his last year at the APA. I had just finished my Postgraduate Certificate in Laws at the University of Hong Kong, and was starting as a trainee lawyer at McAllen Dune in two weeks. Neither of us had class or work the next

Monday, which is why we wanted to sing on a Sunday evening, when it was half price. After corralling a group of high school friends, we checked in that afternoon to the Neway in Sugar Street in Causeway Bay, each hiding in our bags a bottle of Chivas bought at the 7-Eleven across the road.

Our phones started lighting up just after 6 pm. The videos were surreal: tear gas in Admiralty, umbrellas floating through the fog. They were crazy scenes, but none of us in the room were especially political, and we kept drinking and singing. Every half-hour or so we would see more from Admiralty; some of Mo's APA classmates were there, WhatsApping photos to him non-stop, urging him to join them, but to bring face masks and goggles.

I could tell he was considering it, from the fear of missing out more than anything else. Between songs, his thumbs would hover briefly over his phone, thinking twice about what to type. But as soon as another one of his go-to ballads would come up—and he had many—he was back at the mic, diaphragm pumping, neck veins straining to burst free.

It was always close to the end when Mo and I would start a run of Beyond songs. We weren't normally sentimental, but being drunk and tired tended to remind us of our father, and his Beyond CDs stacked beside our stereo at home in Ap Lei Chau. One of my first memories is our father slumped in the massage chair in our living room, listening to a rock song louder than I knew sounds could be, and wiping away tears with his shirt sleeve. When I was older and asked Ma about the memory, she told me it was the day Wong Ka Kui died, after falling off a TV stage in Tokyo and into a coma. The song was 'Glorious Times', the Beyond ode Wong wrote to Nelson Mandela.

Our father died of nasopharyngeal cancer almost four years later to the day, on July 1st, 1997. Most people say they spent that night at home or in a bar, celebrating or commiserating. I remember sitting on my father's bed in Queen Mary Hospital at midnight, watching the TV in the ICU ward as Chris Patten sailed away in the rain and the People's Liberation Army tanks rolled across the Shenzhen River into Hong Kong. It was way past visiting hours, but Ma convinced the late shift nurses to let me and Mo sit with our father in his last hours. The next thing I remember is Ma nudging me awake and telling me it was time to go. The sky outside the window was a light purple, and when I turned my head, there was just Mo in the bed with me. Our father was gone.

'Time to go, Mo,' I remember saying. Mo didn't say anything; he just rubbed his eyes and followed me out.

Whenever we sang 'Glorious Times', Mo and I would almost yell the first line, *The bell chimes the signal to go home*. Sometimes it would make us cry, and sometimes it would make us laugh, and I think our friends always found it a little awkward, even in their drunken state. We usually just kept singing through it, taking each Beyond number as it came, and that morning, September 29th, 2014, we ended with 'Wide Seas, Open Skies' and Mo and I with our arms around each other's shoulders belting the last line, *I'm not afraid if one day it's just you and me*. It was the same way we ended a lot of mornings in Neway, until, in the last few chords of the song, someone banged on our room door and shouted, 'Yeah, fuck C.Y.!'

After we paid the bill, we walked out into the black of predawn Causeway Bay, with Mo skipping ahead in a merry saunter down Sugar Street, swinging a half-finished bottle of Chivas in his right hand. Under the streetlights, Mo's dancing shadow stretched larger than life across the entire width of the street, interrupted only by a parked newspaper van. The air sounded busier than it usually did that time of morning, and when Mo got to the end of the street, his jaunt froze.

'What the heck?' I heard him say.

There were hundreds, maybe thousands, of people just sitting and standing in the middle of Hennessy Road, where there should have been buses and trams ploughing through. And they were singing. I thought I was just drunk, our last song still ringing in my ears, but the closer I got, it was clear, they really were singing 'Wide Seas, Open Skies', like either we had just stepped out into someone else's immense karaoke hall or they just had stepped into ours.

We joined in. What else were we going to do? *Give up on your dreams*, Mo and I sang. *Anyone can do that*.

Two months later, Mo and I were sitting in the stands at Southorn on another Sunday night, waiting for the next game. It was my first day off since starting work, including weekends. The firm had assigned me printer duty: accompanying bankers and accountants at financial printing offices as they prepared to submit initial public offerings to securities regulators. Printer sessions were endless, and trainee lawyers like me had to stay each night until the end, usually 2 or 3 am, waiting for the printers to make revisions and repaginate, then proofreading all the changes. It was a job.

A guy our age jogged over from an opposite court, clearly in our direction. He was trying to get Mo's attention.

'What's up, Mo?' he said. He extended a fist towards us, and Mo bumped it. 'Keep doing it, man,' he said, then ran back to his court.

'Who was that?' I asked.

'I don't know.'

That dark, drunken September morning in Causeway Bay, after we came out of Neway, someone had recorded video of Mo rocking the chorus of 'Wide Seas, Open Skies' and posted it on HKGolden.com. I don't know if it counted as viral, but a lot of people saw that clip. It racked up tens of thousands of views on YouTube and Facebook, and *The New York Times* even did a sleek multimedia write-up about it, about the earnestness you could see on Mo's face and hear in his voice, how it was emblematic of the entire protest movement. They didn't know he was running on almost a whole bottle of Chivas.

The first time he went down to Admiralty, face mask and goggles dangling around his neck, Mo called me from the bus and asked me to explain universal suffrage.

Mo's APA crew were psyched. They told him it was his duty to go to Admiralty, to lead the students in song, give their souls some sustenance before they bedded down in their tents each night. That was okay by Mo. Who isn't happy performing for adoring crowds, being part of something bigger? The first time he went down to Admiralty, face mask and goggles dangling around his neck, Mo called me from the bus and asked me to explain universal suffrage. Not that he didn't get it—he wasn't stupid, he had read up—he just wanted to make sure, if he was going to get up on stage, and someone interviewed him on TV, that he knew what he was talking about.

Ma, who had been the head librarian at the City Hall Public Library since we were in high school, was I think secretly proud of Mo, until she ran into one of his APA friends walking past the occupied section of Connaught Road in front of City Hall and asked her why she wasn't in class.

'No one's in class, Auntie,' the friend said.

Ma stopped leaving dinner out for Mo. She told him in our family WhatsApp group that he could occupy or not occupy Central, but she wasn't going to spend what was left of our dead father's savings feeding a dropout. She also wasn't thrilled I was spending my first night off with him instead of her.

We were still waiting for the next game when another unfamiliar face, this time a girl, sidled up to Mo, closer than a stranger would.

'You going, Mo?' She was about sixteen, thumbs hooked into the straps of her North Face backpack.

'I'm going to finish playing first,' Mo said.

'See you later,' the girl said. As she walked off, she reached into her backpack and pulled out goggles.

'Going where?' I asked. I tried not to sound accusatory.

'The last stand.'

I had read up too. I knew what they were talking about. The movement was fading. The core protesters still blocked Connaught Road, but their perimeter was eroding, and, according to the newspapers, so was public support. I sometimes scanned the forums on HKGolden, and in a final bloom of protest threads, students were circulating and refining battle plans to hold the Connaught Road base, a kilometre down the road from where we were sitting in Southorn that Sunday. They were anticipating a move by the police that night to retake it, and were hoping not only to push back, but outflank the police behind enemy lines, as it were, and reoccupy the plaza outside government headquarters. Some were planning to seize the tunnel section of Lung Wo Road between the PLA garrison and the chief executive's office.

Earlier in the day, my Facebook feed had crawled with comments on a warning the chief executive had issued to the protesters.

'Don't mistake tolerance', he said, 'for weakness.'

I knew Mo was going. I still wanted to hear it from him.

'I don't know,' he said. 'This could be it.'

Mo buffered up the live stream of the protest zone on his phone. Others sitting in the stands with us at Southorn were doing the same.

The police—several hundred, it looked like—were already assembling in phalanxes around government headquarters, rows of round riot shields squared up. There was suddenly the noise of commotion, and I thought at first it was coming from the phones.

'Oh shit,' Mo said. He looked up from his phone and turned his head west, in the direction of Connaught Road. That's where the noise was coming from. The confrontation had started, and we could hear the sounds—sticks and shields and metal clanging, but mostly the rumble, people yelling and thousands of feet pounding the ground—echoing through the canyon of buildings running down Hennessy Road. The live stream had a four- or five-second lag, and when it caught up to all the phones in Southorn, there was this frenzied bustle reverberating from all sides, like the surround-sound checks at cinemas. The guys still on the court all stopped mid-game. Some in the stands starting packing their things and walking west.

'Let's go, Mo,' someone said, a statement more than exhortation, like it was a given. They didn't look back to see if Mo was moving.

'I'm going,' Mo said, but I wasn't sure to whom. He turned to me.

'Come with me,' he said. He had to ask, at least.

I didn't say anything. I wasn't conflicted, or angry. I wish I had had something to say, but I didn't. Mo didn't plead, not even with his face.

'I've got work tomorrow,' I finally said, filling the space. It meant nothing. I don't know what was the real reason I didn't go, but I know work wasn't it.

'Okay.'

Mo was off the bench and on the street in one leap. I remember being distracted for an instant by his Nikes, an almost animal instinct, admiring the reflective swooshes flash back and forth. Then the Nikes were out of sight.

I think we both knew something was transpiring in that moment, something pivotal, but it is hard to go there with your brother, to do anything more than understand each other and, though you always regret it later, resist whatever emotion is trying to break that easy, cool surface where brothers usually stay.

'Okay,' I said, to no one.

Until the internet was censored, it was the most viewed YouTube video ever uploaded from Hong Kong: the Assailant—still no one knows his name—charges out of the Lung Wo Road tunnel, umbrella raised but not opened. Contrary to what some of his defenders first said, he does not look delirious; beneath his hood and through his goggles, he looks clear-eyed, knows his target. You can tell from his pace and his stride, like an Olympic hurdler, his brain has already plotted out his steps; he sees the water drum in front of the wall and he knows he can launch himself off it and over the wall of the PLA garrison.

As his front foot clears the metal hooks that serrate the wall, his back pant leg gets caught on one of the hooks; it might actually have pulled him back down onto the road. Instead you see his shoulders snap forward in midair, collapsed by the force of the two bullets simultaneously puncturing his chest. His body falls onto the road spine first, limbs floating up.

In any other moment, any scenario but this one, someone being shot in Hong Kong ends everything. No one in Hong Kong knows what someone being shot looks or sounds like. The shock, the piercing of our social veil, normally would have left the crowd mute and still. I don't know if that was the intent behind the order to shoot, or if it was simply the rules of engagement for any intruder scaling the garrison walls, but if only the crowd *had* been mute and still, I wonder; everyone wonders.

Though no gunshots had been fired until that point, I think the protestors and media had, justifiably or not, talked themselves into the possibility of a violent suppression. As much as the students tried to distinguish their movement from the 1989 Tiananmen Square demonstrations, even I couldn't help seeing and fearing the parallels. Between the tear gas and pepper spray and 'DISPERSE OR WE FIRE' police banners, it felt like the protesters—and maybe the authorities, more so—had convinced themselves of the inevitability of violence, even gunfire, so that the moment the Assailant was shot, suspended above the PLA garrison wall, it registered not as shock but more like a charge, like cardiac defibrillation.

I felt it too; I didn't know which side I was on, or if I was on any side, but when I saw on TV the Assailant's back buckle in midair, I yelled—I don't remember what—and I wanted to hit something. All these years later, since the night my father died, the PLA still felt like intruders, never protectors. I searched for the gunmen on the screen as if on a hunt, as dozens of protesters sprang forward, trying to scale the wall, climbing on top of each other, never noticing—never conceiving—the PLA snipers stepping out from their hiding spots and firing in rhythm, pop pop pop pop pop. It is hard for me to see it this way, but I can understand why foreigners likened the scene to a zombie film. The snipers picked off four protesters at the top of the pile clamouring at the wall before someone gave them the ceasefire order, likely judging from the now finally-subdued crowd that the emergent threat had expired.

> The PLA snipers stepping out from their hiding spots and firing in rhythm, pop pop pop pop pop.

I have to think the Hong Kong police were shocked too. But their training seemed to activate their crowd control instincts, and one troop, taking advantage of the crowd's stunned paralysis, hurriedly immobilised the remaining protesters who had tried to jump the wall. The police then ringed off those protesters and the ones who had been shot from the rest of the crowd.

A Reuters photographer standing on top of a news van was able to capture at that instant the image that went full-screen on the homepages of every major news website in minutes: a policeman kneeling on the ground, looking up with one side of his face in the shadows, the other side lit by a streetlamp to reveal the tracks of his tears on one cheek. His mouth is agape, the veins in his neck protruding like Mo when he reaches for high notes, and his arms are extended straight down as he performs CPR on the Assailant. There is blood all over the policeman's hands.

Across the top of the photo, on that week's cover of *Time* magazine, was the headline, 'DEATH IN HONG KONG'. All five protesters who were shot were dead either on arrival or within minutes of reaching the hospital: Benson Chan Yip-sing, Karen Choi Kwong-yuen, Leung Wai-hing, Frank Liu-chau, and the Assailant. No one from the Assailant's family ever came forward to identify him; neither did any of the other protesters. He seemed almost a ghost, and the common theory that sprouted across message boards in HK-Golden's last hours was that he was a plant, someone with a reason to die, embroiled in chicanery on the mainland and promised by authorities that his family would be taken care of if he did this.

The other four were all under twenty-five. Karen, the only woman, was a drama student at the APA. Mo hadn't known her, but he came home early the next morning—I had been instructed to work from home—eyes shrivelled from goggle marks and what looked like hours of crying.

We had stayed on the couch watching TV all night, Ma and I, without saying anything to each other, except, 'There he is,' whenever we spotted Mo among the protesters, usually in a corner of the screen. When Mo walked through the door, he was sniffling. The T-shirt and shorts we had played ball in hours earlier were streaked with dried blood in a few places. Ma put her hands on his cheeks, looked into his eyes for a few seconds, then went to the kitchen to fry some eggs for him.

I didn't know what to say. There had, amazingly, been restraint on the scene. A few of the student leaders, choking up as they spoke, had implored the protesters to sit down and sing out their grief, and let the ambulances through. They started with 'Wide Seas, Open Skies', but soon moved on to 'Glorious Times', and that was the only time we saw Mo up close, as a cameraman zoomed in on him singing the first line, *The bell chimes the signal to go home*. I tried to resist a fleeting bitterness that he wasn't singing it with me.

The police were in control. The PLA snipers slid back into their shadows just as quickly as they had emerged, and no one came out from the garrison to inspect what had happened, although reporters noticed several windows on the top floors of the main building light up.

Around half an hour after the shootings, word spread that all the victims were dead, and that, after an apparent confrontation at the hospital, some of their parents were making their way to Admiralty. You could see in the faces on TV a cascade of anguish fall over the protesters, and then a rising venom; deep breaths at first smothered with tears, visibly evolving into something glaring and raw.

At some point the protesters looked up from their phones, where they were watching replays of the shootings, and looked west towards IFC. A news camera caught two taxis stopped under the glowing bitten apple of the IFC Apple Store, where the entrance to Lung Wo Road was blockaded. Two middle-aged couples stepped out of the taxis—the newscaster surmised these were parents of some of the victims—and walked past the barriers. They began running.

That was when the lights were cut and, two seconds later, the newscast. I tried to load up the video feed on my phone, but both my WiFi and 3G were timing out. Ma and I both dialled Mo's number, but there was no signal. SMSes wouldn't go through, either.

A message suddenly flashed on the TV and when I refreshed my browser. 'Due to a critical public security emergency', it read, 'all broadcast, telephone and internet communications have been temporarily suspended. They will resume at 7 am for the chief executive to inform the public of recent events and how public order will be restored.'

According to whatever foreign media later trickled in via Immarsat satellite phones and FireChat over the following weeks, hundreds of protesters had rushed the PLA walls as soon as it went dark, boosting each other clear over the wall and the metal hooks. Some climbed over the main gate of the garrison. They had no discernable aim other than vengeance. One foreign correspondent counted forty-two shots fired. Dozens were believed to be killed, but no one knows for sure, because everyone who made it inside the garrison grounds never came out; they were reportedly either shot or detained.

At home in Ap Lei Chau, we knew nothing. I told Ma I would go look for Mo, but out of obligation, not courage, and I was glad when she refused. She moved in front of the doorway before I had even reached for my sneakers.

'It might be just you and me,' she said.

'You don't know that.'

I don't know what happened to Mo over the next few hours, what he saw or did after the lights were cut. For the short time he was home that morning, I didn't ask. He walked through our door minutes after the chief executive's public statement, and Ma and I were still trying to process that. I guessed Mo had watched it while he sat on whatever transportation brought him home.

At 7 am, the message broadcast on TV had cut to the chief executive, standing in front of the back doors of Government House. It was not a press conference; he spoke directly to the camera, with no live audience. The first thing I noticed was that he was not standing in the middle. He was off to the left; in the middle was a man in military uniform I didn't recognise, and on the right was the Central People's Government Liaison Office director, Zhang Xiaoming.

After recounting, in Cantonese, the 'provocation' of the protesters attempting to scale the wall and explaining that the PLA had strictly followed its rules of engagement, the chief executive stated that in the minutes following the shooting, 'security assets'—he did not specify if they were Hong Kong police or Chinese military—had observed a profusion of terrorist activity on popular Hong Kong internet forums, with specific plans to inflict deadly harm on Hong Kong residents and affirmative responses to carry out those plans. At the same time, recent surveillance of what the chief executive called 'known subversive characters' had revealed the unauthorised possession of arms.

'In light of these grave circumstances, I have determined that the turmoil currently affecting Hong Kong endangers not only the stability of the Special Administrative Region, but also national unity and security, and is beyond the control of the government of the Region. I have shared my determination with the Standing Committee of the National People's Congress, which has agreed with my determination and invoked Article 18.4 of the Basic Law to declare a state of emergency in the Hong Kong Special Administrative Region.'

The chief executive took a breath.

'In accordance with Article 18.4 of the Basic Law, the Central People's Government has issued an order applying national laws in the Hong Kong Special Administrative Region, namely the Martial Law of the People's Republic of China, following a submission by the State Council and a proclamation by the president to that effect.'

The chief executive cleared his throat, then jarringly switched to Putonghua.

'As instructed by the president, and in accordance with Article 9 of the Martial Law, I am hereby relieving myself of the administration of the Hong Kong Special Administrative Region and, effective immediately, transferring it to the martial-law-executing organ to be headed by Lieutenant General Tan Benhong, Commander of the Hong Kong Garrison of the People's Liberation Army.'

The man in the middle, in the military garb, began speaking.

'Hong Kong compatriots, please rest assured, it will be my solemn responsibility to restore order and stability to the

Hong Kong Special Administrative Region. This is a temporary measure.'

I couldn't clearly understand what came next, not only because of the Putonghua, but also the legalese. General Tan outlined what I understood to be restrictions on public assembly and 'street speeches and other mass activities' and imposed a 'press and telecommunications embargo' until such time as the terrorist elements could be suppressed.

Other than these restrictions, the General said, 'Please go about your normal routines.' He said to continue going to work and to school, and to 'enjoy leisure activities'. The courts, he said, would continue to function as normal, 'except with regard to cases related to the current turmoil'. The Stock Exchange, due to open in two hours, would suspend trading for the entire week, and reopen the following Monday, December 8th. All property transactions were likewise suspended for one week. Media outlets and the internet would go live again following the statement, but, in order to prevent 'rumours and fear-mongering', would be restricted from publishing information, once again, 'related to the current turmoil'.

'Please do not panic,' General Tan said. 'Your way of life will not substantially change.'

After Ma finished frying the eggs for Mo, she went into her room. She came out fully dressed, pulling her carry-on trolley suitcase behind her.

'What are you doing?' she asked me. I was checking my BlackBerry; emails were coming in detailing our business contingency plans. Mo was absent-mindedly eating the eggs, not hearing Ma.

'Get your backpack,' she said. 'Come with me.'

After waiting ten minutes for the lift, by the time we finally made it to the street, there were dozens of others, also rolling suitcases and carrying backpacks, heading in the same direction across the street to the shopping centre. It wasn't yet 7:30 am; ParknShop wouldn't open for another half an hour, if it was opening at all, but already there were at least a hundred people gathered in front of the gates.

'Go to the ATM,' Ma whispered in my ear. She gave me her bankcard. 'The PIN is your birthday. Take out the maximum.'

I skipped down the escalators back out the street and around the corner, but the line for the HSBC ATM already stretched at least 100 metres, curling around the block. There wouldn't be any cash left by the time it was my turn. I remembered there was another ATM in a nearby 7-Eleven that no one ever used because it only dispensed credit card cash advances, and most people didn't know it existed in the first place. I walked briskly to the 7-Eleven, not wanting to inspire anyone else to follow me, but when I got there, it had been completely stripped. Every shelf was deserted; no snacks, no Panadol, no drinks in the refrigerators, no ice-cream in the freezers, not even plastic ponchos and disposable underwear. Everything was gone.

But the ATM was still on. I could tell from several dents that someone had tried to crack open the shell, to no avail.

I looked over my shoulder, then inserted my mother's bank-card and keyed in 2-4-0-2-9-0. I tapped the screen for the maximum credit advance, twenty thousand dollars, and received an error message.

'There are not enough funds remaining to process your request. Would you like to withdraw a smaller amount?'

I tapped yes. The machine spit out twelve thousand dollars, which I stuffed into my briefs. I speed walked back to the ParknShop, where the crowd had swelled to several hundred. It was becoming clear no staff were coming to open up.

'Just break in,' someone yelled.

'We have to do this in an orderly fashion.'

'Go fuck yourself, General Tan.'

I found Ma close to the gates, struggling to negotiate her short, squat body through others, to get even closer. Her suitcase was gone.

'Someone took it,' she said, when she saw me looking for it.

'Let's go,' I said. 'It's not worth it.'

Ma looked back at the gate.

'My birthday,' I said. 'It worked.'

We went home.

The looting went on for two days, but it was ultimately contained—those caught were sent immediately and indefinitely, without trial, to Shenzhen No. 2 Detention Centre—as the six thousand PLA troops stationed in Hong Kong fanned out across the city and reinforcements from the Guangdong Military Region were trucked in across the Shenzhen River.

'Like the day your father died,' Ma said, while we watched it on TV.

The heads of large companies and all government departments received phone calls the afternoon martial law was enacted, instructing them to carry on with business as usual. So on Tuesday morning, I went into our office in Hutchinson House even though we were 'pencils down' because no one knew how the market would react when the Stock Exchange re-opened the next Monday, and Ma went to City Hall even though not a single person would show up at the library all week, other than Ma and her staff.

Ma and I took the bus together to Central. Mo was still sleeping when Ma looked into his room before we left. The bus was full, but quieter than the usual morning commute. Passengers were looking out the windows more than down at their phones. Nothing appeared out of the ordinary for the first half of the journey, but when we emerged from the Aberdeen Tunnel on the overpass above the mausoleums in the Hong Kong Cemetery, the passengers on the right side of the bus let out a collective 'Wah' as they saw hundreds of troops lined up conducting drills in the middle of the Happy Valley Racecourse. There were two helicopters parked on the infield, and a tank was motoring in through the underpass from Wong Nai Chung Road. Down at street level in Causeway Bay and Wan Chai, a couple of PLA soldiers were stationed at nearly every corner, rifles at attention.

When we turned onto Gloucester Road, I saw an elderly man come out of the Mormon temple and begin berating the soldier posted at that street corner. The soldier, who looked younger than me, stood motionless, but I could see two other uniformed men approaching. Our bus stopped almost right in front of them, and I could see the People's Armed Police badges on their uniforms.

'Military police,' someone on the bus said. As the bus pulled out of the stop, the two PAP officers each grabbed one of the elderly man's arms and dragged him away. A young woman in business wear sitting behind me and Ma started sobbing.

'There's no need to be like that,' Ma said to her, gently.

I imagined a sea of wreckage, blood stains, mangled bodies. I was prepared for the worst. As government headquarters came into view, Ma squeezed my hand.

All the passengers were anticipating what we would see when we passed Admiralty. I imagined a sea of wreckage, blood stains, mangled bodies. I was prepared for the worst. As government headquarters came into view, Ma squeezed my hand.

But there was nothing. Not just no sign of the carnage from Monday morning, but no sign of the protests whatsoever, except a few stray pastel Post-its on the 'Lennon Wall' staircase, and some yellow umbrella stickers half scraped off the asphalt. Traffic went both ways. In under twenty-four hours, they had cleared everything, and everyone. I don't know if I was horrified or relieved.

Ma and I rode the bus home together that first Tuesday night, and when we opened our door, I noticed Mo's Nikes were gone. Ma walked straight to his room, without taking her own shoes off, opened his door, and just stood in his doorway for a few seconds, looking at his empty bed. Mo never came home again.

Our WhatsApp chat group had disappeared from the app. Ma and I could still message each other, which is how we got on the bus after work at the same time, but neither of us could get a message through to Mo. Other chat groups I was in with friends were still active, but only those Mo hadn't been in. When I searched for FireChat in the App Store, nothing turned up. I had tried browsing at work that day and HKGolden was obviously down, but all other local news sites, even *Apple Daily*, were live, just sanitised. The headlines were mostly about Ukraine and Bill Cosby, along with some city stories on new IVF treatments and a small fire in Ho Man Tin. CNN, BBC and all other foreign news sites timed out. I had received a work email specifically instructing me not to try a VPN or google anything remotely sensitive on my work computer, but even when I tried on my phone or later at home, everything still timed out.

Mo dropped us signs of life every other day or so, a WhatsApp message from an unknown number we knew was him because the message would be one of our birthdays or the name of a cat we had when we were little. It seemed like he was shuffling through SIM cards and phones, able to fire off a few messages from each one before being detected and shut down. I couldn't ask any friends if the same thing had happened to any of their family members, because I could never be sure if we were being watched, in the office or at lunch or on the bus. Mo's singing videos during the protests made me particularly vulnerable to being labelled an 'Occupier', and Ma and I, even in our own home, tried not to talk about Mo explicitly. To be honest, that might have made it easier. When you're forced—or think you're forced; we didn't really know—not to think about someone, it lessens the guilt, and the anger.

In bed, trying to sleep, I burned when I thought about Mo, about the bullets in the Assailant's chest slicing through Mo instead. I started picturing him coming home. I imagined shoving him against the wall and slapping him, trying to rip his cheek off his face. What did he think he could do out there? Was he going to sing the Chinese Communist Party into submission, like it was some pretty girl in his palm? Did he think about what *we* would do if anything happened to him? Did he stop to think about Ma having to scatter the ashes of her younger son? Had he forgotten about our father, about the hole already gaping in our home? How could he put himself in that position, that he might abandon us? How could he be so selfish? Why did he go? And why did I do nothing to stop him?

There was this detached sense of normalcy that permeated the city that first week, forced but resigned. We complied with largely unspoken rules that most of us assumed to be in force, knowing the proclivities of the Chinese authorities, even if we had never experienced them directly. Maybe we could have all tested the water a bit more, or at all, but at what cost? All we knew was that people had died, and we were now under martial law. Whatever lines needed to be crossed had been crossed.

But the façade crumbled at 9:30 am the next Monday, December 8th. The Hang Seng Index dropped 18 per cent in the first three minutes of trading, then another 28 per cent by the noon lunch break. Nearly half of Hong Kong's paper wealth had been wiped out in two and a half hours. General Tan appeared on TV to say the Stock Exchange would not reopen after lunch and trading was suspended indefinitely, as were property transactions. Thousands had been consummated in the morning at prices up to 80 per cent less than the market had been two weeks before. People were desperate to liquidate their assets and get cash out of Hong Kong immediately. Someone at work told me most diamond merchants didn't even bother trying to gouge buyers; unless they had customers with foreign currency, they simply absconded with their goods altogether, placing no faith whatsoever in the Hong Kong dollar. At least that was before all border points were closed, except to foreign citizens who could affirmatively prove they were not Chinese nationals. A Chinese Canadian colleague of mine, who wasn't born in Hong Kong but had three stars on his ID card because of his ethnicity, spent the whole week at the office trying to find ways to remove the stars. When he thought he had done the best he could, he headed to the airport. I don't know if he made it out or not, but he didn't come back to the office the next day, or ever.

Nearly all the city's expatriate judges fled in the following weeks, leaving the judiciary at half-capacity and court dockets overflowing. Local judges said they anticipated delays of up to two years in processing the normal crimes that were ostensibly still being prosecuted and tried according to normal judicial procedures. Anticipating impunity, triad groups went on a racketeering spree, and, with nothing to lose, boldly threatened and bribed PLA unit commanders in various districts to allow them to run what effectively became small but strictly confined fiefdoms in Tsuen Wan, Mong Kok and Kowloon City. To keep children from falling into these enclaves, a curfew was imposed on children under sixteen; they had to be in their homes by 6 pm every day, including on weekends. Witnesses were encouraged to report seeing children out after 6 pm.

On New Year's Eve, Ma and I came home early. We were still taking the bus together every day to and from work. There were no public celebrations permitted, no countdowns or fireworks. All bars and karaoke halls were ordered to close at 6 pm and, in any case, once all the expatriates had left, half of Lan Kwai Fong had gone out of business in a matter of weeks, unable to pay the next month's rent. I hadn't sung K since the night at Neway the protests started, but some friends had told me all Beyond songs had been deleted from the song lists.

Ma steamed a small fish for the two of us for dinner. We spooned out its flesh, even slices of it falling easily off the bone, and layered it over our rice. In one of those random connections your brain sometimes makes, I thought of an aggravating Jay Chou song Mo used to sing at karaoke just to annoy me, called 'Sailors Afraid of Water'. There is a line in the song, at the beginning of the second verse, about not being able to eat seafood, and I suddenly felt this deep ache, a hollowing out of my chest. I needed to hear Mo sing again.

I was reminded of the bottle of Chivas we only half-finished that night at Neway. I got up from the table, went into Mo's room, and dug it out of a stash of clothes piled on top of his desk. A waft of his scent lifted through the room.

'Happy new year, Ma,' I said, showing her the bottle.

'No,' Ma said. 'No. I can't.' She put her chopsticks down, wiped her lips, and went to her bedroom.

I can't see where Mo is exactly. His voice is coming from behind me, from the other side of the fence where an alleyway leads from Southorn to the MTR entrance.

'That's why I never pass to you.'

'How long have you been watching me?'

'Long enough to see you still can't shoot.'

It's true, I couldn't make a basket. In the fifteen minutes since the Adidas kids ran off, I had probably taken at least fifty shots, and only two had gone in. I don't have a great shot, but I'm better than that, and it annoys me, instantly, that Mo is going to give me shit about this abysmal performance. For a moment, we are just brothers. I've almost forgotten what that feels like.

By Chinese New Year, neither Ma nor I had received one of Mo's cryptic messages for over two weeks. My first day back at work, February 23rd, I received an envelope from a courier that I thought was for the bankruptcy proceeding I was staffed on after all our IPOs died. I casually opened it in our firm's reception area, but as soon as I pulled out the single sheet of paper and saw Mo's all caps English handwriting across the top, I put the paper back in the envelope and went to the bathroom. I waited for someone in the stall next to me to flush and wash his hands, and then read Mo's message.

'BIRTHDAY', he had written, in English, and below it, 'BALL'. Then, in Chinese, 'dinner time'.

I tore the paper into pieces and flushed the scraps down the toilet. I went to work the next day, my birthday, carrying all my gear in my backpack and a ball, so I would look like I was going to play basketball after work. I changed out of my work clothes at the end of the day and took the tram to Southorn.

Mo steps into the moonlight. He is wearing a baseball cap, and his hair flows out of it, nearly down to his shoulders. He's grown a beard too.

'Happy birthday,' he says.

'Are you okay?' I ask.

'Yeah.'

'What's going on?'

'Come with me.'

'Where?'

'Just come.'

He steps out of the moonlight again. I grab my bag from under the basket and walk in his direction, into the alleyway. As soon as I am behind the fence, an arm reaches around my neck and holds me still as another arm throws a blindfold across my eyes.

'What the fuck?'

'We need to make sure you don't see where we're going,' Mo says, from a couple metres away. 'For your own good.'

We move south down the alleyway, I can tell, so when we get to a road and into a van it should be on Johnston. The drive is short, four or five minutes, and when we get out, someone buzzes an intercom before the building gate clicks open.

We walk up six flights of stairs, then there is another buzz, another click, and the blindfold comes off. I had thought I was being taken to some kind of insurgent war room, but instead this is more like a college party: dim lighting, soft jazz playing, and a couple dozen coeds sinking into and around plush IKEA sofas, half of them huddled over laptop screens, the other half listening attentively to a woman in the middle speaking above the music. I can't understand her clearly at first, until I realise she is speaking Putonghua, but not like a mainlander. There is something more true to her accent, resonating in a lower register; she is Taiwanese. She's briefing the crowd about something technical, like an engineer, explaining caches, I think I hear her say, and prices and shipping routes.

'Come here,' Mo says, drawing my attention to two guys sitting at a bench table by the window, the screens of their MacBooks illuminating their adolescent faces. The curtains, of a grey, light fabric, are drawn, but a breeze blows them to the side for an instant and I can make out a slice of a brightly lit sign box several floors below, an incomplete arrangement of yellow brush strokes I've seen before, but am not sure where. My first thought is of the PLA banners now slung along sidewalk rails, calling on Hong Kong compatriots to 'Uphold the rule of law and bring Occupiers to justice.'

'Who is she?' I ask, turning my head in the direction of the Taiwanese woman.

'She was a Sunflower leader,' Mo says. 'She's helping us link up with an arms dealer.'

'What?'

'They think they can smuggle in some weapons by boat.'

I look back at the woman. She has bangs brushing the top of large retro frame glasses, and wears an oversized flannel shirt and black leggings. She looks like a film critic.

'Look at this,' Mo says. He points at a browser window open on one of the MacBook screens. I recognise it immediately: it is the McAllen Dune remote desktop login page.

'How'd you access that?' I ask the guy behind the MacBook. He doesn't respond.

'One of your firm's clients is a media company financed by the PLA,' Mo says. 'There should be documents on your servers that have their bank account information. These guys could hack into the accounts, siphon out some of the money—random amounts at random times, so they wouldn't notice for weeks—to pay for the weapons from Taiwan.'

'What?' I say.

'Listen to me. Even better, who knows what these bank accounts are used for? They might already be used to buy arms, maybe from Russia. We could place orders and no one would know the difference. The PLA would be buying weapons for us to use against them.'

'Are you fucking serious?'

'Just type in your login details.' The guy behind the MacBook pushes the keyboard in front of me. 'Once you're logged in, B-Boy can guide you to find the documents. I'm up now. I'll be right back.'

Mo walks away before I can respond. He takes the film critic's place in the middle of the sofas, and someone hands him a guitar. I didn't know he could play. He starts strumming a few chords.

'Hey,' B-Boy says. I pretend not to hear him. Mo starts singing an unfamiliar song. For a moment, his voice is a salve, smoothing over the grating cognitive dissonance of this whole scene, which has been disorienting, almost nauseating. But the song itself is unkempt; it sounds like bad grammar, the errors amplified by Mo's strident voice. It is an original composition, I guess, and it is terrible.

I think about our father slumped in the massage chair, listening to Beyond, eyes wet. I want to ask him what he thinks.

I want him to shut Mo down, shut it all down, this absurd room, our fallen city. How did we get here? How was the turn so swift, so sweeping? All these years without our father, we kept going, me and Mo, we just kept going, together at least. Until now. Now I know what we missed, now I need an adult in the room. Someone needs to be the adult.

B-Boy pokes his finger into my arm. I turn and with both hands shove his whole body backwards, and his chair falls in a clatter against the window. Mo stops singing. I look back at him.

'What are you doing?' I yell. 'This is insane. You're singing songs between smuggling arms? You think you can take on the PLA from an underground coffee shop? You're all going to end up dead. This doesn't help anyone!' I am drawing in deep breaths. 'The song's not even good.'

I start walking towards the door. Mo jumps in my way.

'The song's not even good, Mo.'

'We need your login,' he says.

'That's why you wanted to see me.'

'Yeah.' The two other guys who had brought me here move to Mo's side.

'You don't ever contact me or Ma again. This is it. You're dead to us.'

'Fine.'

I walk back to the table by the window, and type in my login details.

'Get me the fuck out of here,' I say.

They blindfold me and drop me back at Southorn. I go home and don't say anything to Ma, but when I walk past her sitting on the sofa, she catches the trail of air I displace.

'You saw him,' she says.

'It wasn't him.'

When I go into work the next morning, I report that I noticed suspicious activity on my remote desktop the night before and believe my account has been hacked. I had gone to bed half-dreaming of ripping Mo's cheek off and woken up that morning with the same urge gnawing in my stomach: I wanted them to get caught. Within minutes of my report, two uniformed men appear at my cubicle and ask me to follow them to a breakout room. One is a Hong Kong policeman; the other military police. The Hong Kong policeman speaks the entire time, asking if I know who might have done this. I want them to get caught, and yet I say I have no idea.

'What about your brother?' the policeman asks.

'What about him?'

'We know he's an Occupier.'

'Yeah.'

'You don't think he did this?'

'Maybe. I wouldn't know.'

'He's never tried to contact you?'

'No.'

'You've never tried to contact him?'

'He's dead to me.'

The policeman leaves his card with me, and asks me to call if I notice anything else suspicious, or think of who might have been able to access my account details.

Going home that night, on the top deck of a bus with Ma next to me, we stop for a red light at the junction with Burrows Street. I look out the window and down at the empty pedestrian crossing. There is a 7-Eleven at the corner, with a soldier standing guard outside. It doesn't look like anyone is in the store.

The light changes, and as we roll across the intersection, I look down Burrows Street to the right and see a familiar glow of yellow: an illuminated Café de Coral sign box. I glance up across the street from the sign, counting six floors up, and see a grey curtain flapping in the breeze just before the building disappears from view.

When we get home, Ma goes into the kitchen and flicks the switch on the rice cooker. I go into my room. When I hear the hiss of her dropping a bundle of *pak choi* into the wok, I reach into my pants pocket. I take out my phone, and then the policeman's card. *Time to go, Mo.*

Time to go.

Castaway

Jason Y. Ng

W*ake up, sir.*
Wake up.

Those were the first words Chu had heard in what felt like years.

But it hadn't even been three weeks. He knew that because since Day Six, he had adopted the daily ritual of etching a deep incision on one of the tree trunks at every sunset. If he hadn't been found by the Government Flying Service that afternoon, he would have just completed the fourth five-stroke *zing* (正) hieroglyph—the way every child is taught to tally scores in Hong Kong—to mark his twentieth day as a castaway.

Sir, can you hear me? Could you tell me your name?

'My name?' Chu thought to himself, unable to comprehend the relevance given his present state. All his life he had insisted on going by his family name. Whereas his friends had given themselves English ones like Thomas, Stanley, Sylvia and Queenie, he was content with being just Chu. The word means scarlet, the colour of courage, passion and joy. It is the colour of the Ferrari, *lai see* envelopes, blood and the new China. Unfortunately, *chu* is also a homonym for the Chinese word for pig, and he grew up with the pet name 'Chu-zai,' which means piglet. When his Secondary Four English teacher put *Lord of the Flies* on the reading list, all hell broke loose and for the whole term everyone called him Piggy, even though he never wore eyeglasses and was skinny as a rake. He had hated the book ever since.

Can you hear me, sir? We need you to respond before we can get you to safety.

It was that booming baritone again. There were other voices, younger and more agitated, chattering in the background. The youths were arguing over what to administer to the res-cued man: an electrolyte drink, a candy bar, or a shot of mor-phine. *Did someone bring morphine?*

'For God's sake stop bickering and get me a drink of water,' Chu thought. But he was in no position to protest, as he had been slipping in and out of consciousness, unable to even open his eyes or stop his head from spinning like a top. He wanted to throw up, as he frequently had in the last sever-al days. That's what a mono diet would do to someone, he figured. Other than coconut flesh, he hadn't eaten much of anything since the day he was washed up on the south shore of this barren rock of an island.

Chu's mother had told him many times not to go on the boat trip. 'Trifle with mountains but never the sea,' she had warned him, invoking the Cantonese saying. His mother was right—after nearly forty people lost their lives in the

Lamma Island ferry collision a few years earlier, many in Hong Kong had become gun shy about taking boat rides at night. But Chu didn't think lightning would strike twice and decided to press ahead for fear of being left out. His bosses had chartered a thirty-foot yacht and invited the entire staff. They had planned the handover anniversary junk party down to the minute. The group would depart from Central Pier Nine at 6:30 pm on July 1st and sail clockwise around Hong Kong Island. By 8 pm, they should have docked in the middle of Victoria Harbour just in time for the fireworks show. Dozens of iPhones had been at the ready for group selfies. Bottles of 2007 Dom Perignon had been chilling in the cooler on board.

Their boat had just passed Cyberport off the southwestern coast when it all went wrong. Chu remembered hearing a loud bang, like one of the fireworks had gone off prematurely, before everyone on board, including the skipper and his deputy, was flung to one side of the boat like a rag doll. People were too shocked to scream or react at all. The only sound was dark water lapping restlessly against the capsized boat. Chu figured their yacht must have hit another vessel but he wasn't sure. All he knew was that he was one of the lucky passengers who managed to find his way to the stack of life jackets stowed behind the cockpit. As he was doing up the last buckle of the orange vest, a big wave tossed him into the water and knocked his head on a metal bar bolted to the half-submerged boat. Next thing he knew he was bobbing fifty feet from a non-descript shoreline, visible only because those white caps gave off an eerie blue glow as the sea waves crashed on the beach. His instinct sent him flapping his arms and swimming like a frightened animal towards the rocky shore, all the while his head was throbbing like a beating drum and his heart was telling him that he had every reason to panic.

If you don't wake up now, sir, you may not make it off this island.

'It isn't nice to threaten a barely conscious man,' Chu grumbled to himself. Twenty days on this Godforsaken island and he expected some compassion from his rescuers. He wished those young'uns would stop crowding him and give him some space. However well-intended they were, they didn't seem trained for this kind of rescue mission. 'Isn't today a school day?' he remembered his markings on the tree. 'Shouldn't these kids be in class?' Even the older man—the presumed leader of the pack—appeared to be making it up as he went along. Half an hour after discovering a victim, none of them had had the good sense to offer him food and fluids. Once he was back in civilisation, Chu swore, he would write a strongly worded letter to the Ombudsmen.

But he mustn't be bothered with them. His own survival was the only thing that mattered. He needed to focus on opening his eyes or wriggling one of his fingers to show the baritone that he wasn't beyond saving. He strained to breathe a bit more heavily, sucking air into his flared nostrils to make a sound. Sadly the subtlety was lost on his rescuers, for the youths continued to argue with one another.

For days, Chu had struggled to understand why it was taking the government this long to find him. A high-profile shipwreck, with this many victims involved, would have been front-page news and fodder for tabloid newspapers. He could imagine the *Apple Daily* headline in fifty-point type: 'DOZ-

ENS PERISH IN HANDOVER DISASTER; MANY MORE STILL MISSING!' Surely after the divers failed to recover all the bodies, a search and rescue team would have been dispatched, leaving no stone unturned and no island unscoured. Surely his mother would have formed a makeshift alliance with families of other missing passengers and been holding daily press conferences to plead with the authorities to double down on the rescue effort. He should have been found and airlifted off the island in a matter of days.

Unless the government had given up on him and other survivors. He was familiar with the so-called 'golden forty-eight hours'—the critical window of time within which the chance of finding survivors after a natural disaster was greatest. Beyond that, survivability would drop precipitously and the mission would switch from rescue to recovery. He remembered all that from the wall-to-wall coverage of the 2008 Sichuan Earthquake and from each time a coal mine exploded somewhere in mainland China. In his case, it was possible that still-missing victims like him were presumed dead two days after the accident, their bodies forever lost in the shark-infested waters.

He tried to save himself of course. Hong Kongers may not be the most athletic or knowledgeable about the wild, but they are pragmatic. Chu took great pride in his no-nonsense philosophy towards life, which he applied to both work problems and personal dilemmas. He stayed clear of politics, religion and other useless things and focused his energy on making himself more competitive, taking night classes and even getting an insurance agent license in case his marketing firm downsized and laid him off. Life wasn't a walk in the park but there was always a way out, as long as he was willing to think outside the box and, if necessary, make some compromises here and cut a few corners there. He was the human embodiment of the 'okay' hand sign.

Chu decided to treat Mother Nature like one of his clients and put his business training to work. On Day Two, he slipped into his orange life vest in late afternoon when the water was warmest and began swimming east, away from the sun. But things didn't feel right: the water was colder than expected, the current was pushing against him, and he lacked the basic means of navigation. Without his iPhone or Google Map, he had no idea where he was heading. For all he knew, Hong Kong Island was in the opposite direction and he was swimming further and further into the South China Sea. Worse, there might be jellyfish, sharp rocks and other hidden dangers. His scuba diving coach had warned him about grey reef sharks and hammerheads that occasionally stray into local waters during the summer months. And so before the sun started to set, he turned around and headed back to the island. Shortly after he crawled his way to shore, the sky suddenly darkened and a thunderstorm shook the island, whipping leaves and branches into a frenzy. Gusting winds sent waves two, three feet into the air. He told himself never to make the same futile and deadly excursion again.

Having given up on swimming his way home, the castaway had only one option left: stay alive on the island for as long as he could to maximise the chance of being rescued. The lack of alternatives gave him a renewed sense of purpose. Once again,

He was willing to think outside the box and, if necessary, make some compromises here and cut a few corners there. He was the human embodiment of the 'okay' hand sign.

his can-do spirit kicked into high gear and his mind switched to a problem-solving mode. A decade spent in marketing as a project manager had now found new applications in life's most unexpected predicament.

The first rule of tackling an assignment is be organised. On the next morning, Chu mentally drew up a to-do list:

1. *Survey the island*
2. *Find food and water*
3. *Find shelter*
4. *Make a fire*
5. *Make a 'HELP' sign.*

Then he applied the second rule: pick the proverbial low-hanging fruit. He swiftly skipped to the last two items on the list, which he found the most achievable out of the five. After all, there was no shortage of rocks on the island and, within an hour, he completed task no. 5 by lugging the darkest colour rocks he could get his hands on and meticulously arranging them on the white sandy beach. He had chosen to write in English because the Chinese characters for 'save me' had too many strokes and would be difficult to read from a distance. Roman letters, on the other hand, would be visible to any fishing boat or rescue team hundreds of feet away. He took a step back and admired the sign—his first accomplishment in three days—with deep satisfaction.

Task no. 4 was a different story. Nothing happened, not even the faintest sign of white smoke was visible, when he rolled a twig back and forth rapidly on a piece of flat wood—the way he had seen it done countless times in disaster movies. He rubbed so hard that some of the skin peeled off his palms and his hands started to bleed. He had to stop before he got an infection from the open wound, which would certainly be worse than not having a fire. He tried to figure out what had gone wrong: was it the subtropical humidity or that he wasn't using the right kind of wood as a spindle? If it weren't for the balmy July weather, he certainly would have frozen to death at night or at least caught a cold and developed pneumonia.

But no matter which way he cut it, failure still stung. For the first time in his life, Chu wished that he were short-sighted. Throughout primary and secondary schools, he was one of the rare few who escaped the nickname 'four eyes' or didn't have to go blind in gym class. All his life he had prided himself on having 20/20 vision and never requiring eyewear or expensive Lasik surgery.

Perfect eyesight turned out to be a handicap on a deserted island. He remembered how Piggy in *Lord of the Flies* used his precious eyeglasses to light a fire. The fat boy deserved to be killed for his own stupidity, Chu had thought at the time. If *he* were put in that situation, he certainly would have been smart enough to split his glasses into two, saving one lens for his own allies and offering the other to the rival gang in exchange for peace. Poor Piggy could have easily prevented war and his own demise. Not very pragmatic, was he?

Chu shook his head to clear his mind. This wasn't the time for literary critique. To restore his injured pride, he recalled the third rule of project management: never point fingers when things go wrong. He told himself that the fire was only a small setback. Perhaps he would have better luck tomorrow when he found dryer twigs. He patted himself on the shoulders for holding up much better than he thought he would under these dismal circumstances. Just look at that beautiful 'HELP' sign. Besides, the weather on the island was so pleasant that he didn't technically need a fire. With that, he went back to his to-do list.

The other tasks were clear enough: explore the island and find food and shelter. Still, knowing what one should do and actually doing it are two very different things. Chu let several days go idly by without making any progress on addressing his most urgent problem: hunger. By then he had fallen into a mental rut. In his most lethargic and delusional moments, he would laugh out loud over the incredible luck that had befallen him. He felt special not only because many of his co-workers had died in the shipwreck and he alone had survived, but also because he now had the entire island to himself. He wasn't used to all that open space and free time. Of all the things to be number one in, Hong Kong had to pick the worst categories: the world's most unaffordable housing and most overworked people. Like everyone around him, he had spent his adult life chained to his desk like an indentured slave, only to pour his entire savings into the down payment for a shoebox-sized apartment. But now, not only did he *not* have to show up at work and slouch over the same computer screen, every morning he woke up to an unobstructed ocean view that even his best-paid bosses would kill to have. If only he had food and water.

Each thought of eating would give him a sharp pang in his stomach. Out of everything he missed being away from civilisation, food was the one thing that he craved the most. His heart bled just thinking about beef *chow fun* and iced lemon tea. He would gladly 'shorten his life by ten years'—as the popular Cantonese expression goes—in exchange for his mother's steamed pork patties or braised chicken wings. For the first time since the shipwreck, Chu was seriously homesick.

It'll be three weeks tomorrow. How has he managed to stay alive without food and drinking water?

The voice this time sounded fainter. Chu figured the baritone must be addressing his trainees from a distance. The rhetorical question was followed by noisy footsteps both near and far. The rescue crew was surveying the area looking for clues to their leader's question.

For five days now, Chu hadn't drunk anything other than rainwater and dew collected at dawn from large fronds. He had been subsisting on tiny crustaceans hiding under the rocks and a nameless plum-like fruit in nearby bushes. Both tasted terrible and were difficult to find. He wasn't sure if either was even safe to eat. In fact, the diet hadn't agreed with his stomach and he had been losing water massively as a result. His eyes had sunk into his skull and his ribs were beginning to show. He never thought he would complain about losing weight, but the sight of his rapidly shrinking body scared him.

To occupy his mind, he tried to remember how long a person

could survive without food. He vaguely recalled a conversation after watching that Tom Hanks plane crash movie, when a co-worker's know-it-all girlfriend mentioned that Mahatma Gandhi, the world's most famous hunger striker, had survived twenty-one days of complete starvation. Another acquaintance, an avid trekker and a bit of a show-off, had chimed in with the factoid that fifty days without food was the absolute upper limit for any human being. That was as good an estimate for Chu as anything else. And so he gave himself an expiration date: Day Fifty. If he failed to locate a food source by the time he completed the tenth *zing* character, it'd be the end of him.

Hunger hung over Chu like a storm cloud and it took a toll on his immune system. On Day Six, he woke up mid-morning with a bout of fever and shortness of breath. He couldn't stop shivering and had to cover himself with his life vest and a nest of tree branches. He figured he must have caught the flu after the rainstorm the night before. With only the flannel shirt on his back, which had become crusty and frayed, it was a matter of time before his body gave out. But this was no ordinary flu, it felt more severe and acute than any respiratory problem he had ever had. He couldn't walk a few steps without coughing his lungs out or falling over himself. He knew that if he stayed where he was both physically and mentally, he would end up dead before anyone would rescue him.

Chu's condition forced him to reassess his situation and take action. On that same day, he summoned all the strength left in him to begin his journey to the other side of island in search of better prospects. He tucked his life vest under a rock and lumbered up the hill, stopping frequently to catch his breath. The island, he quickly realised, was a glorified hunk of rock the size of a football stadium. The peak was roughly ten floors high and by late afternoon he had reached the top and, for the first time since he was washed ashore, he could see the island in its entirety. He took in the views and started to sob like a small child despite himself. Even at the highest point of the island, he couldn't see anything other than ocean and sky. There wasn't a boat, a buoy or another island in sight. The combination of despair, isolation and finality hit him like a sledgehammer and he fell to his knees, a broken man.

Just then, out of the corner of his eye, Chu spotted a cluster of coconut trees on the north shore of the island. Tears of joy began to stream down his sunken cheeks when he saw plump coconuts hanging under the crowns. One of the trees leaned at a 45-degree angle to the horizon like a bowing servant, its canopy of broad leaves providing a natural shelter against the blazing sun. The thought of food and shade sent him running downhill towards the grove, his illness suddenly forgotten. He had planned on returning to the south shore to retrieve his life vest—his sole possession on the island—but that seemed no longer necessary. The flu virus turned out to be a blessing in disguise, for he wouldn't have made that life-changing discovery if it weren't for his desperate state. He was grateful for Mother Nature's unexpected gift.

Boys and girls, I think I have the answer. The gentleman has been gorging on these for some time.

The baritone's conclusion was followed by what sounded like castanets. Some of the young ones must have picked up fragments of coconut shell and clicked them against one another.

The coconut trees had changed Chu's life. For starters, he no longer woke up every morning wondering when and what his next meal would be. Coconuts provided a ready source of food and fluids—all he needed was a large rock to crack the shell. If he felt particularly energetic, he would even climb up to the tree crown and yank a ripe fruit off with the free hand before dropping it to the ground and letting gravity do the work. A stable source of food offered him more than comfort, it had in essence extended his life expectancy to well beyond fifty days. With a new lease on life, he quickly built another 'HELP' sign just like the one he did on the south shore. He also started marking the day on the base of the leaning coconut tree with a sharp stone.

Chu had taken to the all-coconut diet like a duck to water. Even though it was never his favourite fruit—he had always avoided the flavour when choosing ice-cream and other desserts—and even though eating the same white flesh and drinking the same nutty water day in and day out had got dull after a while, it was far better than the alternatives: briny crustaceans and bacteria-laced water. He smiled at the thought that circumstances could so easily change one's position on things. He credited his adaptability to being a true Hong Konger.

Instead of worrying about what to eat and drink, Chu now spent his days learning how to make a fire. He hadn't given up on task no. 4 and he wasn't going to let it defeat him. It bothered him slightly that there was so much he didn't understand about his surroundings. He couldn't read the night sky to get his bearing or tell which plants were edible and which would kill him. He didn't know what to do with those giant coconut fronds in front of him, although he suspected that a handier castaway would have made thatched roofs or at least a hat out of them. Being in the sun all day, his face and limbs had been badly burned and there were growing concerns about permanent damage to his skin.

Chu blamed his present helplessness on his upbringing. At school, even in college, he was never taught to ask questions or think for himself. He would learn just enough to get through the next exam, of which there were many. Reading the stars or telling plants apart would have been considered 'outside the syllabus' and therefore a distraction from what really mattered: good grades. He had been a straight-A student, because he understood the system and gamed it expertly. But there is no gaming Mother Nature—you either survive or you don't.

Even so, there was no point in beating himself up now. Regrets wouldn't get him home any sooner and, ever the pragmatist, he decided to focus on the tasks at hand. Besides, he had completed two 'HELP' signs in record time, he would soon master fire-making, and he had singlehandedly discovered the coconut trees which had saved his life.

The sun continued to be a serious nuisance to Chu and he prayed for cloudy days—despite not being a religious man. He had counted on the coconut trees for shade, but he quickly realised that their sparse leaves still left him exposed to UV rays. He also suspected that extensive sun exposure might have something to do with his light-headedness and a general lack of energy ever since he moved to the north shore. Sometimes—usually after a meal—he would black out for a few minutes and wake up lying prostrate under one of the coconut trees. He attributed it all to heat exhaustion.

Things became progressively worse as the days wore on. Chu had been passing out at a greater frequency and had to splash seawater on his face just to stay awake. Cracking the hard coconut shell had become increasingly challenging as he lacked the energy to either pick up a heavy rock or climb a tall tree. On Day Twelve, when the second thunderstorm hit the island, as violent rains buffeted his shelter and blustering winds stirred leaves and sand into a vortex, he mustered the last ounce of energy left in him and hugged the leaning coconut tree like a koala. He watched helplessly as the storm swept his precious pile of firewood into the dark.

Another few days passed. The beach was now a messy pigsty strewn with coconut shells and human waste. Chu's physical state had gone from bad to worse—no amount of coconut water seemed to make him feel better. He wasn't sure how much longer he could hang on and began to have serious doubts about his work. Was his 'HELP' sign not big enough? Was it facing the wrong direction? Should he have written 'SOS' instead?

Then, just before sunset on Day Seventeen, Chu was awakened by the sweet sound of a foghorn. Although he was too weak to get up and run to shore, he managed to move his head towards the general direction of the low hum and, there it was; a custard-yellow container ship the size of a small city passing by in slow motion. Dense white smoke billowed from the main funnel as the ship came into full view. He couldn't believe his eyes or contain his excitement. It was as if the gates of heaven had been flung open, and the possibilities of a new beginning were suddenly within reach. Overcome with emotion, he drew a deep breath and willed himself to stand up. He quickly set ablaze the firewood he had restocked after the second thunderstorm, covering his mouth with his flannel shirt to avoid smoke inhalation. Within minutes, a huge bonfire was sending black fumes into the sky, echoing the exhaust from the ship funnel.

A few more minutes passed and the smile on his face gradually narrowed to an open mouth of disbelief. Euphoria gave way to disillusionment as the vessel slowly sailed out of sight. The thought that his best chance of getting rescued had come and gone cut him to the bone. He started to vomit, although not much came out besides coconut water and stomach acid. He fell to the ground and blacked out. That was the last thing he remembered before the baritone and his crew showed up three days later.

Listen up, boys and girls, this man needs our help. His heart rate is dangerously low and he doesn't have much time left. From what I can see, he has been living off these coconuts for days, even weeks. Consider this Survival 101 for all of you: coconut water is potassium-rich and potassium can be dangerous if consumed in excess. They call it hyperkalemia and it can cause light-headedness, loss of consciousness and even death.

How could it be? The very thing that had kept him alive was also killing him slowly.

What the man said shook Chu to the core. How could it be? The very thing that had kept him alive was also killing him slowly. He felt cheated, betrayed and utterly embarrassed. But what choice did he have? He did what he had to do.

We don't have the proper equipment to treat this gentleman on site and so we need him to work with us. We need him to wake up before we lose him forever. You remember your CPR lessons, don't you? Who wants to give it a try? After this, there are still dozens of other islands we need to check to look for survivors just like him.

'There were others like me?' Chu was surprised and relieved. He hoped the others had known the truth about coconuts. Then he remembered his mother taking him to the supermarket after his final exams and letting him choose whatever ice-cream he wanted. That must have been Primary Three. He pointed at a flavour through the freezer door—was it coconut?—and looked at his mother, wondering if he had picked the right one …

Chu found himself drifting further and further into the distant past. Childhood memories and odd realities continued to blur, until faded images and muffled dialogues disappeared into an abyss of numbness. There was something seductive about this semiconscious state, and, like a potent dose of anaesthesia, it compelled him to abandon defences and surrender. In his final throes of life, he heard the baritone again, delivering more diagnoses that might or might not matter to a man who no longer cared.

Care Home

Harry Harrison

Notes

1. The essay 'The Mix-ups' by Louisa Lim is an excerpt from her forthcoming book about Hong Kong.

2. The essay 'On Anger and Love in Post-Occupy Hong Kong' by Timothy O'Leary was previously published in *Cha: An Asian Literary Journal* (2016).

3. The poems 'Groundwork', 'Don't Ask' and 'Negative Capability' by Eddie Tay were previously published in *Dreaming Cities* (Math Paper Press, 2016).

4. The poems 'Mother Turns to Cantopop, and Waits for the Narrative to Turn to Her' and 'Re: work' by Nicholas Wong were previously published in *Iron Horse Literary Review* (2016) and *Diode* (2016), respectively.

5. The poem 'Two Systems' by Sarah Howe was previously published in *Law Text Culture* (2014).

6. An earlier version of 'Umbrella Poetics' by Jennifer S. Cheng was published on the blog *Kundiman Fireside* (2014).

7. The poems 'TWO ZERO FOUR SEVEN', 'How the Narratives of Hong Kong Are Written with China in Sight' and 'Maybe' by Tammy Ho Lai-Ming were previously published in *Asia Literary Review* (2016), *Radius* (2014) and *Berfrois* (2017), respectively.

8. The poems 'An Old Colonial Building', 'Images of Hong Kong' and 'Postcards of Old Hong Kong', by Leung Ping-Kwan, were previously published in *Eight Hong Kong Poets* (Chameleon Press, 2015).

9. The two essays from 'Key Strokes by Loong Hei' by Xu Xi were previously published in *Evanescent Isles: from My City-village* (Hong Kong University Press, 2008).

10. 'City of Darkness' by Michael Braga is excerpted from his forthcoming novel *Orphan City*.

11. All three satirical cartoons by Larry Feign were previously published in the *Independent* in 1997.

12. Two of Harry Harrison's satirical cartoons 'Umbrella' and 'Care Home' were previously published in the *South China Morning Post* in 2014.

13. Gérard Henry's author photo credit: Sonia AU Kalai.

14. Tammy Ho Lai-Ming's author photo credit: Sha'ianne Molas Lawas.

15. Leung Ping-Kwan's author photo credit: Wong Wobik 王禾壁.

16. Louisa Lim's author photo credit: Leila Navidi.

17. Xu Xi's author photo credit: Paul Hilton.

Contributors

 **Michael Braga** was born and raised in Hong Kong where he attended Island School. After boarding school and university in Australia, he returned to Hong Kong and worked in journalism for some twenty years. He is a descendant of two old Macau families. 'City of Darkness' is a version of a chapter from the manuscript of his first novel, *Orphan City*, set in the weeks before the handover. Braga lives in Sydney.

 **Mary-Jean Chan** is a poet from Hong Kong. She won the 2017 Poetry Society Members' Competition and the 2016 Oxford Brookes International Poetry Competition (ESL), whilst being shortlisted for the 2016 London Magazine Poetry Prize. Her work has appeared in *The Poetry Review, Ambit, The London Magazine, Callaloo Journal, The Rialto, Bare Fiction, The Scores, Tongue* and elsewhere. A Callaloo and VONA Fellow, Chan is currently a research associate at the Royal Holloway Poetics Research Centre at the University of London, and is a co-editor at *Oxford Poetry*.

 **Jennifer S. Cheng** is a poet and essayist with MFA degrees from the University of Iowa and San Francisco State University. She is the author of *House A*, winner of the 2015 Omnidawn First/Second Poetry Book Prize, and *Invocation: An Essay* (New Michigan Press, 2011), an image-text chapbook. Her writing has received multiple Pushcart Prize nominations,

along with fellowships and awards from the Ful-bright programme, Kundiman and the Academy of American Poets. Having grown up in Texas and Hong Kong, she currently lives in San Francisco. For more, visit *www.jenniferscheng.com*.

Kris Cheng is the editorial director of Hong Kong Free Press. He is a Hong Kong journalist with an interest in local politics. His work has been featured in *The Washington Post, Public Radio International, Hong Kong Economic Times* and others. Cheng has a degree in sociology from the Chinese University of Hong Kong.

Chow Hon Fai, whose pen name is Bohemia, is a writer of poetry and essays and a Christian. He graduated from the Open University of Hong Kong. Chow won the 2014 Young Artist Awards for Literary Arts and several other literary prizes in Hong Kong and Taiwan.

Larry Feign is a writer and artist based in Hong Kong, where his work was blacklisted for several years straddling the handover, following a high-profile episode of political censorship. He has published fifteen books; his cartoons and writing have appeared in publications around the world, including *Time* and *The Economist*; and he has received numerous awards and fellowships. Previously he directed animation for Disney. Feign currently lives and works in a village on Lantau Island. For more information (and a free cartoon book), visit *www.larryfeign.com*.

Harry Harrison is best known for his daily cartoons in the *South China Morning Post* where he is political cartoonist, his work appearing there six days a week since 2001. Among various other publications, he regularly produces cartoons for Thomson Reuters' *International Finance Review* and he was a regular contributor to *The Guardian, Time, The Wall Street Journal Asia* and *Far Eastern Economic Review*. Over the years, Harrison's work has won various awards including the Human Rights Press Award for Body of Work and most recently the Award of Excellence in Editorial Cartooning at the 2015 SOPA Awards.

Gérard Henry has lived in Hong Kong since 1981. He is a writer, art critic and Paroles magazine's chief editor. He has written on China, Hong Kong art and culture, and on French visual arts for exhibition catalogues and magazines. Henry also practises drawing and sketching and held a solo exhibition of his drawings in Hong Kong and Macao entitled 'Interior Landscapes'. In 1999, he was awarded Chevalier des Arts et des Lettres by the French Minister of Culture for promoting cultural exchanges between the Chinese and French communities.

Louise Ho is one of Hong Kong's most-recognised contemporary poets in English. Born in Hong Kong and raised mostly in the territory, she has lived in Mauritius, England, the United States and Australia. She was an associate professor of English at the Chinese University of Hong Kong, where she taught English and American poetry, Shakespeare, and briefly, creative writing. She has four collections of poetry: *Sheung Shui Pastoral* (1977); *Local Habitation* (1994); *New Ends, Old Beginnings* (1997); and *Incense Tree* (Hong Kong University Press, 2009). Her poems have been published internationally in literary journals. She is retired and now lives and writes in Australia and Hong Kong.

Oscar Ho Hing Kay was formerly the exhibition director of the Hong Kong Arts Centre and founding director of the Museum of Contemporary Art of Shanghai. He is one of the founding board members of the Asia Art Archive, founder of the Hong Kong chapter of the International Art Critic Association and chairman of Art in Hospital. Ho is currently the director of the MA programme in Cultural Management at the Chinese University of Hong Kong.

Tammy Ho Lai-Ming is the founding co-editor of the first Hong Kong-based online literary publication, *Cha: An Asian Literary Journal*, and an editor of the academic journal Hong Kong Studies. Her translations have appeared in *World Literature Today, Chinese Literature Today* and *Pathlight*, among others. She is currently an assistant professor at Hong Kong Baptist University, where she teaches poetics, fiction and modern drama. Her first poetry collection is Hula Hooping (Chameleon Press, 2015). She was the winner of the 2015 Young Artist Award in Literary Arts. For more, visit *www.sighming.com*.

Sarah Howe is a poet, academic and editor. Her first book, *Loop of Jade* (Chatto & Windus, 2015), won the T.S. Eliot Prize and The Sunday Times Young Writer of the Year Award. Born in Hong Kong to an English father and Chinese mother, she moved to England as a child. Her pamphlet, *A Certain Chinese Encyclopedia* (Tall-lighthouse, 2009), won an Eric Gregory Award from the Society of Authors. She is the founding editor of *Prac Crit*, an online poetry journal. She has held fellowships at the University of Cambridge, Harvard University's Radcliffe Institute and University College London.

Law Lok Man, Louise has a BA in philosophy and an MA in English from the Chinese University of Hong Kong. She is currently the Executive Director of *Fleurs des lettres*, an acclaimed literary magazine. She also contributes to *City Magazine, Ming Pao Weekly* and *Hong Kong Economic Times*. She was manager of the Hong Kong International Literary Festival and LitStream, the first literary festival initiated by the Hong Kong Arts Development Council. She was one of the first runners-up of the Third Li Shing Wah Modern Poetry Award for Young Poets.

Arthur Leung holds an MFA in creative writing from the University of Hong Kong. His poems have been published in print magazines, anthologies and online journals. Besides giving talks and demonstrations in schools, he was invited to participate in 'Shall We Jam—A Recital of Leung Ping-Kwan's Poetry in Song, Dance & Music' as a performing artist and in Hong Kong Baptist University's International Writers Workshop as a local writer. Leung serves as an associate editor for *Cha: An Asian Literary Journal*. He was a winner of the 2008 Edwin Morgan International Poetry Competition.

Leung Ping-Kwan (1949–2013) was one of Hong Kong's leading poets, novelists, essayists, photographers and scholars. He published twenty-four volumes of poems, and his poetry has been translated into Swedish, Japanese, Korean, English, German, French and Portuguese. He wrote profusely on the urban cultures of New York, Paris, Berlin, Zurich, Seoul, Tokyo and Hong Kong. He was professor of comparative literature at the University of Hong Kong, and chair professor of Chinese and director of the Centre for Humanities Research at Lingnan University.

Louisa Lim is the author of *The People's Republic of Amnesia; Tiananmen Revisited* (Oxford University Press, 2014), which was shortlisted for the George Orwell Prize and the Helen Bernstein Award for Excellence in Journalism. She is an award-winning journalist, who grew up in Hong Kong and reported from China for a decade for NPR and the BBC. She now teaches journalism at the University of Melbourne. Lim has recently been named a George Orwell Fellow.

Shirley Geok-lin Lim won the Multiethnic Literatures of the US Lifetime Achievement Award and the University of California, Santa Barbara (UCSB) Faculty Research Lecture Award. She has published ten poetry collections, three short story collections, two novels and a children's novel. Her memoir, *Among the White Moon Faces* (The Feminist Press at CUNY, 1996), received the American Book Award and her poetry collection *Crossing the Peninsula* (Heinemann Press, 1980) received the Commonwealth Poetry Prize. She served as UCSB Chair of Women's Studies and as chair professor of English at the University of Hong Kong, and is a research professor at UCSB.

Lui Wing Kai, Eric obtained his PhD from Hong Kong Baptist University. He has published three volumes of poetry, *Doldrums* (2006), *But We Walk* (2011) and *I am Elephant but You are Whale* (2017), and two collections of prose writing, *Park of the Afternoon* (2009) and *Look Down from the Bridge* (2015). He received numerous poetry awards including Hong Kong Biennial Awards for Chinese Literature. He was a high school teacher, an editor, and a judge for the Youth Literary Award.

William Nee is a China researcher for Amnesty International's East Asia Regional Office in Hong Kong. He carries out research on human rights in China, particularly on freedom of expression, human rights defenders and the death penalty. He also monitors the situation in the Xinjiang Uighur Autonomous Region. Nee's commentary has appeared in *The Diplomat, Hong Kong Free Press* and *Open Democracy*, and he is frequently quoted in news outlets such as *The Guardian, The Washington Post* and *The New York Times*, and on TV news programmes, including the BBC, NBC and ABC.

Jason Y. Ng is the bestselling author of *Hong Kong State of Mind* (Blacksmith Books, 2010) and *No City for Slow Men* (Blacksmith Books, 2013). His latest work, *Umbrellas in Bloom* (Blacksmith Books, 2016) is the first book in English to chronicle the Umbrella Movement and the last instalment of a Hong Kong trilogy that tracks the city's post-colonial development. As a columnist, Ng contributes to *The Guardian*, the *South China Morning Post* and *Hong Kong Free Press*. He is also an adjunct associate law professor at the University of Hong Kong and the president of PEN Hong Kong.

Margaret Ng is a barrister in private practice, a writer and a former member of the Hong Kong Legislative Council (1995–1997, 1998–2012).

Timothy O'Leary is a professor of philosophy and head of the School of Humanities at the University of Hong Kong (HKU), where he is an elected member of HKU Council. He co-founded the group HKU Vigilance, dedicated to defending academic freedom. He has written extensively on the work of Michel Foucault, especially in relation to ethics, aesthetics, and the powers of fiction. He is a co-editor of the book series *New Critical Humanities* published by Rowman & Littlefield International.

Michael O'Sullivan teaches English literature at the Chinese University of Hong Kong and is a co-editor of the academic journal Hong Kong Studies. He writes creatively on literature and education and also through poems and short stories. His recent book is

Academic Barbarism, Universities and Inequality (Palgrave Macmillan, 2016).

Ilaria Maria Sala is an award-winning journalist and writer. She has lived in East Asia since 1988, and calls Hong Kong home. Sala has written for a number of international publications, and is now a staff contributor for *Quartz*. She is also a ceramicist, and is passionate about tea and the Qianlong emperor.

Mishi Saran is the author of *The Other Side of Light* (HarperCollins India, 2012), which was shortlisted for the 2013 Commonwealth Book Prize. Her travel book-cum-memoir, *Chasing the Monk's Shadow: A Journey in the Footsteps of Xuanzang* (Penguin, 2005), was shortlisted for India's 2006 Hutch Crossword Book award. Her short stories have won prizes and been broadcast on the BBC. Saran returned to Hong Kong in 2014 after a decade away. She is fluent in Mandarin, French and Hindi. She is writing a novel set in Shanghai. For more, visit *www.mishisaran.com*.

Shahilla Shariff is the author of a collection of poetry, *Life Lines* (Proverse Hong Kong, 2012), which was a finalist in the 2011 International Proverse Prize. Her poetry has been shortlisted for the 2013 Bridport Prize. Her work has been featured in various anthologies, most recently in *LSF Poetry Anthology* (2017), and journals such as *World Literature Today* (2014 and 2017). A lawyer who lives in Hong Kong, she was born in Kenya and is Canadian. She was educated at Harvard College, Harvard Law School and Cambridge University, where she was a Commonwealth Scholar.

Shen Jian is a lawyer and contributor to the *South China Morning Post*. His writing has been nominated for a Pushcart Prize and recognised as notable in *Best American Essays*.

So Mei Chi has worked in journalism for more than twenty years, previously with news media such as *Ming Pao*, Cable TV news and *Ming Pao Weekly*. At present, she works independently and takes a special interest in reporting on social issues and family dynamics. So is the author of *Strangers at Home* (Joint Publishing (H.K.) Co. Ltd., 2015), which explores the complicated layers in foreign domestic workers issues in Hong Kong. The book won the Ninth Hong Kong Book Prize.

Tang Siu Wa 鄧小樺 writes poems, essays, and critiques. She is an editor of several Hong Kong literature collections, a founding editor of the literary magazine *Fleurs des lettres*, and a co-founder of the House of Hong Kong Literature. A curator and human rights activist, Tang teaches creative writing at various Hong Kong institutions and contributes columns and criticism to a variety of local media.

Eddie Tay is a street photographer, a poet and an associate professor in the Department of English at the Chinese University of Hong Kong. He is the author of four poetry collections. His most recent poetry collection, *Dreaming Cities* (Math Paper Press, 2016), features both poetry and street photography.

Chip Tsao is a Hong Kong-based radio broadcaster and columnist and editor of CUP Media. With an English degree from University of Warwick and a diploma in world politics from the London School of Economics, he claims to be, apart from a vagabond world citizen, a happy pessimist and the one-eyed person (that means: man) who takes pleasure in provoking and offending those who deserve to be provoked and offended in the world.

Stephen Vines runs companies in the food sector combined with working as a columnist, writer and broadcaster. He was the founding editor of Eastern Express and founding publisher of Spike. In London, he was an editor at The Observer and in Asia has worked for other international publications including *The Independent*, *The Guardian* and *The Daily Telegraph*. Vines is the author of several books including: *Hong Kong: China's New Colony* (Aurum Press, 1998), *The Years of Living Dangerously* (Texere, 1999), *Market Panic* (Wiley, 2003) and *Food Gurus* (Marshall Cavendish, 2012). Vines hosts a weekly current affairs television programme in Hong Kong.

Marco Wan is an associate professor of law and honorary associate professor of English at the University of Hong Kong. His research focuses on law and literature, law and film, gender and sexuality, and legal/critical theory. He is the author of *Masculinity and the Trials of Modern Fiction* (Routledge, 2016). He received his BA from Yale University, his first law degree and PhD from the University of Cambridge, and his LLM from Harvard Law School.

 **Wawa** (also published as Lo Mei Wa) is a Hong Kong poet. She received her degrees in philosophy in Hong Kong and the Netherlands. She is also a soprano, a lyricist and a cowherd. Some of her work can be found in *Cha: An Asian Literary Journal, Guernica Daily, The Margins, Hawai'i Review, Apogee Journal* and the anthology *Quixotica: Poems East of La Mancha* (Chameleon Press, 2016). Her collaborative work with artists has been featured in various art exhibits in Hong Kong and Glasgow. She is the author of *Pei Pei the Monkey King* (Tinfish Press, 2016). She now lives in Honolulu, Hawai'i.

 **Kate Whitehead** is the author of two Hong Kong crime books: *After Suzie* (Corporate Communications, 1997) and *Hong Kong Murders* (Oxford University Press, 2001). She was on staff at the *Hong Kong Standard* and the *South China Morning Post* and editor of Cathay Pacific's in-flight magazine *Discovery*. Whitehead is now a freelance journalist and has written for many international media outlets, including Acumen, BBC Travel, CNN, Forbes, Publishing Perspectives, *Time, Travel & Leisure* and *Women's Wear Daily*. She also writes for local publications, chiefly the *South China Morning Post*.

 **Joshua Wong** is the secretary-general of Demosistō, a new-generation political party he co-founded in Hong Kong in 2015. Wong came to the world stage in 2012 as the fourteen-year-old student leader in an effort to oppose the implementation of a patriotic education curriculum and in 2014 as a core student organiser for the Umbrella Movement. That year, he

was nominated for *Time*'s Person of the Year and was named one of the twenty-five Most Influential Teens in 2014 by Time, one of fifty World's Greatest Leaders by *Fortune* and 100 Leading Global Thinkers by *Foreign Policy*.

Nicholas Wong is the author of *Crevasse* (Kaya Press, 2015), the winner of the Twenty-eighth Lambda Literary Award in Gay Poetry and the 2016 Hong Kong Young Artist Award in Literary Arts. Wong is a vice president of PEN Hong Kong and teaches at the Education University of Hong Kong.

Xu Xi 許素細 is the author of eleven books, most recently the novel *That Man in Our Lives* (C&R Press, 2016) and *Interruptions* (HKU Museum & Art Gallery/Columbia University Press, 2016–2017). Forthcoming are a memoir *Dear Hong Kong: An Elegy for a City* (Penguin Australia, 2017), *Insignificance: Stories of Hong Kong* (Signal 8 Press, 2018) and an essay collection *This Fish is Fowl* (Nebraska University Press, 2019–2020). An Indonesian-Chinese Hong Kong native and US citizen, she currently lives between New York and Hong Kong, and co-directs Authors-at-Large. For more, visit *www.xuxiwriter.com*.

Marco Yan is a Hong Kong-born poet, who earned his MFA degrees from New York University and the University of Hong Kong. His poems have appeared in the *Pinch*, the *Adroit Journal*, the *Louisville Review* and elsewhere. For more, visit *www.marcoyan.com*.

Chris Yeung is a veteran journalist in Hong Kong. He is the chief writer for *CitizenNews*, a Chinese-language website, and founder of the *Voice of Hong Kong*, an English language opinion website and a part-time journalism lecturer. He worked at *Hong Kong Economic Journal* and headed its English website, *EJ Insight*. Prior to that, he had worked with the *South China Morning Post*. Yeung writes regularly on Hong Kong politics and Greater China issues.

Douglas Young is a Hong Kong native, deesigner and artist. He is also the CEO of and the creative force behind Goods of Desire, an original Hong Kong lifestyle brand whose designs are inspired by the vibrant culture of the city he calls home. Young is a leading voice in design, arts, creativity and entrepreneurship in Hong Kong and is often called upon to share his views on local culture and identity. In 2015, he was named one of Debrett's Hong Kong 100 in the field of art, architecture and design.

About PEN Hong Kong

PEN Hong Kong 香港筆會 is one of the 148 centres of PEN International. It is a bilingual society of Hong Kong-based writers, poets, publishers, editors, translators, journalists and academics. The mission of PEN Hong Kong is to bring together individuals working in the field of the written word to celebrate and promote literature and defend the freedom of expression in Hong Kong and the rest of China.

An English-language-only PEN Hong Kong Centre was founded in the 1980s by a number of Hong Kong-based expatriates. In the 1980s and 1990s, the organisation was widely recognised for its work providing assistance to writers who were Vietnamese refugees. The centre became inactive after key members of the organisation left the city.

In 2016, a number of writers, journalists and academics came together to revive the Hong Kong centre, motivated in large part by the rapid erosion of press freedom, academic freedom and the freedom of expression in general in Hong Kong. High-profile incidents, such as the knife attack on then-Ming Pao editor-in-chief Kevin Lau Chun-to, the Causeway Bay Books disappearances and the University of Hong Kong pro-vice-chancellor selection controversy, have bolstered the need for a bilingual platform that brings together the Chinese language and English language literary circles, which, for years have been segregated due to the differences in language and readership.

On November 13th, 2016, PEN Hong Kong was officially launched at the Foreign Correspondents' Club, Hong Kong, in conjunction with the Hong Kong International Literary Festival.

For more information about PEN Hong Kong, visit our website at *www.penhongkong.org*.

EXPLORE ASIA WITH BLACKSMITH BOOKS
From retailers around the world or from *www.blacksmithbooks.com*

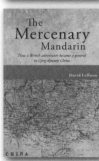

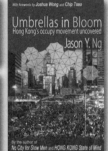

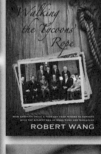

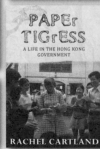